"You're a cold-hearted man, Denny."

"No, Kate," he said, "I'm a realist. I can't afford to be anything else. If I start thinking like an optimist, a lot of people are going to die. Our agents need to be human, too. So do we for that matter."

"There's a difference between being a hopeless optimist and having hope," Kate said, her voice soft. "I'd like to believe that a big part of what Room 59 does is finding that difference."

"Maybe it is," Denny said. "But in the meantime we have a job to do, and sometimes that means that we have to use people in some not-so-nice ways, even our own agents. Especially when it means they're better agents for it in the long run."

"We all get used," Kate said. "That comes with the territory. But that doesn't mean we always have to do the same to our own people."

"Kate," Denny said, "unless I miss my guess, by the time he lands in Anchorage, Jason will have already figured out that he may have to die in order to achieve some level of success on this mission."

Other title[s] in this series:

ROOM 59

THE ties THAT BIND

cliff RYDER

A GOLD EAGLE BOOK FROM

WORLDWIDE®

TORONTO • NEW YORK • LONDON
AMSTERDAM • PARIS • SYDNEY • HAMBURG
STOCKHOLM • ATHENS • TOKYO • MILAN
MADRID • WARSAW • BUDAPEST • AUCKLAND

First edition October 2008

ISBN-13: 978-0-373-63268-8
ISBN-10:   0-373-63268-1

THE TIES THAT BIND

Special thanks and acknowledgment to
Garrett Dylan for his contribution to this work.

THE ties THAT BIND

PROLOGUE

Most days, Denny Talbot, the head of Room 59 for the United States, enjoyed his job.

Throughout his careers in naval intelligence and the SEALs, the corporate world, politics and espionage, he'd learned the skills necessary to manipulate events and people with a calm precision that many others found disconcerting. And he'd learned to enjoy the games required by his position in an international espionage organization: the push and pull of compromise that got things done, the cloak-and-dagger efforts required to kill those who needed killing or remove a threat to the world. In this job, Denny knew he made a difference, helped make the world a better place. Each mission was both professional and personal, because it often meant the difference between a safe world and a world gone mad. And so most days, he enjoyed it.

Today, however, was not one of those days.

Part of his frustration was that he was supposed to be taking a few days off—and instead of being outside, riding his Tennessee walkers and enjoying the fresh air, he was inside. Working. And the work was on the far, distant side of the universe from enjoyable or fun.

An amplified scream of pain brought Denny's thoughts back to what had interrupted his time off. Most of the time, he lived and worked in New York, but he liked to escape to his small ranch outside of Nashville for his downtime. Most of his life had been filled with the noises of cities or combat or meetings in small offices filled with intense people. His ranch was quiet, secluded and—barring an emergency situation— private. But when you worked for Room 59, downtime didn't always equate to time off. The organization was too large and too involved in the shadowy underside of the world for any of its leaders to truly take time off. What they did was too important to ever let the events shaping the post-9/11 world stray too far from their minds.

Created after the horrific events of that fateful day, Room 59 represented an effort by most of the major countries of the world to stop threats *before* they happened, and to do so in a way that couldn't be traced back to any one specific nation. The countries involved poured millions into the project through shadow corporations that no longer existed, and the organization itself reported to the independent International Intelligence Agency. Yet, as large a joint venture as Room 59 was, its members were invisible to the outside world. Very few people in even the highest levels of government knew who they were. Everything they did—from daily operations to assassination missions to intelligence gathering—was done behind walls of encryption and secrecy. Meetings were held in virtual-reality conference rooms, where people were represented by electronic avatars that might, or might not, represent their true appearance.

Room 59 had important work to do, and discovery by the media or an opposing interest might mean the end of the organization itself.

Denny was seated in a secure office, hidden inside his ranch house. His eyes were covered with a pair of highly advanced glasses that connected to his computer and launched his avatar into the virtual world of Room 59. In that world, his avatar was seated at his desk, too. He tried to make his virtual office very similar to the one he used in the real world. It was comforting to him and seemed to put visitors at ease, as well. People who were comfortable, Denny knew, were more likely to let their guard down.

Floating directly in front of him was a video recording. In the virtual world, no monitor was needed—images, videos, recordings and other data could simply be pulled from icon files and launched into view. The video was poor quality, but clear enough to be seen. The audio track was a little too good for Denny's taste.

The man's screams, the slap of a heavy fist against flesh, the slow *pit-pat* of blood hitting the concrete floor…these were sounds that Denny knew all too well. He knew torture was a necessary part of espionage, but that didn't make it pleasant. If a man came to enjoy it, he needed to find a new line of work.

In the video, a Russian man was manacled to a chair. His brown hair was wet with sweat and blood, and his deep-set eyes seethed with pain and rage. His lips were swollen, his nose was crooked and thin rivulets of blood ran from both nostrils. Naked from the waist up—his captors obviously hadn't gotten to the more drastic forms of information extraction yet—his chest was crisscrossed with the marks of his interrogation. From the look, Denny guessed they'd been using some kind of heated metal to sear the man's skin.

Denny suspected that the people who were questioning him were CIA, probably black ops, but they weren't on camera and even their voices had been changed on the audio track. With time, they could probably be found, but the interrogators didn't really matter. What mattered was what the Russian was telling them.

Between sobbing breaths, he hissed, "You…fucking barbarians. I've told you. That's all I know."

"Yeah, right," an off-camera voice said. "But here's the problem, Yusiv. I think you're lying. *We* think you're lying. We think your story is bullshit. Mother Russia hasn't had the money or the technology to develop anything like that."

"I do not lie!" the Russian screamed, then his body sagged in exhaustion. The scream had taken the last of his strength. "They have it and they will use it," he whispered.

"When?" the other voice snapped. "Where?"

The Russian shook his head. "I have told you all I

know. They are testing it in the Bering Sea. I don't know how it will be used, but you can be sure that they will. There are powers in Russia who are not happy with the changes in our country. They want to go back to the old ways."

"The old ways?"

"They want to be a world power again," the beaten man said. "Bring back the arms race, the Cold War, all of it. Then, we were feared. Now, we are a joke to the rest of the world."

The interrogators laughed. "That's true," one of them finally said. "So, your story is that someone over there has developed an Oscar-class nuclear submarine capable of supercavitation…and they're testing it in the Bering Sea."

"It is not a story," the Russian said, his eyes blazing once again. "You make it sound like a children's fable."

"We think it is," one of the men said. "We think you didn't like serving in the Russian navy and now you want to defect. Isn't that closer to the truth, Yusiv?"

The Russian spit blood on the floor and shook his head. "I have nothing else to say."

The video cut out at that point, and Denny saw that the communication icon was flashing. He tapped it with an outstretched virtual hand and a small window opened in front of him, revealing the face of Kate Cochran—his boss and the woman who ran Room 59.

Despite her platinum-blond hair and her ability to be lighthearted from time to time, when it came to work, she was all business. "What do you think?" she asked. In Denny's experience, Kate tended to be direct, to the point and have high expectations. When she wanted answers, she wanted them immediately.

Denny leaned back in his chair. He assumed she knew more than she was saying and was looking to him for additional input before reaching any conclusions. "What do you think?" he countered. She was used to his asking questions in response to hers. It was how they worked.

"You know those new biometrics tools our research folks put together?" she asked, then continued without waiting for his reply. "I had the video and audio tracks scanned using those. They're more reliable than any polygraph machine. At the very least, the Russian believes he's telling the truth."

"Then," Denny replied, "we've got a serious problem. A nuclear sub capable of supercavitation is no joke."

Kate sighed heavily. "When don't we?" she quipped. "So, you're the ex-navy man. What does that mean in layman's terms?"

"This is an oversimplification in a lot of ways, but put simply, imagine a nuclear-armed submarine that can travel at twice the speed of anything we've got in the water right now. That means twice the distance. It also means that we'd have virtually no warning at all if they decided to park one off the West Coast and launch. They could be there, launch and be on their way home before we'd have a chance to do anything about it except tell the president to get in his bunker and push the button."

Kate was silent for a moment, then said, "Shit."

"That's one way to put it," Denny said. "We need an operative up there and fast. If it's true, it means that the U.S. is going to have to move back toward Cold War footing. Everything changes if the Russians are rebuilding their arsenals."

"They've started doing long-range patrol flights again," Kate said. "Where the hell are they getting the money for all this?"

Denny shook his head. "I don't know. A lot of money has been pouring into Russia since the collapse of the Soviet Union. It's hard to trace it all. Right now, all we really need to know is if they've actually got a sub with this kind of capability. And if they do, we need to have it, too."

The very idea of resuming the arms race made him grit his teeth. There was no win for anyone in that scenario. "Or we need to make sure that it's destroyed," he added.

"I agree," Kate said. "I'll take it before the IIA representatives today, and they'll green-light the mission, even if I have to break arms to get the votes."

"Understood," he said. "Do you want to assign the agent or do you want me to do it?"

"Do you have someone specific in mind?" she asked.

Denny tapped a glowing icon in front of him and a folder appeared. He tapped it again and it opened. "One of our newest recruits," he said. "Jason Siku."

Kate scanned the folder's contents. "Why him?" she asked. "This would be his first official op. Pretty intense work for a newbie."

"Normally, I'd agree with you," he said. "But this guy isn't our usual recruit. He's had a ton of espionage experience, speaks fluent Russian, and with his ancestry, he'll be able to fit right in up there. This isn't a kill assignment—though his final training mission was. This is recon only. If we need to step up to a search-and-destroy, we can reassess the situation then."

Kate nodded. "Do you expect any other complications? We can't afford any mistakes here."

"None," Denny said. "Siku is a straight arrow. He worked for the CIA before he came to us. He has no family and no real ties to anyone. His mission success rate with the Feds was perfect, and he doesn't wander off track. He'll get the job done."

Denny paused, thinking for a moment. "Besides that, we've got an off-radar employee already in the field up there," he said.

"Who's that?" Kate asked.

"A local who translates intercepted Russian communications, that sort of thing. There's some minor weapons smuggling going on up there, and the agent keeps us apprised of that situation, too. It's not a full-on field agent, but we'll know the score and be able to keep an eye on Siku."

"All right," Kate said. "I'll get the ball rolling and get back to you later today. You can expect a mission assignment within four hours."

"I'll be standing by," Denny said.

Kate laughed quietly. "No, you won't. You'll be back out riding your horses and playing cowboy. I'll call you direct and give you the thumbs-up. Go back to your rest and relaxation. Though what you call relaxing, I call being bounced around and risking a broken neck."

"Ah," he said, smiling. "You just haven't ridden the right kind of horse."

"And I'll be keeping it that way, thank you very much," Kate said. "Gotta go."

She signed off and Denny studied the video again. He didn't need to see the biometrics results. The Russian was telling the truth, but the submarine was only part of what made the story disturbing. The very idea of the Cold War starting up again—a war that he'd already survived once—chilled him to his core.

The first Cold War had been a quiet one of buildup, cat-and-mouse games and political posturing. The players in the game now would be far different than those faced before. Sooner or later, the players would include extremists who wouldn't hesitate to use any of the weapons in their arsenals to start a truly global conflict.

And in that kind of war, Denny knew, there were no winners at all.

There was only a world filled with death and ash.

1

Jason Siku slipped the modified shooting glasses over his eyes. From his perspective, the yellow-tinted lenses were more than just a coloration that brought out contrasts in the landscape. The lenses used a tiny microprocessor built into the frames to work in tandem with the high-tech rounds he was testing tonight.

The indoor firing range was almost empty, and Jason was enjoying the relative peace of practicing without the interruption of other people talking and shooting at the same time that he practiced. He dropped an empty clip from his porcelain-framed Glock 17 and slid in a new one. Setting the weapon down, he attached a new human-shaped target sheet to the clips, then moved it out to a distance of fifteen feet. Picking up the gun once more, he set his feet and turned on the laser sight with a tap of his thumb.

A red dot appeared on the target's chest region. He

took one steadying breath, then began shooting. A few seconds later, the last round was fired and the slide sprang open. During these sessions, Jason didn't think or reminisce, and he rarely spoke to anyone when he was here. An excellent shooter, he knew, thought of nothing during the moments of pulling the trigger but his weapon and the target. Everything else was a distraction that could prove deadly or cause a miss.

He removed the empty clip and was reaching for the next one when a hand on his shoulder startled him enough to almost cause him to jump. He felt his muscles tense momentarily, then he relaxed them. He turned to see the owner of the range, Jim Miller, staring at the target. Jason pulled off his ear protection and offered a slight smile. "Hi, Jim," he said. "Everything okay?"

Miller continued to gaze at the target. "Fine," he said, then shook his head. "That's…that's some good shooting. Even taking the short range into account, I don't know too many people who can shoot like that."

Jason nodded. "Thanks. I practice at ten, fifteen and twenty feet," he said. "Every once in a while, I'll go out farther, twenty-two or twenty-five feet, but it's really kind of pointless beyond those ranges."

"How's that?" Miller asked.

"Most shootings with a handgun occur inside twenty feet," Jason said. "Being a crack shot at fifty won't help you much if the other guy is ten feet away and shooting back."

"I suppose not," Miller admitted. "Those are some nice patterns, too. Two to the chest, one to the head. You didn't miss once. We've got a couple of shooting-club champions that come here that don't get groupings like that."

Jason smiled. "I practice a lot."

"I've noticed," Miller said. "You've been in here often." He shrugged. "Anyway, I didn't mean to interrupt you. I just wanted to let you know that we're closing in about fifteen minutes."

Jason glanced at his watch. "Thanks for the reminder. I was kind of in a zone."

Miller grinned. "I noticed that, too." He headed back down the firing lane and said, "Have a good night."

"Thanks," Jason said. "You, too."

He considered running a few more rounds through the weapon—it was also new—but he'd already done over five hundred this week. The gun felt comfortable in his hands and his accuracy with it was solid. The fact that the rounds he was using were specially made for Room 59 agents wasn't something anyone needed to know.

Working with information processed by the shooting glasses, the modified rounds were autocorrecting. A tiny microchip tracked the previous round and the shooter's visual response and made adjustments on the fly. If you were off by a half inch with the first shot, the second shot would be dead-on. It was a marvelous modification, but Jason didn't like to count on it, so he'd practiced with the weapon until he felt that he wouldn't need the rounds to adjust for him more than a quarter inch at twenty feet or less.

He reloaded and placed the weapon in the ballistic

holster under his left arm, then pulled on his jacket. He took his extra clip and slid it into the spare magazine slot on the holster, reeled in his target and policed his area clean. He knew no one would bother to look at the casings too closely. There were thousands of them in the area, and it would take more than a cursory examination to notice anything different about them anyway.

Jason crumpled up the target and tossed it into the trash can, then started walking toward the front of the building, where Miller sold guns and other sporting goods. Just as he reached the door leading into the shopping area, he brought himself up short. Even through the heavy sheet metal, he could hear the sound of raised voices.

Cautiously, he eased open the door wide enough to slip through. The voices were clearer now.

"Just give us the money, man, and we're outta here. No muss, no fuss." It was a young man's voice.

"Do it now!" another voice yelled. "Stop fucking around, old man!"

"I'm doing it," Jason heard Miller say. "I have to turn on the computer first. I already shut it down for the night. The cash drawer won't open unless the computer is on."

"Oh, freakin' bullshit, man," the first voice said.

Jason eased his way up one aisle, cut sideways, then began working his way forward. What kind of idiot would choose to rob a gun shop? he wondered. Miller had to be armed or have a weapon behind the counter. Why wasn't he fighting back?

"Look, you owe us, man, and now you're gonna pay up. Stop with the excuses."

Jason was finally close enough to peer over a large stack of shotgun shells that were on display. The two men talking to Miller both looked to be in their twenties. The one with the calmer voice held a revolver in his hands, while the screamer was carrying a sawed-off shotgun. Both of them wore gang colors, which meant that they were at least used to the idea of violence, if not used to doing it themselves. Both of them had various tattoos and piercings—anonymity was not a part of their world.

It didn't matter to Jason what Miller supposedly owed them; what they were doing was robbery.

He decided to play it straight and see what happened. Room 59 agents weren't supposed to get involved in this kind of thing—they were supposed to be invisible—but he wouldn't let a good man die or be robbed for no reason. Stepping out from behind the display, he pulled out his wallet and kept his head down. "Hey, Jim," he called. "What do I owe you for tonight?"

"What the fuck is this?" the screamer said. "Don't move a freakin' muscle!"

Jason stopped in his tracks. "Whoa," he said. "Easy, kid. I don't…hey, I don't want any trouble."

"Too late for that, man," the first guy said. "It found you."

Jason risked a glance at Jim, saw his hand easing toward the underside of the counter and gave a slight shake of his head. "It usually does," he said, putting his wallet back into his jeans. "Are you boys giving my friend Jim here a hard time?"

"Ain't none of your damn business. Don't move, don't get hurt. We'll finish up what we gotta do and be on our merry," the calm one said.

Jason went still. He turned his gaze on the calm one first, then the screamer. "In exactly thirty seconds," he said, his voice low and deadly, "I'm going to kill both of you. And not in a nice way, but in a slow, painful way." He kept his hands out, palms open and visible. "Or you can leave and never come back. It's up to you."

"What the fuck you talkin' about?" the screamer said. "I'll shoot you down, man, and sleep like a baby."

"Twenty seconds," Jason said.

"Man's crazy," the first guy said. "Got a death wish or something."

"Fifteen seconds," he said. "Your time is running out, boys."

"Just give us the damn money, Miller!" the second guy yelled. "Your boy done took out a loan to pay for his habit, and since he's not around no more, you get to pay up."

Miller's eyes met with Jason's. "Fuck you," the shop owner said. "My boy *died* because you got him hooked. If anyone owes, it's you."

"Guess they both want to die," the calmer man said.

"Wrong again," Jason whispered. In the blink of an eye, he had the Glock free from the holster and he fired a single round into the forehead of the kid carrying the revolver.

He fell over dead, the back of his head a gaping, gory hole.

"Grinch!" the screamer said, then turned his rage toward Jason. "You fuckin' said thirty seconds!"

Jason shrugged. "I lied," he said, bringing the Glock around. "Drop the gun, kid, or you'll be just as dead as your buddy Grinch."

Jason watched as the boy considered his options, saw him make his sad decision and begin to raise his shotgun. Before he could squeeze the trigger, the Glock spoke twice more, and the boy dropped the gun and began to scream in earnest. His knees were gone and he writhed on the floor, crying and bleeding.

"Jesus," Miller said.

"He doesn't have much to do with this kind of thing," Jason replied. "Lend me your belt."

"What?"

"Your belt," he snapped. "Unless you want that boy to bleed to death."

Miller whipped his belt off and handed it over.

Jason kicked the shotgun away and knelt down by the wounded boy, using Miller's belt and his own to make tourniquets on each leg. "Shut up," he snapped as the boy continued to scream and moan. "You could be dead."

"You fucker," the kid said. "You shot us both. You killed Grinch and my legs are all messed up. I'll never walk again. You said you'd kill me."

"I lied about that, too," Jason said. "Besides, walking is a privilege, you know. By the time you get out of prison, who knows what kind of shape you'll be in."

"Prison?" the kid said.

Jason stood up quickly, then turned to Miller. "You carry the Glock 17 model?" he asked.

"Sure," he said. "Why?"

"Get me one," Jason said. "With a loaded clip. Be quick."

Miller was moving on automatic pilot, but he did as Jason told him. Jason took the weapon and jogged back to the range door, firing the weapon three times. Then he brought it back to the shop owner.

"Take this," he said, handing it to him. He glanced around. "Do you have video surveillance of any kind here?"

The man shook his head, still stunned. "No," he said. "Never figured on anyone trying to rob me."

"I don't suppose," Jason said. "Listen, Jim, I've got to get out of here and fast. As soon as I'm out the door, you call the cops and tell them what happened…but leave me out of it. Don't mention my name or my involvement." He leaned forward, his eyes boring into the other man. "I was *never* here. They came in, tried to rob you and you defended yourself, got it?"

"I…I got it," he whispered, looking at the carnage. "Who…who are you?"

"I'm nobody," Jason said. "I'm a ghost."

"A ghost," Miller said. "You're pretty good in a fight for a ghost."

Jason laughed quietly. "That wasn't a fight," he said. "That was just practice."

"Jesus," Miller said again. Then he added, "The boy will talk."

"Probably," Jason said. "But he's loaded on drugs—

crack or meth probably—and they'll never believe him. Just stick to your story and give them the Glock, okay?"

"Yeah," he said. "Okay."

Jason turned and moved for the door.

"Hey!" Miller called.

Jason stopped but didn't turn around.

"Thank you," he said. "Thanks for saving my life." He sighed. "They got my son hooked on meth and it killed him. I couldn't get him to stop, couldn't save him no matter how hard I tried."

"That happens sometimes," Jason said. "You can't save everyone."

"Well, you saved me, so thank you. My son is dead, but I still…I want to live."

"You're welcome," Jason said as he stepped out into the night.

The parking lot had only a few vehicles left in it and was poorly lit, but Jason found his own brown Volvo without any problems. He moved quickly, knowing the police could arrive any moment. He hit the remote unlock button on his key tab before he got to the car, skipping his usual quick walk around to ensure that no one had managed to get inside. It was always unlikely, but he never took chances with his safety. Now was the time to get moving.

He lived an orderly kind of life. His car was the safest one on the market—even safer after he'd added some additional aftermarket accessories. His apartment was sparsely furnished, meticulously neat and held no real clues as to who he was or what he did for a living.

He climbed into the Volvo, started the engine and

headed for his apartment. In the distance, he could hear the telltale sound of police sirens. Clean action had felt good, despite breaking an operative rule. Of late, he'd felt strangely conflicted. When he'd worked for the CIA, he had very little downtime. Room 59 operatives had mandated time off between missions. He'd been surprised by the intensity of the training period, including his first posttraining assignment—a final exam, of sorts—that involved him assassinating a target. It had been a simple assignment, really. More the kind of thing assigned to a rookie than an old hand like himself.

In the darkness of the car, Jason laughed to himself. Home was just a place to sleep between jobs. He wondered if any agents had a wife and kids in this line of work. He shook his head. It didn't make sense to have a family. Not for people like him.

And yet…family was on his mind more and more lately. Despite his son's death, Jim Miller had wanted to live. He probably had a wife, maybe other kids—people he counted on and who counted on him. When he'd left the orphanage, Jason had no idea who his real family was or even if they were alive. All he had was his last name, which was on his birth certificate. He'd tried to find out more a couple of times, but other than learning that his mother had been an Inuit from somewhere in Alaska and his father was unknown, there'd been precious little information. After a time, he'd given up on the idea and, considering his profession, it was probably the wisest course of action. Being responsible for his own life, taking his own risks was one thing, but adding a wife or a child or some other family member to the mix, putting them at risk, seemed the very height of irresponsibility.

Still, he was alone and, he admitted to himself, lonely. It would be good to have someone he could count on. Someone to come home to.

He turned the corner close to his apartment complex and pulled into the parking lot. He shut down the Volvo, locked it and headed inside. He'd grab a quick bite to eat and then rack out for the night. His mandatory downtime was over, and he expected that an assignment would be heading his way soon enough.

Once he was inside, his thoughts turned again to the idea of trying to find his mother, his family. Why had she left him at the orphanage in Seattle? Why didn't he want him? Did he have other family members—a brother, a sister, someone? The questions plagued him even as he heated a bowl of soup and cut a few slices of bread.

He knew he couldn't live the life he did forever. Sooner or later, he'd get older, slip up and get killed or have to find something he could do that didn't involve fieldwork. Would he be able to have a family then, or would it just be more of the same? What kind of woman would ask about his day and accept the only answer he could give—"I can't tell you or I'd have to kill you."

Sitting at the kitchen table, Jason pondered the questions and wondered why they were coming up again now, so soon after starting a new job, but his mind didn't have very long to linger on them. Halfway through his soup, the pager on his belt began to vibrate.

He pulled it free and looked at the display.

His first assignment, Jason realized, was right on time to distract him from these notions.

2

The next morning found Jason up before his alarm clock sounded. It was a few minutes before six. He went through his usual routine—a five-mile run, a quick shower, a breakfast of oatmeal and eggs, with grapefruit juice and a cup of coffee.

He took the time to scan the morning paper and found a short note in the local section on page six about the robbery. Miller had stuck to the story Jason had given him, and the police were calling him a "tough citizen" and a "hero." The man he'd killed was wanted for two other robberies and a suspected homicide. Good riddance, Jason thought.

When it was about time for him to go to work, he sat at the small computer console in his apartment and booted up the system. In all his years as a CIA operative, he had worked with a lot of gadgets and toys, but when compared to the Room 59 equipment, it was apples and oranges. They were years, perhaps decades ahead of what other agencies were utilizing in the often silent war to keep America safe. The virtual conference room used by field agents was just one of the more unique tools in the Room 59 arsenal.

Once the computer was booted up, Jason slipped on a pair of glasses that projected the virtual world onto the lenses. He clicked on the launch icon. This was the first of several layers of security he would have to pass through in order to report in. The icon opened a window that appeared on the lenses rather than the screen itself. All that was visible was a large text block requesting his password.

Jason typed it in, and the launch console flickered once, then vanished and was replaced by what appeared to be a long hallway. The walls glowed a faint green color and reminded him slightly of the look of the old Tron video game. This, of course, was much better. He was now simultaneously sitting at his desk and walking down the hallway. His avatar, which he'd designed himself, appeared much like he himself did. A six-foot-two-inch-tall man with broad shoulders and a narrow waist. His black hair was cut short and neat, and his eyes were a cold, faded blue. He preferred to dress in a sport coat and dress shirt, with pressed slacks and polished shoes. Jason believed that looking professional was the first step to being professional, so he dressed the part every working day. He knew he was considered handsome by most of society's standards, and had no problem finding female companionship when it suited him. He enjoyed the sex, but that was all it ever was.

Love, he knew, was out of the question. Just like family.

He knew that some people created fanciful avatars or added personal touches like wings, but for himself, he saw no reason to change who he was or how he looked. The people who ran Room 59 knew what he looked like, and it was highly unlikely that anyone he might encounter in the virtual world would care how he appeared, let alone actually see him in real life. Part of the job was *not* interacting with other operatives unless a mission specifically called for it.

At the end of the hallway he came to a simple door and next to it, a hand and retinal scanner. As he approached the door, he stopped.

A female voice said, "Place your right palm and eye in front of the scanner for identity confirmation."

Jason raised his glasses and held his hand up to the scanner that appeared on his computer screen.

The voice said, "Please hold still while the scan is in progress." A brief light flashed over both his palm and his eye. The voice said, "Scanning." Then it continued, "Identity confirmed. One-hundred-percent match to existing record for Siku, Jason, field agent. Voice confirm?"

"Siku, Jason," he dutifully said as he adjusted his glasses. "Reporting for virtual conference scheduled for 0800 hours."

"Voice confirmed," it said. "Have a nice day."

In front of him, the door unlocked and Jason opened it, stepping into an office building that extended as far as the eye could see. He'd been told that some of the security protocols were new, but he had to admit that any system that could scan his palm, voice and retinal prints from a distance was pretty impressive. He'd also been told that anything less than a one-hundred-percent match would result in bad things. What those bad things might be, no one seemed to know.

The conference room was down a row of cubicles and to his left, and he moved there, not bothering to greet the other avatars working around him. He stepped into the conference room, and saw that his boss, Denny Talbot, was already seated at one end of the table, talking to someone on the floating screen in front of him. Denny waved him in, and Jason stepped inside, shutting the door behind him.

"He's here now," his boss was saying. "I'll get back in touch right after we're done here." Denny looked up from the monitor, then stood and offered his hand. "Good to see you again, Jason. How was the down-time?"

Jason shook the offered hand. "Boring," he said. "I really don't need that much of a break between jobs."

"You're not the first agent to tell us that," Denny admitted. "But everything we've learned so far suggests that a successful agent is one who does take a break once in a while." He gestured toward the chairs. "Have a seat."

Jason sat down, marveling again at how real this virtual world seemed. It was computer programming on a level the rest of the world only imagined in science-fiction books and movies. "Do you have an assignment for me?" he asked, stretching his legs beneath the table. "I'm ready to get to work."

Denny picked up a file from a small table behind him. "Indeed," he said, sliding it over. "Straight recon, nothing fancy. Get in, confirm the information, get out and bring it back."

Jason opened the file folder and quickly reviewed the contents, committing them to memory as he read. "Supercavitation?" he asked. "No one has that kind of technology yet."

"Not that we know of," Denny said. "But we've reviewed the source carefully, and at the least, *he* believes it's the truth."

"So, you want me to find this sub—if it exists—and bring back as much data on it as possible?" Jason asked.

Denny nodded. "The plans, if at all possible. Our source believes that there are forces in Russia who want to bring the Cold War, the arms race, the whole shebang, back into full swing."

Jason considered it, then nodded. "I wouldn't be surprised," he said. "In fact, it wouldn't even be the first time I've heard the sentiment. A lot of people miss Mother Russia, despite her less-than-charitable ways."

"I suppose so," Denny said. "But we can't afford another war—cold, hot or anything in between. If the Russians have developed this sub, we need to find it, get the plans and immediately make it known that we can build them, too. Hopefully, they'll realize how closely we're watching them and focus their efforts elsewhere like food for their people."

"Why me?" Jason asked. "I'm not usually a straight reconnaissance man."

"According to our intel, they're testing the sub in the Bering Sea. We want you to use the local Inuit villages along the coast up there for cover. You also speak fluent Russian, which makes sending you an even better fit."

Jason glanced through the folder one more time, memorizing the information and calculating what he'd need to accomplish it. "Mission support?" he asked.

"We'll put together an offshore support team by the time you're in place, situate them on an oil barge. Just set up a coordinates beacon somewhere out of the way and within twelve hours, you'll be good to go." Denny tapped an icon and the image of a very attractive woman appeared. "This is Tina Kanut. She's native, knows the area and works for a guide agency up there. We've already arranged for her services."

"Sounds fine," Jason said. "Any other parameters I should know of?"

Denny shook his head. "Nothing critical. Just remember that this is a recon mission, so I'd rather not have a trail of bodies. Get in, get the data and get out. Clean and simple."

"Understood," Jason said. "And if something goes wrong?"

"If you can and there's time, check in with me and we'll decide how to proceed. If not, destroy the sub. That will send a message, too," Denny said.

"Got it," Jason said. "When do I leave?"

"We've got you scheduled on a flight from Minneapolis to Seattle, connecting to Anchorage, tonight," he said. "Your cover documents are being delivered this morning. You'll be going in as an advance man for a geographic-survey team. That should give you a solid reason to be in the villages and along the coast, too."

"That works for me," Jason said. He slid the folder back to Denny and got to his feet. "I'll report in as soon as I've got something solid."

"Just remember that that part of the world is a strange place," his boss replied. "The Russians watch the Bering Sea very carefully and they're always listening, and the Inuit are a people trapped between the need to adapt to the modern world and the desire to cling to their traditions. That's another good reason to send you, Jason. You have a better chance of understanding them, I think, than any of our other agents, and if they can be a help to you, that's a good thing, too."

Jason chuckled dryly. "My mother was Inuit, so I have the blood," he said, "but I'm hardly one of them. I don't believe in family."

"I know," Denny said. "It's one of the reasons we recruited you. Family men get tangled up in personal issues. That doesn't seem to be a problem you have. Still, that doesn't mean you can't use the native people up there if it comes to that."

"I don't imagine it will," Jason replied. "But I'm not above using them to get the job done."

Denny thought about it for a minute, then said, "I know that, too, Jason. I've read your file several times over. You're smart, educated, cold and decisive. It's why you've been so successful and why I think you'll be successful here. That said, beneath the exterior, I imagine that you're as human as the next man. Try not to let the machine take over completely, okay? The best field agents tend to blend your strengths with the ability to be compassionate."

"I'm not a machine," Jason objected, stung a little. "I just don't have much use for other people. They're a burden I don't care to deal with."

"You mean like what happened at the firing range last night?" Denny asked. "You killed one man and injured another."

Jason paused, stunned that his boss knew what happened. "How did you—"

"It's my job to know," Denny said. "And for what it's worth, you did the right thing. We ask our operatives to be ghosts, but there's also a time for doing what's right. That was the choice you faced last night, and you made the right call."

"It won't happen again," Jason said, still trying to wrap his mind around an organization that could know so much about one person so quickly. "I mean…you hired me to be a ghost, so that's what I'll be."

Denny chuckled. "Sooner or later, you'll do the human thing again. I understand why you feel the way you do, why you operate the way you do. Just remember that relaxing once in a while won't hurt you, okay? You are human, after all." He smiled.

"Got it," Jason said. He turned to the door. "I better get a move on if I'm going to be ready to catch that flight."

"Stay safe," Denny said. "And think about what I said, Jason. No man can stand alone forever."

Without looking back, Jason said, "I'll give it some thought, boss." Then he opened the door and slipped out of the room.

All the way back to the log-out screen, he thought about Denny's words. What did they want from him? One minute, he's supposed to be a cold-blooded killer, the next he's supposed to…what? Be a kinder, gentler assassin?

He logged out and put the glasses on the desk, rubbing his eyes to ease the strain. It was ridiculous, he thought. He didn't have time for friends and family. And he didn't have time to deal with any of the feelings associated with those issues today. He had saved Miller because it was the right thing to do, not because of some human bond. Most of the time, there was right and wrong, good and evil. Shades of gray entered into it, but usually that was confined to situations where feelings were involved, where the moralities of a given situation were debatable. He didn't deal too often in those gray areas. His life tended to be black and white and he preferred it that way.

He got up from the desk just as a brown envelope slid beneath his front door. He knew it would contain his travel documents. "I've got work to do," he muttered to himself as he crossed the room. "I'll deal with learning how to be a more compassionate assassin tomorrow."

"YOU'RE CERTAIN of this, Denny?" Kate asked, running a hand through her short-cropped hair. "He's brand-new and this is delicate. We can't afford any mistakes at all."

"I'm sure, Kate," Denny replied. "You've read his file."

"I know, I know," she said. "Ph.D. in psychology from Harvard, with a genius-level IQ. Borderline photographic memory. Well above average blending skills and he excelled in our training program. His final test was a masterwork. That dignitary was about as covered as anyone I've ever seen and Siku got him. My concern is that this could get personal for him. His family is out there…somewhere. We don't need personal right now."

"Sure, it is," Denny said. "But the man obviously does not care. He's ice, Kate, and his record is spotless. My contact at the CIA said that they called him the thinking man's assassin. Do you know why?"

She shook her head, and he continued. "Because he was like a computer. Precise, calculating, no feelings at all. He plans and plans and then does the job. No mistakes. And he's not above using people to meet his mission goals—even if it gets them killed."

"I understand all that, but this isn't an assassination," Kate said. "With any luck at all, no one important will even know he was there."

Denny sighed heavily and wished he could go back to his horse ranch. "Kate, with all due respect, I think you've missed something here."

One eyebrow arched and her lips pursed tightly before she said, "Go on."

"The odds of him finding the sub—if it exists at all—then getting to it, getting on board and getting out again with no one the wiser are about a million to one against. Submarines are very confined spaces, and a stranger is going to be recognized instantly. It's far more likely that he'll be captured."

"So why send him?" Kate asked. "If he's just going to be captured and die, what's the point?"

"I didn't say he'd die, Kate," Denny said. "I said it was far more likely that he'd be captured."

"What's the difference?"

"If he does get captured, Kate, it won't be for long. Certainly not long enough for them to get him back to Russia. The most likely scenario at that point is that he would find a way to destroy the sub and kill the crew, even if it meant his own death."

"How did you reach that conclusion?" she asked. "His psych profile doesn't indicate anything like suicidal tendencies."

Denny shrugged. "He's not suicidal. What he is, Kate, is a man without anything in his life but the mission. That can be a good thing for us, of course, because if he's successful, we win, and if he fails, it's likely that we at least gain some time. Not as big a win, but a win of sorts. It's not a very good thing for him to be that way, but he hasn't figured that out yet. He may live long enough to do so, but I can't really say for sure at this point."

"You're a coldhearted man, Denny," Kate said. "Very cold."

"No, Kate," he said, "I'm a realist. I can't afford to be anything else. If I start thinking like an optimist, a lot of people are going to die. Our agents need to be human, too. So do we, for that matter."

"There's a difference between being a hopeless optimist and having hope," she said, her voice soft. "I'd like to believe that a big part of what Room 59 does is finding that difference."

"Maybe it is," Denny said. "But in the meantime, we

have a job to do, and sometimes that means that we have to use people in some not so nice ways, even our own agents. Especially when it means, they're better agents for it in the long run."

"We all get used," Kate said. "That comes with the territory. But that doesn't mean we always have to do the same to our own people."

"Kate," Denny said, "unless I miss my guess, by the time he lands in Anchorage, Jason will have already figured out that he may have to die in order to achieve some level of success on this mission. As you said, he's not stupid."

"And when he realizes that you've sent him on what could be nothing more than a quick trip to die?" she asked.

"He'll be cranky," Denny said, smiling. "But he'll also have to decide if there's anything more important in his life than the mission—even something as petty as getting even with me. He'll either die or come back a better agent for the experience. He might even come back with some actual feelings."

"Sounds like you've got it all worked out," she said. "But it still feels crappy."

He nodded. "Yes, it does," he said. "But with another Cold War brewing and more international terrorism going on than we can even begin to keep track of, we need better agents than we've ever had—men and women who can find the balance between hopeless optimism and hope, who can think on their feet and decide what is more important to them—their lives or the world. We need agents who can make that choice confidently, Kate."

She thought for several long moments, then nodded. "You're right," she said. "The game is changing, I think, faster than many of us believed it would."

"It always does," Denny said. "And if we don't change with it, we won't be anything more than dinosaurs waiting for a meteor strike."

"I'm not ready to be a fossil quite yet," Kate said, laughing.

"Nor am I," Denny said, "despite how I look. I'll keep you in the loop."

"Do that," Kate said. Then she added, "And you look fine." She cut the connection, her virtual avatar winking out of existence.

Denny leaned back, then returned to the file folders on his desk. He'd already spoken to Tina Kanut and explained the situation. She was to play the native guide and nothing else. Her only job was to keep an eye on Jason and if things began to go wrong, she could step in, identify herself and lend a hand.

Sadly, there was more going on in Room 59 than this one mission, and his attention was needed elsewhere. Win or lose, succeed or fail, there were always threats to be addressed. The threats, Denny thought, never stop. He hoped he was doing the right thing where Siku was concerned, but his agents needed to be human, as much as they needed to be effective. Too much of what Room 59 did involved making human decisions. It wasn't all about killing. Sometimes, it was about choosing the lives of others over your own.

And sometimes, it was just the opposite.

3

The flights from Minneapolis to Seattle and on to Anchorage were uneventful, and Jason spent his time mentally reviewing the specifics of the mission, memorizing his cover story and trying to determine the best way to address the challenges of trying to find a submarine in the icy waters of the Bering Strait. Of course, finding it wasn't the only problem, though that one was a significant challenge in and of itself.

But the biggest problem would be getting to the sub, getting on board and getting out again without being seen or captured. Even the largest submarines in the world had very limited amounts of space, and the entire crew would know one another on sight. The likelihood of capture or death was quite a bit higher than usual, and being sent on what could be either a wild-goose chase or a death sentence didn't improve his mood very much. Denny had to have known this was not a simple mission, possibly even a suicide mission, and Jason intended to have some serious words with him when he returned—assuming, of course, that he survived at all.

As the plane began its descent into Anchorage, Jason thought about the fact that this wasn't going to be his usual kind of operation. He enjoyed missions where planning was almost as important as execution. The proper plans almost always led to the successful completion of an op, and in his experience, failure was usually the result of poor planning. The problem here was that no plan could possibly address all—or even most—of the likely challenges. In other words, he was going to have to wing it. It was an uncomfortable sensation for him at best.

Still, he suspected that these kinds of missions were among the reasons that Room 59 existed in the first place. During his training period, his final test—what they called a mission assessment—was the elimination of a well-protected foreign dignitary who'd been selling state secrets on the black market. It had been an unfortunate situation all the way around. The man had a history of excellent public service to his own country and had built a network of friends within the U.S. government, as well. But he also had a gambling problem that led to a massive debt load. He turned to the only resource he had—selling secrets to both sides and funneling the profits to pay off his debts. Still, the man had a wife, two kids, a family…and he had to die. It wasn't a situation where a slap on the wrist would do the job. His removal had to be quick and quiet.

After reviewing the mission parameters, Jason had flown to Washington, D.C., and attended a party where the man was a guest. He'd slipped through the crowd in a waiter's uniform and removed him with a poisoned appetizer. By all appearances, the man had had a massive heart attack and was dead long before the paramedics could arrive. It was an unfortunate end to what had been a successful career, and his family would suffer grief. Still, Jason didn't ask any questions and he didn't hesitate. His trainers were very pleased, and even Denny had congratulated him on doing a difficult mission without letting it get personal.

"Why would it have gotten personal?" Jason had asked.

"Targets are still people," Denny had said. "The man had a family and was well respected."

"It wasn't personal to me," Jason had said. "He needed to be killed. That simple."

Denny had stared at him for a long moment, then nodded. "You'll find, I think, that many of our missions aren't so *simple,* as you put it. Sooner or later, you'll run into something that makes it personal."

Jason smiled grimly. "Nothing in our line of work, not even death, is personal. What we do is simple because it's necessary. There's no need to muck things up with feelings."

For some reason, remembering that briefing now, Jason thought that perhaps Denny had been right. Sometimes the work could get personal. Even being this close to where his family had come from, where they might still be, made him edgy. He turned his mind back to his work.

Other than his cover story as part of a geological-survey team, Jason didn't see a need to be overly creative with this mission. His real name would work fine and might even be helpful with some of the native people. After the plane touched down, Jason grabbed his laptop case from beneath the seat in front of him and made his way through the terminal to claim his baggage.

Denny had arranged a guide who was familiar with the coastline and knew the native population well. Jason grabbed his bags from the carousel and took a cab to his hotel. He'd chosen the Anchorage Grand Hotel for its central downtown location since he wasn't sure how his guide would suggest they travel up to the strait.

He arrived at the hotel, and was pleased to find a message waiting for him from the local guide. His briefing materials indicated that she worked with a travel agency and came highly recommended. Jason checked in and used his cell phone to call her. He suggested they meet for dinner to discuss his needs and her ideas. She sounded bright and ready to work, and if nothing else, having someone along who knew the area well would be a good thing.

He took a brief nap, then headed down to the dining room to wait for Tina Kanut. When she stepped into the restaurant, Jason did a quick double take. For some reason, he'd expected her to look more like the native guides he'd used for missions in the Middle East or in Africa—weathered, worn and hardened by the conditions of their lifestyle.

In person, Tina looked younger than her picture,

probably in her late twenties or early thirties, with the dark hair and eyes of her native Inuit people. She was breathtakingly beautiful. The photo Denny had shown him didn't do her justice. She moved with the kind of grace usually reserved for dancers, and her frame was tall and lean. He caught her eye and waved her over. She waved back and headed his way.

Jason knew that a woman like this could be a distraction on a mission—he was a man, after all—but if she proved competent, then it would be up to him to control his urges and stay focused. It wouldn't be fair to deny her the job simply because she happened to be knockout gorgeous.

He stood as she reached the table and offered his hand. "Jason Siku," he said, keeping his handshake firm and businesslike. "It's nice to meet you."

"Hi, Mr. Siku," she said. "Tina Kanut. It's nice to meet you, too."

A sexy voice, too, Jason thought, then forced himself to business. "Please, sit down." He resisted the urge to pull out her chair.

They both sat, and he signaled the waitress, who came over and took their drink orders. Scotch on the rocks for him, and a soft drink for her. They made meaningless small talk until the drinks arrived, then turned to business.

"So," Tina said. "The agency told me that you were looking for a native guide, all the way up to the Bering Strait. That's a long haul from here."

He nodded. "Yes," he said. "My thought is to fly to Nome, then head up along the coast."

She considered this for a moment, then said, "That makes the most sense, but it's not an easy trek, Mr. Siku. There are only a few roads leading out of Nome, and even those only go a short distance. After that, it's ATVs and hard work."

"I can handle it," he said. "I've traveled all over the world in some of the roughest country this planet has to offer."

Tina laughed quietly. "I've heard that before, too," she said, then changed tack. "What are you looking for specifically?" she asked. "I might be able to save you a lot of time if I know what you're after."

"Nothing in particular," he said. "The company I work for does detailed, computer-based mapping, combining physical inspections, satellite imagery and aerial photography. They send me out in advance of the regular team so I can get the lay of the land, let them know of any problems the ground team might encounter before they arrive."

"You don't work for an oil company, do you?" Her tone was one of pure suspicion.

"An oil company?" Jason asked, honestly perplexed. "No. Pretty much I'm a what-you-see-is-what-you-get kind of guy. Why would you think I work for an oil company?"

"No reason," she said, her voice filled with doubts.

"Look, Tina," he said. "I need a guide and you're who my company arranged for. The agency says you're the best. I'm not sure where all your suspicions are coming from, but I can assure you that I only want to tour the region and head back home."

"My suspicions are pretty well founded," she said. "You wouldn't be the first native or half native who's come up here, working for one of the oil companies and looking to exploit my people."

Jason chuckled in sudden understanding. "Well, you're right about part of that, anyway," he said. "Yes, I'm half-Inuit. But I grew up in an orphanage and I don't know much at all about my biological parents, where they live or anything else. To be honest, I don't really care. I'm just here to do a job and go home." He let his tone turn more serious. "I don't have any interest in doing anything other than my scout survey job, and then I'm gone."

"Siku is a common enough name, but there is something vaguely familiar about you," she said. "I just…" She sighed deeply, then straightened. "Never mind. And please excuse me. I'm sorry, Mr. Siku. I don't mean to come across so defensive. There are a lot of unscrupulous people in the world and a few of them have turned their eyes to this part of the world, hoping to cash in on the natives. I don't take jobs that will put them in danger or leave them exposed to more problems than they already have."

"Call me Jason," he said. "And don't worry about it. I'd rather you be up-front about any concerns you might have now than have to get a new guide along the way. Good ones are hard to replace and the agency said they were sending me the best. I'm not here to search out my family or take advantage of your people in any way."

She nodded, and then said, "They are your people, too, even if you don't know them."

Her words struck a chord with his own thoughts of the previous weeks, but he knew that family would only be another distraction during a difficult assignment. "Maybe," he said, "but I'm afraid that I've never really seen it that way. And while this trip might present an opportunity to search out my family, I am here for business."

"Fair enough," she said. "I'll be your guide. When do you want to leave?"

It was Jason's turn to smile. "Not so fast," he said. "Now it's my turn to ask some questions of you."

"Of course," she said. "What do you want to know?"

"How long have you been a guide?" he asked.

"I started doing wilderness guide work with my grandfather when I was sixteen," she said. "So…almost twenty years now. Usually, I work with groups wanting to see native villages or the national parks and wildlife, but I've done other types of tours, too."

Jason nodded. "Such as?"

"A lot of corporate folks think that they can make a lot of money if they find the right angle," she said. "For a while, they were willing to pay me really well to tour them around and prove how wrong they were." She laughed. "I stopped when I realized that they were never going to go away. The hunger for land and cheap, exploitable labor never ends. That's why there's so many mining operations up here—but at least they tend to pay well, even if the work is backbreaking and dangerous."

"Fair enough," he said. "What kind of challenges can we expect on our journey?"

"That depends," she replied. "You've picked a good time to come up here. In early fall, the temperatures are decent and the wildlife hasn't gotten really hungry yet. We'll stay in the villages whenever we can. Aside from panic, do you know what kills most people wandering around in the wilderness?"

He shook his head.

"Lack of awareness," she continued. "People don't pay attention to what's going on around them—the way the ice might be cracked or weak in certain areas, signs of dangerous animals, that kind of thing. Up here, it pays to be observant."

"You might be surprised how many parts of the world that rule applies to," he said. "Still, I'll make a point of remembering." He laughed. "Of course, I make a living by being observant, so perhaps we'll do just fine."

"I haven't lost anyone yet," she said. "Is there anything else you'd like to know?"

Signaling the waitress, Jason said, "Just two things. What do you want for dinner and when do we leave?"

"We can catch a flight to Nome tomorrow," she said. "Alaska Airlines has several flights a day."

"And dinner?" he asked.

She smiled and once again he was struck by her attractive appearance, which didn't seem to match her job. "I'm going to have dinner with some friends tonight, Jason. Then I'm going to get some rest. I'll pick you up tomorrow morning and we'll go to the airport."

"You're not going to let me buy you dinner?" he asked, disappointed. The company of a beautiful woman made almost every mission more bearable. No strings, just temporary pleasure.

"No," she said. "I wouldn't want you to think it was my tip. Usually those come *after* the work."

"I was just being friendly," he protested. "Nothing wrong with having a bite of dinner together, is there?"

"Actually," she said, "there is. I don't socialize with my clients. I don't get personal with my clients. I take them where they want to go, show them what they want to see, keep them safe and send them on their way." She finished off the last of her soda, then added, "Just business, okay? I'll see you in the morning. Eight o'clock sharp." Tina nodded to him, then turned and walked out of the restaurant.

While admitting to himself that she looked just as good leaving as she had coming in, Jason found himself a bit flabbergasted. He hadn't made a pass or suggested they go upstairs for a slow tango between the sheets. But it was rare that he got the rough brush-off just like that.

"I just asked what she wanted to eat," he muttered to himself.

"I'm sorry, sir?" the waitress asked.

He looked up, realized that she'd been standing there waiting.

"Nothing," he said. "Never mind."

"The lady won't be staying for dinner?"

"Apparently not," he said. He glanced at the menu again, then said, "I'll have the burger, please."

"Struck out, huh?" the waitress asked, a grin forming on her features. "Don't worry. It happens to the best of them."

"Not to me," he muttered again, then forestalled her asking what he'd said by adding, "I'd also like a salad, but after the main course."

"Yes, sir," she said. "Can I get you anything else?"

"No, thank you," he replied.

"Save room for dessert," she suggested. "Our espresso torte is heavenly."

"I'll keep it in mind," he said. The waitress walked away and Jason turned his thoughts inward once more.

He had a guide, but she was also more than a little uptight. And automatically suspicious. He'd have to be careful to keep her focused on what she believed he was here for. That she was protective of her people was understandable, but the woman herself seemed contradictory. One second she was nice, straightforward and engaged. The next, she was practically telling him off for asking her what she wanted to eat. There was something about her that struck him as familiar, too, but he couldn't place what it was.

Still, so long as he moved carefully, she would be easy to keep distracted. At least until he disappeared while looking for the sub. He would have to try to think of something to keep her from sending out search parties for him.

He sighed. Another complication—and a female one at that—was not what this mission needed. Resigned to making the best of it, he settled in to wait for his meal.

4

The road out of Nome was little better than a rutted concrete path, but Tina quickly proved herself competent. Using a large SUV and a trailer with two ATVs, she guided their vehicle around the worst of the potholes and hazards, while simultaneously pointing out sites of interest along the way. She was a good guide, Jason realized, knowledgeable about the area, its history, people and animals. She didn't talk too much, but kept the conversation light and interesting. And completely impersonal.

The landscape itself was one of harsh beauty. Dark-brown-and-green tundra grasses dominated the view, with distant snowcapped mountains. Birds and rabbits were plentiful, and when he rolled down the window, the wind from the ocean was crisp and cold and hinted of the coming winter. This was not a place for the weak, and those who survived here—in the city or in the surrounding areas—had a good reason to be proud.

Several hours after leaving the small town, the road wasn't even a pretense anymore, but simply a wide gravel trail. Not long after, Tina pulled the SUV off to the side and said, "This is where the going gets rough. We'll leave the truck here and take the ATVs the rest of the way."

"You just leave your truck?" he asked, surprised.

She shrugged. "Why not? It's not like anyone is likely to steal it. Where would they go?" She gestured at the empty scene around them. "Even if they went into Nome, someone would recognize it. Theft isn't very common up here. Everyone knows everyone else."

"Makes sense," he said. He opened his door and climbed out of the truck, stretching his legs. "Can I help you unload everything?"

"Sure," she said. "Do you know how to drive an ATV?"

He nodded. "I've used them many times."

"Good," she said. "Then we can skip the lesson. I've already loaded all our gear onto the cargo racks, so all we have to do is back them down and we're good to go."

Jason climbed up on the trailer, while Tina lowered the gate. "One word of caution," she said. "If you haven't driven one of these with a trailer attached, they don't corner as tightly. Also, there's plenty of icy patches, even some snow in places, so keep your speed down. If you hit an ice patch going too fast, we'll have to bring in bulldozers to find your body."

He grinned and started the ATV's engine. "Got it," he said, putting the machine in gear and guiding it down the ramp. He noticed how she watched him, making sure that he wasn't all talk and actually knew what he was doing. He pulled his ATV over to one side, and watched as she drove the second ATV off the trailer. When it was clear, he lifted the gate and shut it firmly, latching it into place.

He crossed back over to his own machine. "Are we ready?" he asked.

"As ready as we can be," she said. "I'll take the lead. Just follow my trail and we should hit the coast in about an hour. From there, we'll go north. If you want to stop for anything, just honk the horn."

"You're the boss," he said. He slipped a pair of goggles over his eyes and pulled up his hood, fastening it with Velcro. There was no point in starting out cold.

She set off toward the coast, keeping a steady pace, but not going too fast. Even if he'd lost sight of her, the tracks made by her ATV in the heavy tundra grass would be easy enough to follow. Aside from startling the occasional bird or rabbit, there was little to see. Once, in the far distance, he thought he saw a moose, but with the cloud cover and shadowy light, he wasn't certain.

According to the compass, Tina had begun bearing slightly to the north. If she was following a trail, he certainly couldn't see it, but it was entirely possible she didn't need one. Some people had a compass in their head, and were never truly lost. Off to his left and at quite a distance, Jason spotted what looked like some old, ruined buildings. He slowed to a stop and honked the horn.

Ahead of him, Tina slowly circled back, then pulled alongside him. "What's up?" she asked.

He pointed at the ruins. "I'd like to take a look at those," he said. "I find such places interesting."

"There's not much to see there," she said. "It's an abandoned Inuit summer village from a long time ago. They left when the waters near here were fished out by nonnatives."

"Still," he said. "I'd like to see it, if you don't mind stopping."

She shrugged. "You're the client." Turning her ATV in that direction, she set a somewhat slower pace toward the abandoned village. Jason followed in her wake, thinking about what it must be like for people to have to move their homes because others had destroyed their way of life.

Just as they reached the copse of trees that sheltered the buildings, Tina jammed on her brakes and abruptly turned around. Her eyes were wide. "No questions," she snapped. "We've got to get out of here right now!"

Startled, Jason stopped his ATV completely. "Wha—" he began to ask, even as she motored by him, going as fast as she could, the trailer bouncing wildly behind her.

He turned to look at the buildings, wondering what could have possibly set her off like that, when he realized that there were several men coming out of the trees. Dressed in winter camouflage, they were heavily armed and already moving into position to open fire.

"Not the friendliest natives," he said, diving off the ATV to use it for cover as the first shots rang out.

Bullets dug up the turf near his ATV. Jason slipped off his goggles and put on the shooting glasses. Now was as good a time as any for a field test. He drew his Glock from beneath his coat, checked the load, then popped up over the seat of his vehicle, sighting on the closest man, who was running toward him.

Jason exhaled and fired. The lenses of his glasses simultaneously tracked the round and his visual response. The bullet took the man just below the collarbone and punched through the other side, shattering his shoulder blade. He screamed and fell to the ground, his blood staining the grass and the patchy snow a bright crimson.

"Four and a half inches high at twenty-nine feet," he estimated, gauging the feedback that ran in a tiny font along the bottom of his lenses. "And slightly to the right."

The other two men dived for cover of their own, one behind a log and another behind a small cluster of stones. Neither one seemed too interested in retrieving their bleeding friend, whose moans could be heard between the shots they were firing for cover.

They weren't using military-grade weapons, he realized, but heavy-duty bolt-action hunting rifles. When they paused to reload, he risked another glance over the top of the ATV. One man had moved closer, crawling through the scrub grass. He'd drawn a revolver. He popped his head up every few feet to take another look. There wasn't anything special about him that Jason could see. He looked quite a bit like a hunter who'd been caught poaching, but either way, he and his friends seemed serious about doing harm.

As the man low-crawled past his wounded comrade, he muttered, "Shut up, will you?"

The momentary distraction was all Jason needed. He slipped around the front tires, sighted and fired. This time, his aim was perfect—the round entered the man's forehead one inch above his eyebrows and dead center. The force shoved him upright, his features straining with shock, and Jason fired again, aiming center mass and driving him backward into the ground, dead before he landed.

"That's two for me and none for you," he called out to the last man. "I advise you to throw down your weapons and come out where I can see you."

There was a long pause, then, "You won't shoot?"

Grinning to himself, Jason called, "No, I won't shoot. Come on out."

He watched as the man tossed a rifle to the ground, then stepped out from behind the cluster of rocks, his hands raised. His features were unremarkable—fair skin, blue eyes, a mop of sweaty brown hair.

Jason got to his feet and closed the space between them. Behind him, he could hear the sound of Tina's ATV returning. She must have realized that he hadn't followed or had been watching and figured out that the situation was under control.

"Who are you?" Jason barked at the man. "And why'd you try to shoot us?"

The man stepped closer. "No one you know," he

said. His hand was a blur as he reached for the handgun behind his back. Jason didn't even blink, but dropped two rounds into the man's chest, killing him instantly. He fell over backward, his scream of pain cut short as the last of the air left his lungs.

"Stupid fool," Jason said to himself. He looked down at the wounded man on the ground and assessed his condition. He'd lost too much blood and was already fading into unconsciousness. They were too far from anywhere to save him. "Sorry," he said, "but this is the best I can do for you." He shot him once in the head, ending the man's misery.

Behind him, he heard a sharp intake of breath and turned to see Tina staring at him, her eyes wide with outrage. "You…you just shot those men in cold blood!"

"What?" Jason asked, even as he loaded a fresh clip. "I did not!"

"You did! I saw you. The one man surrendered and the other was wounded and you just…you just killed them like it was nothing."

Shaking his head, Jason moved to gather up their weapons. He tossed them in a pile between the three bodies. "The man who surrendered was going for a gun behind his back," he explained. "Roll him over and take a look if you don't believe me. As for the man on the ground…he was going to die, Tina. A slow and painful death. I killed him because we're too far away from anywhere to do anything for him."

"Right," she said, her voice rising an octave. "So now you're a doctor, too?" She stumped over to the second man and rolled him over, then gasped. The gun he'd been going for was on the ground beneath him. Then she turned to look at the last man he'd killed. The pool of blood that had spread from beneath his back was testament to how badly he'd been wounded.

Tina turned back to Jason and nodded. "All right," she said, angry. "Fine, you were telling the truth. But where did you learn to fight like that? You killed three armed men and never even broke a sweat."

"I grew up in a rough neighborhood," Jason joked, then he turned serious when he saw that she wouldn't accept a flip answer. "I've been in a lot of tight scrapes over the years—the Middle East, Africa, Bosnia to name a few. You either learn how to fight in places like that or you die. I learned how to shoot pretty well."

Looking over the bodies once more, she shook her head. "That's the understatement of the year, if I've ever heard one. Now what do we do?"

"Check them out. Look the place over, then move on with our journey," he said.

"We're not going to take them back?"

"To Nome?" he asked. "Why would we? We can let the local authorities know what's happened when we reach a village. Someone must have a phone somewhere."

She laughed. "No, there aren't too many phones out here, but the village we're going to stay in has short-wave radio."

"That should work," he said. "In the meantime, let's see if we can figure out why these guys came out shooting. Even if they were poachers, it doesn't make a lot of sense to attack us the way they did." He turned to move toward the buildings and she followed along behind.

"I have a guess," she said, her voice hesitant. "They were probably smugglers."

"Drugs?" he asked.

"Guns," she replied. "They move them from here and down into Canada, where someone else sells them cheap into the United States. I read an article about it in the paper."

"People are running guns in Alaska?" he asked, surprised. "Seems like a hard way to go about it. There are easier ways to get things into the U.S. than trekking across the Alaskan tundra."

"Maybe," she said, "but think of it this way. Out here, what are the chances of running into anyone, let alone law enforcement? Out here, we're mostly on our own. And there's a whole lot of big empty between here, Canada and the U.S."

"True enough," he said.

They stopped in front of a dilapidated hut. The boot tracks on the ground were fresh and he followed them inside. Sure enough, there were several large crates. He opened the top one to find it filled to the brim with Russian AN-94 assault rifles and clips. They were brand-new.

"Jesus," he whispered. "Why were those guys shooting at me with hunting rifles when they had these?"

Tina's voice was equally quiet. "I don't know, but I've heard rumors that people who cross the smugglers are usually found during the spring thaw. Maybe they didn't have ammunition?"

Jason quickly opened the other crates. He found more rifles and clips, along with one set of the older-style LAW rockets used by the U.S. military forces until the late eighties or so. But no ammunition. "You're right," he said. "No ammo. Just the weapons and the rockets. I suppose I should be glad they weren't able to use one of these on me."

"Yes," she said, "you should. Can we go now? I want to get out of here in case someone comes looking for them. This could be where they were dropping them."

He looked around the ancient building once more, then shook his head. "It's an inconvenient spot for a drop point, but you're right. We need to keep moving. How far is the coast from here?"

"Not far," she said. "Maybe three or four miles."

"Okay," he said. "Go get one of the ATVs and I'll get to work."

"Work?" she asked. "What are you going to do?"

"Trust me," he said, turning away to begin resealing the crates.

She sighed and stomped out of the room. Not long after, he heard the sound of her pulling up on one of the machines. The engine cut out and he called to her, "Come in and lend me a hand."

Tina came back into the building. "Now what?"

"Now we load the crates onto the trailers and haul this stuff to the coast."

"Are you crazy?" she half yelled. "You're going to steal from the smugglers?"

"No," he said, "I'm going to return their merchandise. The rifles are Russian. The rocket launchers are probably black market, sold out of Vietnam or some- where else in Southeast Asia. It's only fair that I put them back into the sea, where they can make their way home."

"Let's just go," she said. "Let the authorities deal with it."

"Help me or not," he said, his voice turning cold. "If this is a drop point, then these weapons will eventually wind up in the United States and that puts a lot of people at risk. I won't allow that to happen."

For a long moment, it looked as if she was going to argue, ask questions or put up a fight, but then she sighed and kept whatever was on her mind to herself. Jason suspected he'd be hearing more about it later.

Without another word, she moved to the end of one of the crates and together, they quickly loaded the trailer. Once all the crates had been loaded, he checked the other buildings to make sure there wasn't anything else left behind.

"All right," he said. "Now, I want you to drive that machine down to the coast and wait for me there. Just give me a bearing. I'm going to make sure our dead friends here aren't left out for scavengers."

She shuddered dramatically. "I'd rather not know. Just head due east for two miles, then bear north. You'll find the coast without a problem. I'll look for you."

"Good enough," he said. "Now get going. We don't have much light left and I want to find shelter before dark."

She nodded once, then left. Jason got to work, dragging the bodies into the abandoned Inuit building and covering them as best he could. The door was long since gone, but with the cold and their winter gear, they might not give off a scent that would attract predators—at least for a little while. Once he was done with that, he returned to his own ATV and headed for the coast.

His mind worked at the situation rapidly. Obviously, Tina knew more about the smuggling going on in the area than she'd read in some newspaper article. Just as obvious was the fact that if these smugglers could get large crates of weapons into this area from Russia, they'd have no problem at all importing other weapons, too. Like bombs.

If a terrorist group decided to infiltrate using this method, there'd be little to no chance of knowing it before it was too late. His mission parameters had suddenly expanded. Now he had to find the sub…and also figure out a way to stop the smuggling operation. He'd have to get word to Denny about what he'd discovered as soon as possible.

Tina had said there were no phones up here, but Jason had a satellite phone and other advanced communications equipment in his gear. At the first opportunity, he'd check in with Denny and Room 59 and find out what they wanted him to do. Surely they would recognize the additional threat and move to put a stop to it.

He clocked the distance and it wasn't long until he found the tracks from Tina's vehicle. There was no way to wipe them out…and if the smugglers wanted vengeance, it was only a matter of time until they found out which direction they'd gone. He could be in for the fight of his life.

What was he truly fighting for? he suddenly wondered.

He shook his head, plagued again by questions that he'd never seriously considered before. None of these questions mattered. Not right now. Right now, he had a mission to accomplish. Everything else was secondary to that.

In the far distance, he saw Tina waving her arms at him. They had a long way to go before they'd reach the village she'd shown him on the map, and already the evening darkness was closing in.

5

Jason pulled up alongside Tina at the edge of the village. He could see the shapes of houses and they moved into the village. They had arrived well after dark and the cold was beginning to seep through the layers of clothing and give his skin that vague itching-burning sensation that came with freezing temperatures. Tina hadn't spoken a single word since they met back up along the trail and argued about her not listening to his instructions. He supposed he should have expected it.

She had gotten rid of most of the weapons, but had kept one crate containing a variety of the arms they had found. She said she wanted to be able to prove to the authorities that what they were saying was real. Jason had been furious, but understood why she hadn't listened. In truth, he didn't plan on dealing with the local authorities at all, but now he'd probably have to.

Either way, ever since then, there'd been nothing but silence between them. The quiet was more worrisome than the millions of questions that he knew must be rattling around in her head.

Tina pulled her ATV to a stop next to a large cabin, gesturing vaguely for him to follow as she climbed off her machine and headed up the steps of the cabin. Shutting his own machine down, Jason stood and stretched, considering the load of weapons that they were carrying. They had covered them with a tarp, but he felt uneasy about leaving them out in the open. Anyone might happen along, get curious and find themselves armed with a Russian assault rifle.

Tina ran back down the steps.

"Leave them," she said, her voice almost as cold as the air around them. "No one is going to bother anything out here, and unless you want to freeze I suggest you get inside."

"Isn't there anywhere safer we can store them?" he asked as the wind began to pick up speed with surprising force.

"It's not like we just pulled into New York with a U-Store-It around every damn corner!" she yelled over the howling winds. "If you want to babysit a crate, you're more than welcome. I'm going inside."

She climbed the stairs again. Jason didn't hesitate this time. He was only half a step behind her as she pushed open the cabin door. He turned as the wind ripped the door out of Tina's hand and slammed it against the wall. Reaching past her, he grabbed it and leaned his weight against it, pushing it shut. The sudden silence was almost as eerie as the sudden onslaught of wind had been.

"I thought the weather didn't start getting danger-ous for another month or so," he said. "Where did that come from?"

His guide laughed harshly. "Why did you think you were wearing all that gear? In case the weather got bad in another month?" She sighed, then said, "Those winds can come off the ocean any time of the year, es-pecially as the season changes and the jet stream along with it. They'll freeze an unprotected person to death in very short order, but they are fairly rare this time of year."

Tina looked thoroughly disgruntled. She pulled the cap from her head and crossed to the fire that was already burning in the fireplace, careful not to stand too close and cause her hands to ache more than they must have been already. She must have arranged for the cabin in advance; the fire had obviously been going for a while, as a nice pile of hardwood coals was already settled into the grate. Jason swept through the rooms doing a security check. The two bedrooms were fur-nished identically, down to the comforter and remotes for the televisions on the dresser. A clean set of towels and a welcome basket with coffee and hot chocolate sat on the dresser.

Jason returned to the living room. Tina still hadn't moved, and the tension in her features hadn't lessened by so much as a single fine line.

"Are you all right?" he asked.

She tilted her head, her lips compressed tightly

together and her eyes narrowed. She no longer rubbed her hands for warmth, but held them fisted at her sides.

"You're fucking kidding me, right? No one gets shot at, sees other men shot and killed, then tows cartons full of munitions through the Alaskan tundra and is 'all right.' Just what the hell is going on here? Who the hell are you?"

"I told you I work for a survey—" he began, but she cut him off immediately.

"Bullshit!" she snapped. "Complete and utter. I've seen a lot of surveyors come through here. They carry maps, advanced GPS systems, charts and notepads, and on occasion a flask of whiskey on their hip." She jabbed a finger in his direction. "What they don't carry is semiautomatic handguns, and they sure as hell don't fight like you did!"

Jason folded his arms across his chest. He had only been in this position one other time in his career. Back when he was doing black ops for the CIA, his cover was blown in Peru while he was trying to get to a double agent. He got caught in the midst of a drug exchange that went sour, and the whole operation had blown up in his face. He ended that situation with the expediency of simply killing the guy, but that man hadn't been necessary for his mission. For right now, Tina was. If necessary, he would kill her, but he preferred not to. And his cover wasn't completely blown; she was suspicious, but it seemed as if that was more of a personality trait than anything else.

He wasn't sure what he should be more concerned about—the beautiful woman scowling at him across the room or Denny Talbot's reaction to all this when he had specifically asked for little to no body count. The three dead men back at the ancient village would not, in Denny's estimation, constitute a minimal body count. One thing he was sure of was that being treated like an errant schoolboy by a woman he'd known for only a day was intolerable. He would worry about Denny tomorrow. Right now, he had to deal with Tina. And he couldn't let his anger at her treatment of him get the better of him.

"Is there anything I can say that is going to make you feel better about any of this?" he asked. "It's not like I planned on running into a bunch of gunrunners."

"You could start by telling me the truth about who you are," she said.

"I don't suppose you would be willing to accept that I acted on instinct?" he asked, allowing a half smile to cross his lips.

"Not with shot groupings like that," she said. "I've been on more hunting trips than I can count and have been shooting most of my life. I don't know anyone up here who shoots with that kind of calm and accuracy." She shook her head. "Especially not when someone is shooting back."

He sighed heavily. "Look, Tina, I'm afraid that there isn't anything much more that I can tell you. I spent some time in the military—Special Forces, actually—though it was a long time ago. Those guys shot at us and I reacted. Call it muscle memory if you want."

He walked toward her, but she held up her hand and backed away shaking her head.

"I'm not buying," she said. "I may not be a genius, but I can tell when someone isn't telling me the truth. What kind of surveyor carries a gun?"

"One who wants to live—" he started to answer, but she held up a hand once more to silence him.

"I'm done for the night. I'm going to bed and tomorrow morning I'm going back to Nome and I'm reporting all this to the authorities. You can finish your so-called surveying without me. I'm not about to get my ass shot off for what I'm getting paid."

Trying another approach, he said, "That would be a shame, it really is such a nice ass…"

She turned and slapped him. Hard.

"Okay, wrong thing to say," he admitted, rubbing his cheek. "Tina, hold on a second. Please."

She arched an eyebrow but kept her silence.

"Look, I need you. You're the best guide around. And I need the best to do my job right. If you won't accept that what happened out there was just pure survival instinct, then I don't know what to tell you. I had no idea that those men were there, but I won't apologize for choosing our lives over theirs. I didn't go looking for trouble and I hope you can believe that. But I'm not very big on turning the other cheek when someone tries to shoot me, either."

"I don't know what to believe," she said. "You sound sincere enough, but something about your story doesn't ring true for me."

"I can respect that," he replied. "But truth often has a lot to do with perspective. The bottom line is that I need your help."

"My help for what?"

"To do my job. I'm not here to hurt you or anyone else. I've told you that before and I meant it. But I'm not going to stand down and do nothing while someone is shooting at me, either. I've been in dangerous situations before, and if those were small-time operators, they would have hidden or tried to scare us off. They're part of a larger group and if they're operating around here, it could jeopardize not just me getting my job done, but a lot of your people, too."

Jason could see the confusion, then defeat roll across her face. He knew he had her, at least for the moment, but he also knew he couldn't push her too quickly.

He ran a hand through his hair, more tired than he'd realized. "Look, just sleep on it, okay? We can talk more in the morning. We're both exhausted. I'll see if I can shed a little more light on the situation for you then. Besides, we'll have to talk to the local authorities and get these weapons in the hands of the right people."

Finally, she nodded. "Okay," she said. "I'll sleep on it. Right now, I'm too tired to think anyway."

Tina stomped to her room and slammed the door. Jason heard the lock click into place. She might be willing to listen to him a little more, but she obviously didn't trust him. He checked the windows in the living room and kitchen, placing small motion sensors on the rails that would send a signal to his watch. He placed another one by the door.

Convinced that the cabin was as safe as he could make it, Jason stripped off his outer layers and sank down onto the couch. Propping his feet up on the table, he rolled his head back, contemplating what a disaster the mission had been thus far.

JASON AWOKE to the smell of fresh coffee. He propped himself up on his elbow and pressed the light on his watch. Five-thirty. He swung his legs over the side of the couch and ran his hands through his hair, then slipped on a shirt and headed into the kitchen.

Tina was standing at the counter. Her red fleece sweatshirt was unzipped, showing off her black tank top and nicely rounded breasts. Her hair was tucked behind her ears, eyes closed, as she took a long sip of coffee. Jason could feel the room heat up—or at least his own body temperature—but put his libido in check, knowing he would have to play nice if she was going to remain an asset to him. He also knew that if this got too complicated, he might have no choice but to eliminate her and for that reason alone he needed to keep his distance. He allowed himself one more glance and then put the foolish thoughts away.

"You're awake," she said, her voice much less tense than the night before.

"I could never resist the smell of fresh coffee."

"Help yourself," she said.

Jason pulled a cup out of the cupboard and poured the coffee. He stood silent. Psychology 101. Most people hate silence and will say anything to fill it, even if what they say is a mistake. He had played human-behavior games too many times and he always won. No matter how calculating or bright his adversary.

Tina took a deep breath.

Here it comes, he thought.

She shifted from one foot to the other.

Oh, yeah. She's mine, he added to himself.

"You know, maybe we should start over," she said.

He tried not to smile in victory, but he knew he was failing when he saw her wrinkled brow.

"I wasn't saying that to be funny," she said.

"I know," he said.

She set her coffee on the counter, reached out her hand and said, "Tina Kanut, guide, trapper and on occasion not a half-bad dancer. And you are?"

Jason grinned and stared at her hand. He put his coffee down, as well, and put both of his hands on hers. He shook his head and she pulled her hand away.

"I could just leave you here," she said.

"You could, but you won't."

"How do you know that?"

"Pretty simple. You know if I was going to hurt you, I would have done so when I was already getting rid of the bodies. You also know that those were not nice men and that I was only protecting my backside. And finally…"

Jason paused, knowing that she wouldn't be able to go on without hearing the last and he did have so much fun with word games sometimes. In a life like he lived, the little amusements were all one sometimes had.

"Finally, what?" she asked.

"Finally I wasn't just protecting my backside. I was also protecting yours."

She pondered for a moment and then looked at him with renewed conviction. "You know, that's one of the few things you've said that I do believe."

"Why?" he asked.

"Because you slept out in the living room on the sofa instead of in the bedroom," she said. "If someone tried to come in during the night, you wanted to be between me and them, didn't you?"

He nodded, surprised that she had even noticed.

"I don't trust you," she said, her tone decisive. "And I don't think you've told me the whole truth. But what I need to know is if you're here to hurt someone. I'm not just taking you to any village. I'm taking you to *my* village. If you can't or won't tell me the truth about your purpose up here, I guess that's your problem, but I have to know that you're not out to hurt the people I care most about."

"Scout's honor," he said without hesitation. "I'm not here to hurt anyone."

She pushed away from the counter and started walking to her room, but stopped in front of him. Her hip brushed his as she said, "I bet you weren't ever really a Boy Scout."

Jason watched the way she walked, her flannel pants perfectly outlining her behind. "No," he whispered to himself, completing the old joke, "but I got kicked out for eating a Brownie or two."

JASON WAITED for Tina in the living room. She came out of her room with a bag in tow.

"How soon can we make it to your village?" he asked.

"It won't take too long—about a half day—but we need to talk to whatever local authorities are here first and turn over those weapons. I imagine that could see us here for an extra day."

"Why don't we take them along with us?" Jason suggested. "Then we can report them to the authorities in your village. You probably know them, and my time-table doesn't get held up. I'm on a bit of a schedule."

"You don't have any intention of giving those weapons over to the police, do you?" she asked.

"If you'll recall," he said, striving to keep his voice calm, "I didn't want you to bring them along in the first place. But the answer to your question is no. I don't have time to deal with local officials right now. You can believe me when I say that those weapons will get turned over to the proper authorities, more so even than the local cops, who would probably just sell them at the next police auction or keep them for themselves."

Tina didn't say anything, but Jason could tell she was considering what he said carefully.

"Not to mention," he continued, "that it's hard to run an operation like that without it drawing notice, especially in small towns or communities where everyone knows everyone else. The odds are good that someone pretty high up on the law-enforcement side of things around here is on the take, maybe even actively partici-pating, and they are not going to take kindly to our taking away a large chunk of their bread and butter."

She tossed up her hands in surrender. "Fine, fine," she said. "But at the least, I want to talk to the local cops in my village. I know them, and I can't imagine any of them are involved. Fair enough?"

Jason nodded his head in agreement, while thinking

about how he could stall her again on the issue once they arrived at her village.

"Can we go, then?" he asked.

"Sure," she said. "The sooner we leave, the sooner we'll get there. I'd hate for your timetable to be off by more than a minute or two." The sarcasm in her voice was cutting, but he ignored it.

Instead, he headed outside, gently pulling her along behind him. "Good deal," he said. He'd picked up his little motion sensors while she was getting ready to leave and had gathered his own things together. The ATVs were right where they had left them. The town was just beginning to wake up and Jason didn't want to get stuck answering questions about missing members of the local population. Before he moved the bodies, Jason had done quick scans of their fingerprints and took digital pictures of their faces. When they settled at the cabin he sent them to Room 59 via a satellite uplink from his PDA. The response had been fairly quick. All three had rap sheets that weren't far from what they had been caught at yesterday and two were from the village that they were currently situated in. Denny had sent a message asking for a mission update as soon as possible.

They warmed up the ATVs and were quickly back on the road. Jason was getting used to the cold. The sun was just beginning to peek through the slate-gray clouds on the eastern horizon. He was thankful that there was daylight available at all. In another couple of months, it would be perpetual night up here. On the other hand, that might have served his purposes better.

In his experience, the environment could help or hinder a mission and there was little predicting what the weather was really going to do from one day to the next. Up here, it could change in a minute, so he knew it would be wise for him to keep an eye on the weather.

Tina had mentioned to him that they would follow a road to the next village, and Jason kept waiting for it to appear, but it soon became apparent that her idea of a road was more like a vague path with some barely visible tire tracks tracing a route of some kind between the vast jumbles of rock they were crossing. Clumps of brown autumn grasses did little to brighten the landscape. The ATV bounced roughly, jarring his tailbone with each bump.

He thought about his guide. She wasn't like anyone he'd ever met. A beautiful distraction for sure, he reminded himself, watching her maneuver her vehicle around the worst of the bumps.

He hoped he could finish the mission and get out of here sooner rather than later. What his life didn't need right now was an additional complication…and women were always complicated.

6

After a couple of hours, they arrived at a small weatherworn wooden building that must have been a frequent stop for travelers along this route. Jason was more than happy to be off the ATV. While he'd traveled via almost every kind of transportation known to man, those experiences didn't make riding the ATV over rough terrain any more comfortable. He went to the small fire pit in the corner and found it stocked with dry firewood, tinder and kindling. He made quick work of getting the fire going and soon had the chill gone from the air.

The only furniture in the shack was a small wooden picnic table with benches. Tina opened her pack and pulled out a couple of cans of soup, popped off the tops and set them on the small grate by the fire. It only took a couple of minutes for them to heat up. She added a couple of apples and a plastic package of crackers. She removed the soup cans from the grate and put them on the table, then handed him a spoon. "Eat up," she said.

Jason couldn't have been more happy if he had been served a five-star meal.

"So how did you get into being a guide?" he asked between bites. "You mentioned your grandfather back at the hotel, but you're obviously bright and capable. Have you ever thought of leaving here?"

"You mean go be someone's gofer and live in the big city?" she asked.

"No, I didn't mean it like that, honest. I'm just... curious."

"I started hunting and fishing when I was a little girl. Of course, as a teenager there was nothing that I wanted more than to get away from my village or any other village up here. My parents died when I was ten, and my grandfather raised me. He indulged in my every whim and so when I said I wanted to go to the big city he was heartbroken but supported me anyway. My grandfather is a man who lives and respects our past and the roots of our culture.

"Anyway, I went to New York. I earned my degree and started working. I got to see and do quite a bit, but after a couple of years, I realized I hated my job. I hated the life I was living—or, more accurately— wasn't living. I went to the top of my apartment building one night and realized that while I might be closer to the sky way up there, I sure as hell couldn't see it. I started missing home. So I quit and came back here, but instead of working for someone else I started our guide operation," she said.

"You? I didn't know you owned the company. I thought the CEO was some guy named Tanuk."

She laughed. "Tanuk is my grandfather. He taught me everything I know about how to do this part of the job. His position is advisory, and he's a very wise man, but he's mostly a figurehead. Still, he's the head of my family and I would not dishonor that by acting like I could have done this all on my own."

Jason realized he'd never really had that kind of connection with anyone. As far as he was concerned his roots only went as far as the file that was sealed when he was eighteen. There were times, like recently, where he desperately wanted to have the foundation that she was talking about. He shook his head, trying to chase away the longing that was starting to fill him.

"What about your family?" she asked. "Do you have any clues besides your last name?"

"Not really," he said. "But I'm not here for that anyway. Maybe someday I'll come back up here and see what I can find out. I can't afford to get caught up in personal stuff when I'm on a deadline."

"So you don't have any family at all?" she asked, the tone in her voice one of sorrow.

"Just me," he said. "But that's all I've ever needed anyway."

"No man can stand alone forever," she whispered, unconsciously echoing Denny's words.

"Maybe not," he said, gruffly. "But he can try."

THEY TRAVELED another three hours before Jason began to see signs of life. As they rounded a small hill, avoiding a cluster of bone-white boulders, he saw the first cabin. Soon, more buildings appeared and Tina brought her ATV to a halt.

"Home," she said, pointing to the village at the bottom of the hill that was made up of buildings lined up in a jagged row that followed the edge of the water, but were far enough back that the occasional flooding wouldn't bother the residents.

Some of the buildings looked as modern as anything in Anchorage, but others showed they were from a forgotten era. Jason raised an eyebrow when he realized that at the far side of town there were a large number of tents erected. His gaze followed the line of tan canvas tents until they disappeared behind a low hill and went out of sight.

"What do you make of that?" he asked, pointing to the row of tents.

"Those tents belong to people who live on the outer rim. They come here to barter and trade for supplies before winter really sets in. Once it does, they have to make do with what they have. They are a beautiful people, living almost entirely off the land and staying close to their traditions."

She guided him to a small cabin on the outskirts of town. It wasn't nearly the size of the one that they had stayed in the night before, but was large enough to suit his needs. Jason set his bag on the sofa and surveyed the room. There was only one door in or out, and there was a woodstove instead of the roar of the fireplace.

"So, will this do?" she asked. "There's plenty of wood laid in, and the kitchen is stocked, too."

"Should be just fine," he said. "Where's your place?"

"Her place," said a deep voice from behind them, "is with me."

They both turned to see an old man standing in the doorway. He balanced his weight on his cane, pulling himself up to his full height, and doing his best to give off a sense of strength and intimidation.

"Grandfather," Tina said, "this is Jason Siku. He's the client I went to pick up in Anchorage."

She walked over to kiss him fondly on the cheek. He shared her eyes, but if he'd once had the same vibrant spirit as his granddaughter, time and the harsh roads he'd taken in life had worn it down to a nub. Still, he held the same air of confidence Jason had seen in many tribal elders. What he lacked in energy, he most likely made up for in hard-won wisdom.

"It's a pleasure to meet you, sir," Jason said. He moved closer to the old man and extended his hand.

Tanuk had a firm grip despite his age, and his dark, leathery skin had been weathered by the tough environment as much as by age. A small tattoo was inked at the base of his thumb, and though there was something familiar about it, Jason couldn't place it. He made a mental note to try to figure it out later.

He took Jason's hand and pulled him closer, his eyes staring at him intently.

"Siku," Tanuk said. "You must be related to Jesse. You look just like him."

Tina snapped her fingers. "You're right, Grandfather! He does look like Jesse. I've been trying to put my finger on why he looked so familiar. It never crossed my mind to consider someone right here in the village."

"Jesse?" Jason asked.

"He lives here," she said. "I'll be sure and introduce you. Maybe he's a long-lost relative or something. Now that I'm aware of it, you two really do look alike." She shook her head. "I can't believe I didn't put it together before. I'm supposed to be the observant one."

"Or maybe," Jason replied, thinking that running into a potential family member would only make this mission more difficult, "you could just show me around the village a little and then we can get some rest. There are a lot of areas I need to look at that could be of interest to my company."

Tina paused briefly, then nodded. "Sure. I'll meet you outside in ten."

Tina locked arms with her grandfather as they walked down the steps. The hard edge that he was coming to know in Tina's personality all but vanished as she walked along with the man who'd seen her through so much of her life. Once again, the thought crossed his mind that the choices he'd made in his life were causing him to miss out on other things, maybe things that were more important than he'd realized.

Maybe this might be the place to find those things, he thought. He shook his head. All of that would have to wait. The mission came first.

Maybe the difference between working for the CIA and Room 59 was that by their nature, Room 59 missions held the potential for more distractions and complications. Quite often, his previous work could have been boiled down to travel here, kill this dictator, come home. Repeat as needed. There were never personal aspects to the missions because it was never personal.

While he was waiting for Tina to return, Jason grabbed his GPS gear and some other equipment and put it all in a weatherproof backpack. He also changed clothes, opting for long silk underwear and multiple layers to try to stave off the cold a little better. He didn't know how long he'd be outside, but he absolutely needed to find a clear spot to set up the drop for his other equipment. His contacts would be expecting the signal and it would be a lot easier to handle in the little bit of daylight that was left rather than having to stumble around in the dark.

He left the cabin and found that Tina was waiting outside, but Tanuk was nowhere in sight.

"You must be tired," she said. "We can do this first thing tomorrow if you'd like."

The dusky horizon showed there was little time left to get the bearings he needed. He shook his head. "Just a quick tour so that I have a basic idea of the landscape and we'll call it a day," he said. "Timelines, you know."

"You keep mentioning this timeline," she replied. "If you shared it with me, I might be able to help you reach your goals."

"Unfortunately, I don't know the exact details myself quite yet. I'll get more information as I go along. The biggest hurry right now is just getting started. Once I do that, I'll know more from there."

"Still not willing to share the details?" she asked.

She made a soft *tsk*ing noise. "You know, my grandfather believes that it's unhealthy to keep everything bottled up inside, but, hey, it's your life." She gestured in the direction of the coast. "Let's take a little walk that way, so you can at least avoid falling into the ocean."

"Well, I don't think I need that much hand-holding," he said. "I can usually tell if I'm at a waterline."

"The waterline isn't the problem," she said. "It's the tundra grasses." She pointed to the small peninsula-shaped fingers of grass that pointed out into the ocean. "The water slips beneath the tundra grasses, eroding the soil beneath but they look safe enough. It's hard to tell where the solid ones are versus the ones that are little more than plants on top of a thick layer of muck until it's too late. Some of them are actually quite deep."

"Deep enough to get swept away in?" he asked.

"Not usually," she said. "But what can happen is that the ground basically turns into quicksand, or even a sort of natural cement. It can leave you stuck out there all night and as you might imagine, it can get downright chilly before the sun comes up. Here, let me show you."

They walked up a slope at the center of the village. People waved and called out greetings to Tina as they walked past, but like any other small village he'd ever been in, they were uncertain of strangers and said little to him. They finished the short climb and came upon a beautiful view of the ocean. The cove below them was empty, waiting for the evening tide to roll in.

"When I was a little girl," Tina said, "my dad would take me down there to dig for clams. We would wade out in the mud up to our hips with little shovels and buckets, searching out our dinner. Look over there." She pointed to one edge of the cove.

The ocean waves that were rolling in at that point took on a life of their own, rising up higher than a normal wave and crashing into the rocky edges.

"When the tide is out, the mud is soft and supple and easy to dig in, but unlike other places, the tide doesn't come in gradually here. It comes in as a wall of water, and in front of it, the temperature is subzero. Just before the tide comes in, the mud turns as hard as cement."

"You're joking," he said, amazed. "That fast?"

"Not in the least and please don't test the theory. More than one person has died in that very cove because they did not get out quickly enough. Our tide charts here aren't just for boats, but for people, too. A lot of folks still get their clams down there. They have to know for sure when the tide is coming in so they don't get stuck out there. A rescue is…difficult at best." She handed him a small sheaf of papers. "Here are the tide charts, which I thought you might want."

"Thanks," he said, taking the papers and slipping them inside his coat. "That's important information and I won't forget it. I'll be sure and include it in all of my data. I can actually set my watch with that kind of information."

Jason took out his GPS tracker. More than just a location device, it had a high-focus laser pointer that could assign satellite-coordinated grid coordinates of anything he aimed it at. It was a lot like using a laser to paint a bomb target, but instead of an explosion, the information he was painting would feed into the handheld device and create a virtual map. From there, he could use it to send the information back up to the satellite and get the data to Room 59. They would use the coordinates to arrange for his supply drop.

As he worked, Tina watched in silence, then said, "That's not like any other GPS system I've ever seen. How does it work?"

He briefly explained some of the device's more basic functions, leaving out that he was actually communicating with anyone, but including that it worked in tandem with a mapping satellite.

She whistled. "Very high-tech," she said.

He nodded, watching the final coordinates upload, and decided to change the subject. "So with the navy and coast guard patrolling these waters, not to mention all the national and corporate interests in this part of the world, how is it that a low-tech group like the one that we encountered the first day can manage to run a smuggling operation without being found out?"

"Easy," she said. "The people around here know the waters and the land. All of this may look small on a map, but it's a vast amount of space and there are limited resources—even for the military. Plus, there are a lot of things that go unnoticed when it comes to the villages. People just assume that we are a bunch of uneducated natives and leave us alone. But what they don't realize is that even if the heart of biological science isn't here, there isn't a single person in the world who's going to know more about the ocean or the creatures that live in it than the people right here in this village. And it's not because they are well read or have some mystic, native powers, but because the information has been passed down from generation to generation."

Jason pulled his binoculars from his pack and peered through them, looking at the next cove over. The houses stopped before then, but a small road led down to the water's edge.

"What's that over there?" he asked.

"The next cove?"

"Yes," he said.

"The villagers call it Blue Whale Bay. The water over there is deep, but sometimes when the tide goes out, animals can get stuck. A long time ago, a baby blue whale was beached there. The mud helped keep it wet, and the villagers did the rest until there was enough water to get him back out to sea. The name stuck."

"Not many people go there?" he asked.

"It's not like this is a hopping tourist spot," she said.

Jason finished inputting his notes into the handheld and marking everything he could until there wasn't enough light left to continue. "Guess that will have to do for a start," he said.

She agreed and they walked back down the slope to his cabin. She stopped at the bottom of the steps.

"What time do you want to start tomorrow?" she asked, a small smile playing over her lips. "I know you've got a schedule to keep."

Ignoring the sarcasm, he said, "How does six sound?"

"Early," she said, "but I'll be here." She waved then turned and moved off into the darkness. Clearly, she was going to try a different set of tactics to get the information she wanted.

Jason watched her retreating form for a minute more and then went into his cabin and shut the door, locking it behind him. He pulled the handheld out of his pack and hooked it to the laptop he'd set up on the small kitchen table. Syncing the data he'd gathered, he quickly created a four-dimensional map of the area. Such maps weren't commonly used, but including the approximate time between each point on the map would make it easier for them to time the drop. He added the tidal-chart information Tina had given him.

The far side of Blue Whale Bay would make for a good drop location. His mapping device showed several small caves in the area and he would be able to camouflage the rest of his supplies underwater. It was likely that Tina wouldn't even know about all the caves, since several were below the water's surface.

Jason chose the exact drop location, accounting for the tide, and transmitted the signal to the offshore team and the satellite, so Denny would know what was going on. He would rendezvous with them a little after midnight to pick up his equipment. Finally, he typed a quick situation update for Denny, including the information about the smugglers, and sent it off via the Room 59 back door that was built into the mapping satellite. Then he closed the computer, locked it and placed his sensors around the cabin.

He wanted to get a couple of hours of sleep before the real work began.

7

Jason looked at his watch one more time as he checked the gear he would take with him. He had to accomplish the drop without being seen or heard. Selecting clothing he'd picked out specifically for this mission, he chose to use the new extreme-cold underarmor that the Room 59 research team had just developed. It was a highly flexible material that would ward off more than just the cold. A set of black BDUs went over the top, and these, too, had been specially designed to reflect heat back to his body. If someone was using an infrared scanner, he would appear as nothing more than a temperature variant within normal range. He had a light jacket that was the same synthetic material as his underarmor, thicker but just as flexible, and capable of protecting him from edged weapons, as well as from small-caliber arms fire.

He pulled on the light pack and grabbed the small kit off the table, then slipped out into the night. He stayed to the shadows until he reached his ATV. Once there, he reached into the kit and removed two small attachments and screwed them into the mufflers of the vehicle. Using a sound-baffling technology unavailable anywhere else, they would render the vehicle virtually silent. He slipped on his sunglasses and switched them over to night-vision mode. With those tasks completed, Jason took off for the bay.

The only sound the ATV made was crunching rocks beneath its tires. He maneuvered it slowly around the outskirts of the village, over the rise and back down to the shore of Blue Whale Bay. No one appeared to be following him. He climbed off the quad and pulled an ultraviolet beacon from his bag, placing it in the rocks. The signal that he sent earlier should have brought the offshore team close, but this would give them pinpoint accuracy.

He sat back on the rocks and waited. It didn't take long before the light of a submersible was moving up the shoreline. It followed the path of his beacon light like a plane would follow lights on an airport runway. The submersible itself was a small vehicle, not much wider than the ATV he'd been driving. Behind it, it towed some of the equipment that he'd requested, including a portable sonar device, which he intended on using tonight for his first scan of the nearby waters.

The submersible was a new design developed by the research division of Room 59 for underwater missions. They called it the Scorpion, and as it crawled out of the water and came to a stop, Jason thought it had been aptly named. It had six retractable appendages: four "walking" legs and two mechanical arms with different attachments for the various jobs it might be called upon to perform. Its outer hull was depth resistant and utilized a sophisticated cloaking mechanism that actually bent light, making it seem almost invisible. It also had a special oxygen-exchange system that could allow him to stay submerged for up to two full days if necessary. The legs themselves could attach to rock, metal and almost any other surface.

Jason shut off his UV beacons and pulled on the two pouches that the Scorpion had brought ashore. One was filled with the diving gear he would need, including a self-propulsion system that would allow him to travel safely through the Arctic waters at a very high rate of speed, while keeping him warm and emitting a signal that would look like a school of fish to any radar system. The other pouch contained the munitions equipment he'd asked for, knowing that it might be necessary to take out the sub completely.

Jason hooked up the sonar to his handhold. He launched several sensors into the ocean that he would be able to track. They would monitor all unnatural movement in the nearby waters, based on a database of marine life in the area. If there was an Oscar-class sub anywhere around he was bound to find it eventually. He wasn't completely convinced that the sub would be here at all.

"New survey equipment?" a voice behind him said.

Jason spun and pulled his handgun in one smooth motion. Tina stood on the top ledge staring down at him, aware of the weapon in his hand, but either unaware of or ignoring the red laser dot that had appeared on the center of her chest. Only his hours of practice kept him from pulling the trigger.

"Damn it to hell, Tina!" he snapped. "What are you doing out here?"

"I think that should be my question, don't you?" she asked.

Jason sighed and reholstered his pistol, and grabbed the gear that he needed to take back to the cabin with him. The submersible had been sent from offshore, but the command controls were now transferred to his handheld device. He typed a quick command and the Scorpion slipped backward into the water. It was remarkably quiet as it disappeared beneath the lapping waves.

When it was safely gone, he turned and stalked up the bank to where she stood, then roughly grabbed her arm and pulled her over to his quad.

"You can't grab me—"

Jason clamped a hand over her mouth and she quieted instantly, her body going tense.

"Listen to me," he whispered in her ear, his tone harsh. "I will try to explain some things to you, but your curiosity could have gotten you killed tonight. Now, you can either shut up and come with me back to the cabin and hear what I have to say or—" he took his hand away from her mouth "—I will have no choice but to consider you a direct threat to my mission and I will treat you accordingly. Do you understand me?"

Tina nodded her head, wisely keeping silent. Jason moved to the quad and pulled her onto it behind him.

If she made another move or tried to raise an alarm he would have no choice but to kill her.

He drove back to the cabin and they got off the ATV. He grabbed his gear and nodded his head toward the door. Tina moved in front of him and opened the door, then stepped inside. He followed behind her, then set his gear down by the door, shutting it firmly and locking it behind him while she moved to stand in the small living room.

"All right," he said. "Who the hell are you?"

"What are you talking about?" Tina asked.

Jason pulled out his Glock and walked toward her until she sat on the sofa. He sat down on the coffee table in front of her.

"I have worked in this business a very long time and I am incredibly difficult to sneak up on. I don't have time for games and I'm not known for my tolerance. I'm going to ask you again, and you are going to tell me the truth. Who are you?"

She started to try to slip off the couch. Jason stuck his boot up on the edge of the sofa, blocking her exit. "It's rude to leave in the middle of a conversation," he said. "It makes me cranky."

Tina stopped trying to move away and faced him again. "Interrogation is more like it," she snapped. "I'm exactly who I've told you I was since the beginning."

"What were you doing following me down to the water?" he asked.

"You *are* arrogant, aren't you? I didn't follow you. There's a lookout point I go to on the bluff above the cove. I like to watch the whales as they come in and out of the bay. I saw someone moving down there and I realized it could only be you. No one else in the village is dumb enough to fool around down there at night."

"Oh? Why's that?"

"The rocks aren't stable. They can shift about with the tides. I was coming down to warn you when I saw your creature crawl up on the rocks."

"You were whale watching in the middle of the night?" Jason asked.

She looked a little sheepish and her cheeks filled with a blush. "I go out there when I need to think. I wasn't able to sleep. I've had a lot on my mind."

Jason raised an eyebrow.

"I just had to go and sort something out in my mind, okay?"

He still remained silent, knowing that she would finish her confession, whatever it was. It was the silence game all over again.

Finally, she waved her arms in exasperation. "Fine! Fine! I needed to go and think about, work out this…this attraction that I have for you! I can't explain it and it bothers me, all right?"

Jason couldn't help himself. He started to chuckle.

"Why are you laughing?" she demanded.

"You've made it clear from the very beginning that you wanted nothing to do with me in that way, and you've done nothing since that would indicate otherwise," he said. "You've hardly been a portrait of warmth and desire."

She stood up then. Jason didn't prevent her this time.

He watched her every movement, every breath, trying to separate the truth from the lies. Was she working for the smugglers? Could he trust her?

"So have you worked out your…attraction?" he asked.

"Yeah," she said. "I realized that it was simple. The guy I was attracted to is a complete liar and a killer, so there is no attraction." She was shouting now. "There! Problem solved! Can I go now or do you still want to shoot me?"

Jason ran his hands through his hair. How could one mission get so completely and utterly screwed up before it had even really begun? He watched her pace around the room. There was no hint that anything she'd said was a lie. No indrawn breath, no pause in her speech pattern, no pupil dilation, nothing.

"Sit down, Tina," he said quietly.

"If you're going to kill me you might as well do it while I'm standing," she said.

"I'm not going to kill you. We're going to talk and then I'm going to try to figure out what to do."

She sat on the edge of the sofa.

"Okay," he said. "I can only tell you so much, but I'll try to give you enough so that maybe we can get through this, all right?"

She nodded and he continued. "I work for the government. There have been reports of a submarine operating in the Bering Strait that has some special capabilities. I'm here to find out if it really exists."

"Why not come in as an official? Why not just come in with navy boats and find it?" she asked.

"If it were that simple, then I wouldn't be here," he said. "They don't send people like me for simple missions. Now, the fact of the matter is that I think that there are people using your village and maybe others as a cover and that those people intend great harm. Whether they are connected to this supposed submarine or not, I don't know yet. What I do know is that if you want to help your village, you'll keep silent and help me. The sooner I have the information I need, the sooner I can leave…and the sooner the people smuggling weapons into this part of the world can be stopped."

She sat and pondered the information that he had given her for a minute. Then a small smile crossed her lips. This was followed by a full-on grin a moment later.

"What are you smiling about?" he asked.

"Are you telling me that I snuck up on a spy? An honest-to-God, *professional* spy?"

"Damn it!" he yelled. "Tina, this is serious. I need to know if you are going to help or if I'm…going to have to do something I'd probably regret. I don't want to hurt you, but—" His tone turned deadly cold. "If you represent a threat to my mission, I will. So what's it going to be?"

"You would have killed me before now if that's what you wanted to do," she said.

"I already said I didn't want to, though that option is getting more appealing by the second," he gritted out.

"Of course I'll help you," she said. "It beats dying by a long shot anyway." The grin lit up her face again. "But just admit it. I snuck up on a spy."

"Fine," he sighed, waving a hand in surrender. "You snuck up on a spy."

"Grandpa would be so pleased. He used to take me on hunts and taught me how to walk silently. He didn't hold out any hope for me for so long. He would be so proud."

"Tina!" he growled.

"I'm not going to say anything," she said. "Scout's honor."

"Girls can't be Scouts," he said.

"No, but I bet you did have some luck with those Brownies."

He hadn't realized she'd heard his earlier remark and felt the tension in the room ease as they both burst out laughing.

"Okay," she said. "So what do we do now?"

"Now," he said, holstering his Glock, "we wait."

JASON AWOKE to the enormous blast of a foghorn. He pulled his handheld off the nightstand and accessed the data streaming from the sensors he'd had the Scorpion deploy. They'd detected a large ship, probably a cruise liner of some kind, which had just pulled into the village harbor.

A message in response to the update he'd sent Denny the previous night was also waiting for him.

Original mission priority unchanged. Secondary missions involving recent developments approved. Use of local assets conditionally approved. Standard cleanup measures will apply if risk assessment increases beyond tolerance levels.

In other words, if things got out of hand, he would be ordered to kill Tina and anyone with whom she'd possibly spoken. Perfect.

He dressed quickly in heavy, flannel-lined jeans and a wool sweater, then set out to meet Tina at the one little restaurant in town. Most of the locals looked at him with suspicion, but that was the nature of most small native villages the world over. Newcomers were distrusted until they'd proved themselves. Jason knew the dilemma that they faced with strangers. Always at cross-purposes, few that came were interested in accepting the people here for who they were. They were either profiteers looking to exploit the resources of the environment or the people, or protesters looking to stop the profiteers, but often just as unfamiliar or unaccepting of a way of life that had been passed down from family to family for generations. The old Inuit ways were passing, and holding on to those that remained was a grim, desperate task for many of the elders.

The small restaurant had windows overlooking the water, but nothing that could truly show off the spectacular view offered by the nearby cove. Practicality won out over aesthetics, and keeping the heat in and the cold out was more important than showing off the view.

The setup was very like any coffee shop in the lower forty-eight states, a counter in front of the window and booths that lined the walls. The deep-brown wood textures of the booths contrasted oddly with the yellowish-orange fabric that covered the seats, and Jason suspected that rather than pay to have upholstery sent up from Anchorage, the owner of the place had used the fabrics available locally—which meant fewer choices and no sense of aesthetics at all.

Tina was sitting at a booth at the far end, stirring her coffee absently. She didn't look at him as he approached, but he could tell by the tense set of her shoulders that she was aware of his presence. Obviously, the events from the previous night were still weighing heavily on her mind—maybe as much as they were weighing on his. The thought that he might have to kill her was more disturbing to him than he wanted to admit.

She was a study in contradictions—smart, beautiful, well educated, but living the rough life of a guide in the wilds of Alaska. Was she really as unaware of the criminal activities in the area as she claimed, or was she right in the middle of it, trying to keep him off the scent? Despite it not being his primary mission, he would have to find out the truth about the weapons smugglers, and if she was involved, he would have no choice but to bring her down along with the rest of them.

He strolled to the booth and sat down. She didn't bother to look at him, but unfolded a map on the tabletop and pointed out several trails and areas on the map. "If you want to get to the next village to the north, this is probably the best route—"

Jason placed his hand on the map. She looked up at

him and then back down at the map. She pushed his hand away and kept talking.

"I'm not sure exactly what information you need," she said quietly. "But I'll help in any way that I can."

She looked him in the eye as she spoke the last. A spark of determination lit up her face, and Jason was more confused by that than ever. So far this woman had seen him kill three men, get rid of dangerous weapons, and now she knew that he was a spy and she was still willing to help him. If he didn't end up killing her, he just might ask her out to dinner. She had guts and intelligence, and that was worth a lot.

"I appreciate your help," he said. "What I really need are lookout points to different harbors that are deep enough for a large submarine to enter or that a large ship could dock in, but that might not be thought of as typical places for seagoing vessels. I also need to meet anyone in town that you think might be involved or could get involved with the weapons smuggling. That needs to stop now, before they find a way to import something truly dangerous."

"Jason, you have to understand that the people here are loyal to the village and each other. We're not part of any country. Not really. This part of Alaska is more like a forgotten borderland. The only way for us to survive is to stay out of the politics and keep our minds focused on our people's survival."

"So what are you saying?" he asked.

"I'm saying that guns from Russia, or submarines, or lots of things that wouldn't normally be seen in the U.S. or in waters near the continental part of the country are more normal here than you might think. We've got more important things to worry about."

"How is that possible? I know that these waters are patrolled."

"Sure, they are, but there is a lot of water and a lot of space and not very many people to patrol it. The coast guard does a lot, but they spend more time and energy on rescues than they do anything else. A major storm that wiped out every village along the coast would probably be a sidebar in *National Geographic* about how the Inuit culture had finally died off."

Her voice was understandably bitter. This place, these people, mattered to her. Maybe more than anyone or anything had ever mattered to him.

Jason nodded. "I understand what you're saying, Tina. I really do. But here's what I want to know—how involved in the weapons smuggling are you?"

She raised her hands defensively. "I'm not," she said. "I swear it. My grandfather would never tolerate it. But I do know some people who are, and I—"

"You what?" Jason interrupted.

"I just know people that are and I wouldn't betray their trust any more than I would yours."

"Even if it meant saving lives? What if the next thing they decide to import is a nuclear warhead?" he asked.

She started to reply, but he forestalled her answer.

"Listen, I'm not asking you to betray anyone," he said. "But I still have a job to do. All I'm asking is that you introduce me to a few people and let me draw my own conclusions. In the meantime, you can think about what I said. Sometimes the only way to keep people safe is to protect them from the ones they love."

"Well, in any event, you're about to get your wish," she said. "Here comes someone for you to meet right now."

8

Jason turned to see a man walking toward their table. He was tall and lean, and walked with the smooth stride of a predator. His gaze was focused, but he didn't miss anything around him, either. That, however, was where the resemblance ended. From his clothing, he looked more like he should be panhandling for loose change on some dirty street corner rather than living in an Inuit village. His dirty blond hair and blue eyes made him stand out even more in a village filled with dark skin and even darker hair and eyes.

"Tina, my love, you didn't come to see me this morning," he said as he reached them. "I thought you would want to take a trip out to see the pretty new cruise ship that's parked herself in the harbor."

"Sorry, I've been occupying her time this morning," Jason said.

The man ignored Jason and directed his next comment to Tina. "Maybe you have some time this afternoon," he said.

"Chris Marley, this is Jason," Tina said. "I'm afraid that you'll just have to miss out on my company. I'm busy today."

Reading her body language, Jason could tell that she was uncomfortable with the man. She got to her feet and motioned with her hands. "If you'll excuse us."

Jason stood quickly, purposely crowding Chris to make him step back. He wanted to give Tina room to walk by without getting any closer to someone who made her so obviously uncomfortable.

Jason took a cue from Tina's reaction to the man. On a hunch he said, "Excuse us," in Russian.

"No problem," Chris replied in English.

Jason didn't say anything else, but turned and followed Tina outside.

"Who was that guy?" Jason asked.

"One of the local dregs of society," she said. "Just the sort you're looking for."

"He's obviously not Inuit. What's he doing here in the village?"

They walked to a Jeep she had parked outside. Jason didn't realize that it was their mode of transportation until he heard the beep of the alarm being turned off. He looked back at Tina in surprise.

"You did notice that there were other cars here, right?" she asked.

"Yeah, I just wasn't sure you owned one."

"Believe me," she said, "when winter hits, no one wants to be stuck with just a snowmobile or an ATV."

She climbed into the Jeep and Jason got in the passenger's side. She started the vehicle and pulled away from the curb, then resumed their conversation.

"Chris showed up here about five years ago. He came in with an oil outfit trying to convince the village to allow exploration drilling. The company did everything right. They promised the town council that if the right amount of oil was found no one in the village would have to work again, while promising the village elders to respect the land and our culture. They drilled two test holes. First one showed nothing, but the other looked like it had struck the mother lode. Chris was on the drilling crew."

She laughed bitterly.

"Anyway, one night he got drunk in the bar and started spouting off how it was all a scam and basically the rights that people were going to give up weren't to have a couple of oil pumps in the backyard, but an open-pit gold mine. The oil test had been rigged to show a large deposit of oil, but there really wasn't any. This village sits on a rich mineral deposit. The company was run out of town and Chris was the hero, even though he didn't really remember it the next day. The company he worked for had brought in a boat to tour their investors around the coastline. Since they were in such a hurry to leave, they left it behind. Chris uses it to fish and on occasion takes out a tour group. No one from the company has ever asked about it and no one out here cares. I suspect that he has nowhere else to go."

"Do you think he uses his boat for other things besides fishing and tourists?" Jason asked.

"You mean like smuggling?" she asked. "I wouldn't doubt it. He's not burdened with a particularly strong moral compass. The only direction his compass in life points is straight to him."

"I know the type," Jason said.

They drove along the coast and Tina pointed out the areas on the map that might be useful. Jason took digital images of the sites they visited and downloaded them. There were several spots he planned to revisit when he didn't have company and had time to explore a little more.

Once they were back in the village, Tina maneuvered the Jeep into a parking spot in front of a small mechanic shop.

"What are we doing here?" Jason asked.

"There's someone else I want you to meet."

They went into the main office and waited for an attendant. The wait wasn't a long one. A man who looked a lot like Jason stepped out of the shop and came to a sudden stop behind the counter.

Jason's sharp indrawn breath was the only sound in the room. He couldn't have been more stunned if he had walked in and seen the president. The man, who had been wiping his greasy hands with a rag, stared at what might as well have been his own reflection.

"Who the hell are you?" he growled.

"Jesse, this is a friend of mine, Jason. I thought you two might want to meet."

"Why would you think that?" Jesse asked.

"Isn't it obvious?" Tina said. "You two look almost identical. You could pass for twins. And you have the same last name."

"Lots of people look the same in the world, Tina," he said. "What is it they say? We're all supposed to have a twin somewhere or another. I guess you found mine. Congratulations." He stuffed the greasy rag into a pocket of his coveralls. "If that's all, I'm busy."

Jesse went back into the garage and left the two of them standing at the counter.

"Come on, Tina, let's go," Jason said.

"Don't you want to know more?" she asked.

He shook his head. "Not right now." He glanced in the direction Jesse had gone. "And even if I did, he clearly isn't interested in finding out more, either."

Tina offered him a look of exasperation and he sighed. The woman could say more with a look than many could with four sentences, he thought.

"Hey," he said, "at least now I know where to go when I have the time to look for answers, okay?"

She nodded once, and he followed her out of the shop.

JASON SAT in his cabin syncing the information stored in his PDA to his computer. The activity in the water for the area all seemed normal, and there were no signs of a submarine showing up on the Scorpion's radar. If the supercavitation specs were accurate, the water displacement alone would set off multiple sensors. He was beginning to feel as if the whole mission was a wild-goose chase. What were the odds that the Russians had actually come up with the money *and* the technology to pull off something like that anyway?

Plus, the meeting with Jesse had thrown him more

than he wanted to admit. The other man really could have been his twin.

He tapped some keys on his PDA and used a Room 59 back-door access to the FBI's computer system. He wanted to look up Jesse and see what he could find out. The files quickly loaded on the small screen and he read the summary notes.

Siku, Jesse. Age: thirty-two. Current state of residence: Alaska. Family history: mother, Cressa Siku, deceased. Father, unknown. Siblings: unknown. Criminal record: misdemeanor possession of a controlled substance, two convictions prior to age eighteen. No other convictions. Alert: current suspect in small-arms smuggling from Russia. Field investigation pending agent availability.

Jason sat back and looked at the computer screen. A copy of his birth certificate held the name of his mother. Cressa Siku. It was the only information he had—the orphanage had given it to him when he turned eighteen—but now that name meant something more. He had a brother. At least by blood. But what did it really mean?

He leaned back in his chair, stretching his back and rubbing a hand over the aching muscles of his neck. The real work of this mission hadn't even begun, and he was already tired. The discovery of a brother he'd never known he had—who happened to be a suspect in the weapons-smuggling operation that Room 59 had just authorized him to take down—was an added complication he didn't need. Brother or not, he had a job to do. The man was a total stranger, so why should he feel anything for him?

He picked up the PDA and looked through the oceanic-activity logs again, comparing them to the map Tina had shown him that morning. There was one area showing some boating activity that she had said was usually pretty dormant. Jason decided to go check it out. At least that way when he reported in to Denny what a dismal failure the mission had been so far, he could show that he'd made a reasonable effort. Plus, he admitted to himself, he was dying to try out the Scorpion.

Jason left the cabin and rode his quad down to the water's edge, then signaled the submersible, which climbed onto shore. The one nice thing so far about being a Room 59 agent was the plethora of cool toys that he had to play with. The Scorpion came to a stop and Jason keyed the entry code on the exterior and climbed on board. He had worked with the controls in a virtual-reality simulation during his training period, but that hadn't really prepared him for the experience of being inside the actual pod. The controls glowed indigo and silver, giving the cockpit an almost supernatural feel.

He closed and locked the hatch, then turned on the air-exchange system, giving it time to engage before he headed for the water. A light flashed on the control panel indicating that the system was ready, and he guided the pod to the water. The way it moved on land reminded him of riding a camel, which he'd done on several occasions in the Middle East. They were temperamental, nasty animals. But once he guided the pod into the water, it suddenly felt as if he'd entered a whole other world. The jerky motion he'd experienced on land completely vanished. The vehicle had been designed to react to both the hand controls and his body movements, which made it much more agile and responsive.

"All right," he said to himself. "Let's see what this baby can do."

Deep enough now to have the guidance lights on along with the radar, Jason sped along the bottom of the ocean floor, disturbing sea creatures as he went. Curving around rocks and using the legs to push off any shoals that were in his way, he was having the time of his life. It was like driving a sports car underwater.

He made the last curve to head into the cove that was supposed to be dormant. His radar showed three boats in the water. He shut down the external lights and switched the view screen to dark mode: a combination of infrared spectrum and night vision that allowed him to steer clear of obstacles while being able to see sources of heat without being seen himself. He approached the shoreline and, using the Scorpion's radar tools, began to assess what was going on.

He quickly discovered there were a number of people on land, which meant that was where he needed to be, as well. Jason quickly moved the Scorpion to an isolated spot and maneuvered it out of the water. He switched from sonar to straight audio pickups, which, along with the night vision, would give him plenty of information.

There were twelve men surrounding several crates. The audio feed could pick out each individual voice and he could tell they were speaking Russian. The infrared scan showed weapons signatures pretty much identical to the ones he and Tina had found in the abandoned village. Although he couldn't see their faces, Jason recognized two of the voices right away—Jesse and Chris.

The conversation moved quickly as they satisfied themselves that the weapons were suitable and arranged to meet the smuggler in the village the next day to deliver his payment. As the meeting wound down and the dealer and his men returned to their boats, Chris's and Jesse's voices died out.

As tempting as it was to take the Scorpion in close and blow up the weapons that were piled on the beach and—presumably—in the nearby boats, Jason needed to know if these guys were just run-of-the-mill smugglers or if their plans included something far more sophisticated and dangerous than rifles. If he took them out now, he'd never find out the whole truth.

A better plan, despite the urge to unleash destruction on the smugglers, was to go back into town and then tomorrow stop by the garage and have a chat his long-lost brother.

At that point, actions would speak much more loudly than any words they could exchange.

"YOU KNOW," Jason said as Jesse stepped through the door into the shop, "I've thought about this moment many times in my life."

Startled, Jesse jerked to a stop, dropping his keys onto the floor and spilling his coffee. "Ah, shit!" he said.

Jason stood up from the chair he was lounging in and leaned forward on the counter. His gaze took in the coffee cup on the floor and he shook his head in mock sadness. "Look at that mess you've made. You should get someone to help you clean that up." He added a *tsk*ing sound with his tongue. "It's too bad you don't have any *family* that could help you out around here."

Jesse kicked the cup out of the path of the door and snatched up his keys, slamming the door shut behind him.

"I don't know what the hell you're talking about," he said. "Maybe I should just call the cops and have you arrested for breaking and entering."

Jason chuckled softly. "Oh, I don't think that you're going to do that," he said. "I think that maybe the two of us should have a talk."

"Look, I don't know you," Jesse said, "or anything about you, but I didn't exactly have a Norman Rockwell upbringing. I don't have any desire to go digging up the past. Maybe we're related, maybe not, but it doesn't matter to me either way. I don't have a family." There was a cold finality to his voice.

"You're not even a little curious?" Jason asked, then continued without waiting for his answer. "Tell you what. Just indulge me a little and tell me a bit about yourself."

"I told you, man, I don't want to get into all of this. I don't have a family and I'm fine with that."

"Hmm...now that's interesting," Jason said. "We

could probably pass for twins—a fact that would make most men stop and wonder for a minute. That you appear to be indifferent to that tells me that you either knew about me or…" His voice trailed off, then he laughed. "There is no 'either,' is there? You knew about me, didn't you?"

Jesse dropped his keys on the counter and said, "Yeah, fine. I knew I had a brother out there somewhere. Big deal. And maybe it's you and maybe it's not. Lots of people look alike. What I know is this. My mother was some slut who dropped me off the first chance she could find—an orphanage in Anchorage, if it matters to you—and she split. I heard that she's dead. I did some digging when I was a teenager, asked around when I first got up here, so I knew a brother existed. But let me be clear—I don't care."

"Sorry," Jason said. "But I'm not buying it." He stepped out from behind the counter and headed for the door. He decided to try a different approach. "Look, I don't know for sure who you are to me," he lied, "but I do intend to find out. Maybe, deep down, you'd like to know, too."

Jason pulled on the door.

"Jason." Jesse's voice was deep and quiet, barely above a whisper.

"Yeah?"

For a long minute, silence held them both, then he said, "My life is complicated. I don't know that you want to get too close. It might be better for both our sakes if you just left it alone."

Jason watched him carefully, wondering if his words

represented a threat, a warning or genuine concern. Maybe a little of all three.

After another moment, he nodded, then said, "Everyone's life is complicated, but maybe helping with that is what families are for."

9

Jason left the shop and returned to his cabin to find Tina waiting for him.

"What've you been up to?" she asked.

"Oh, just wandering about, really," he said. "Come on. I've got something to show you."

They started up the quads and Jason led the way back to the beach where he had seen the smugglers the night before. The tide had washed away most of the tracks, but not all of them.

She knelt down to examine what was left. "There were quite a few people here," she said. "What was going on here?"

"Another arms deal," he said. "I need to figure out where they're storing all this stuff and who is paying for it. I haven't seen this many illegal arms deals since I was in the Middle East. This is a real hot spot."

"One of the advantages to living in the middle of

nowhere," she said, looking around, "is that no one sees anything. From the tracks, it looks like two larger trucks and maybe a couple of smaller ones left from here. How many people were there?"

"About a dozen," Jason said. "But some of them went back to the boats that were anchored out there. Three of them."

Tina nodded, keeping her thoughts to herself.

"Tina," he finally said, "where are they taking the weapons? What's the drop point?"

She blushed slightly and had the grace to look at him sheepishly.

"I know we've covered this," he said, keeping his voice gentle. "But if you're involved somehow, you need to tell me or this is going to get really ugly. You know my mission, and I've revealed far more to you than I should have. I'm not after you and even the smugglers are really a secondary consideration for me. But I do have a duty to fulfill, too."

"I already told you," she said. "I'm not involved. I just can't help but feel that I'm betraying some of my people by helping you."

"Tina, this can't just be about your loyalties or where people are getting the money to survive in hard times. These weapons aren't heading for soldiers or warriors. They're going to end up in the hands of criminals who will hurt people. Maybe a lot of people." He felt himself tensing up again and purposely took a deep breath. "These aren't small shipments. The whole situation is bordering on a major business. If someone is planning something big, do you really want your village to be seen as the staging area for whatever ends up happening?"

She nodded her understanding. "I know you're right," she said. "But I don't want to see people prosecuted who don't deserve it. Most of them are just trying to get by."

"No worries there. I'm just a surveyor, remember?" he said, grinning. "Whoever is helping them on this side is not who really needs to be stopped. Most likely, they are just a pawn in a much bigger game. The person I need to find is the one setting up the deals and supplying the contacts and help. A couple of dock lackeys—for want of a better expression—aren't that interesting to the government. Most of the people involved or helping are probably already flagged and their activities are being monitored to see if they become a bigger threat."

"If federal law enforcement—like the FBI—knows that some of them have been doing illegal things, why not shut them down?" she asked.

"For a couple of reasons, really," he explained. "First, why settle for the little fish when, with a little patience, you can catch the big one? As of right now, what they probably know amounts to a few misfits in the far frozen north smuggling a handful of Russian rifles into the country for small-time profit. In other words, why bother?"

Tina glared at Jason, her dark-brown eyes flashing.

"What?" he asked. "Now what's got you riled up?"

She held up a finger in accusation. "In the last few sentences, you've equated everyone in the village to misfits, lackeys and pawns. Do you really think that everyone here is that ignorant?" she asked, then continued before he could get a word in edgewise. "I'll have you know that there are a lot of sophisticated, intelligent people here. They might not know how to build a computer or a space shuttle or do neurosurgery, but what they do know has kept our culture going for as long or longer than almost any other on the planet."

She paused for a breath and Jason took the opportunity to break in. "Whoa! Whoa! Hold on a minute. That is not what I think. What I was trying to illustrate is how this is going to be seen by the law-enforcement community in the continental United States. If you'll recall, you were the one who pointed out to me that it's my heritage, too, so I don't have any reason to start slamming the people in the village. What I do know, however, is how perceptions work and when they can be an advantage or a disadvantage, depending entirely on how they're utilized."

"I'm not sure I understand what you're getting at," she admitted.

He took a seat on a dry log and gestured for her to sit down. When she did, he continued. "Think of it like this. The village is small and—by population—is largely uneducated in the same sense as most communities down south. The government isn't going to see this place as either a threat or a significant asset. It's a place—a dot that's not even visible on most maps. Can you agree with me on that?"

"Sure," she said. "It's not a really accurate perception of the place, but I can see how people might view it that way."

"Okay," he said. "The danger happens when people assume those views or perceptions *are* accurate. In general, I don't think that the people in the village are dangerous, but I do know that it would be really easy for a dangerous person to hide up here among the people and never get picked up. The reverse is also true. I wouldn't think to ask most of the people here for help with advanced calculus, but I'd trust almost anything they had to tell me about the environment in this part of the world, the waterways or really anything having to do with the area itself. To me, this is a huge asset. A resource that many people would overlook, based on those inaccurate perceptions we've already established."

"I see what you're saying," she said. "In other words, you aren't going to take a resource for granted any more than you're going to utilize that resource for something that it isn't suited for."

"Exactly," he said. He got to his feet and motioned for her to follow him. They moved back up the hill, following the tracks made by the smugglers the night before. At the top, the tracks split, with one set heading in the direction of the village and the others heading northeast.

"Where would that set be going?" Jason asked, pointing to the second set. "They'll get stuck in those trucks."

"If they were regular trucks I would agree, but you aren't the only one with cool technology," Tina said. She knelt down and examined the tracks again. "I've seen these trucks. They're built with a track system that can be fitted over the wheels. They'll drive through or over just about anything, kind of like a tank or a snowmobile. I bet if we followed the tracks they would go pretty quickly from wheel marks to the track ribbing they use over the wheels themselves."

"So where would they go?" he asked.

Tina shrugged. "I don't know the answer to that one, but we could go find out. How much gas do you have?"

"I've got plenty. You go back to town, I'll go check it out and meet you back in an hour or two."

"And what happens when you get lost?" she asked. "Should I just leave you out there to die or would you like me to send out a set of sled dogs?"

"I don't get lost," he said, chuckling and tapping his temple. "I'm one of those people with a built-in compass."

"Maybe so," she said, "but you don't even know what you're up against at this point. I'll tag along and if something starts going down, I'll get out of your way. I'm a guide, but you aren't paying me enough to take a bullet for you. Either way, I can't let you wander off into the middle of nowhere without your guide. If you died, it would play hell on my business."

"Tina, I'm not going to argue," he said, his voice firm.

"Good," she said. "That will save us a lot of time because I'm following the tracks whether you are or not. Curiosity and all. You coming?"

She didn't wait for his reply, but jumped on her quad and took off without him.

Jason had difficulty catching up at first. The ground was boggy in places, rocky in others, and Tina knew how to avoid the obstacles easily. Once Jason fell in behind her, he made a point to stay directly in her tracks to avoid any problems.

They traveled for the better part of an hour before they crested a ridge and Tina rolled to a stop. Jason pulled up next to her.

"That was a dirty trick, driving through that boggy area," he said.

"It wasn't a trick," she replied. "Just a friendly reminder that you may not be able to instantly recognize when and where the dangers are. That's part of the reason you hired a guide, remember?"

"Vaguely," he said, smiling. "My reasons for doing that come and go from my mind, depending on your behavior."

She laughed and then pointed down into the shallow valley below them. "What do you make of that?"

Jason could see the outline of several trucks and a small building. He grabbed his binoculars and took a harder look. The building looked like a large tin structure. Four men milled around outside, heavily armed. The trucks that had been on the beach were sitting outside and appeared to be heavily loaded.

"You had to know about this place. It's not that far from the village," he said.

"Far enough," she said. "No one comes out this way, Jason."

"Well, there sure is someone here now. Have a look," he said, handing over the binoculars.

She peered through them. "Oh, my God. Those guys have guns." She paused. "A lot of guns."

"Do you recognize any of them?" Jason asked.

"Yeah, that's Chris coming out of the building now. I'm not sure who the thugs with the guns standing around outside are. The other guy coming out of the building is…holy shit! That snake, that dirty rotten snake!"

"What?"

"His old boss is there. Boris Ambros—the one that I told you left town. He's there. Chris must have been working for them the whole time. What the hell do they want?"

"I don't know," he said, filing the name away. "You didn't mention before that the oil company was Russian."

"No, I didn't," she said. "I guess…I didn't think it was important. Every other company that tries to break in up here is Russian." She peered through the binoculars again, then added, "He had lots of different people working for him—locals, whites, Chinese, Russian. It was a pretty mixed crew."

Jason took the binoculars back and watched as the men climbed into vehicles and left, while Chris and the older man Tina said was his boss walked behind the building. A moment later, it was Jason's turn for a surprise. "Holy shit!" he said, echoing her comment. "I don't believe it."

"What?" Tina asked.

"Do you know what that is?" he asked, watching in stunned amazement as it lifted up beyond the building.

"That?" she asked. "Unless they've invented a new type of flying can opener, that's called a helicopter."

"That, my dear, is not just any helicopter. That thing makes my underwater craft look like a bath toy. It's not even supposed to exist yet!"

"What do you mean, it's not supposed to exist?"

Still stunned, Jason explained. "That helicopter is an XJ6, developed under the prototype name Asp. It's the most advanced combat helicopter in the world. It has rotor dampeners that adjust as it flies to make it virtually silent and an advanced weapons system that is pinpoint accurate. It doesn't show up on most forms of radar, because it uses light- and signal-bending technology that the rest of the world doesn't even know exists."

"Is it too much to hope that his boss is some eccentric rich guy who likes to collect odd military equipment?" Tina asked.

"You don't understand," he said. "The Asp doesn't exist. The only reason that I know about it is…" His voice trailed off, suddenly aware that he had already said too much. If she ever decided to get out of the guide business, she'd make a hell of an interrogator. People would just talk to her and not even know it.

"Long story short, I was asked in an advisory capacity to look at some of the designs and give input on what would work tactically in the field."

"Well, just because you didn't see it built doesn't mean that it didn't happen. How long ago were you asked?" she asked.

"Three weeks," he said. "They told me it was a prototype." His mind was working quickly. Someone inside Room 59 had either sold or leaked the plans even before he'd seen them. Or they'd been stolen. In either case, Denny had to be notified immediately of a possible security breach.

The helicopter took off and, as Jason promised, it was virtually silent. It flew off into what Jason knew from his premission review was a military-only fly zone.

With the compound below deserted, Jason knew he had to see what else was there. These had to be the guys. There was a very good chance they were involved with more than just weapons smuggling. If they had the helicopter, it wasn't a huge leap to imagine that they also knew about the sub. He needed to know where they were getting their technology and more importantly still, where they were getting their intelligence.

"Tina," he said. "I need you to go back. I have to see what else is down there and now is the perfect time to do it. The place is practically deserted."

"If it's deserted, then I should be able to come along."

"Practically doesn't mean entirely," he said. "They won't leave it unguarded." He held up a hand as she started to object. "Please," he added. "I can't do my job if I'm worrying about you, too."

She looked as if she wanted to argue some more, but said, "All right, but if you aren't back in town in two hours, then I'm calling in the cavalry and we're coming out to find you."

He chuckled. "There isn't a cavalry within two

hundred miles of here, but…if I'm not back in two hours, a cavalry will come whether we want it to or not, because I'll be dead. I can promise you that wouldn't go unnoticed."

"Good to know," she said. "Stay safe." Then, without another word, she turned her quad around and headed back in the direction of the village.

He waited until Tina was out of sight and then planned his approach to the compound, looking for the best way in.

His plan crystallized in his mind, and he said, "Bingo," then headed for his destination.

10

Rather than risk being spotted, Jason left his quad where it was and set out on foot. There were enough trees, shrubs and grasses to give him adequate cover, especially if his approach was at more of an angle rather than straight ahead on the rough track the trucks had followed. He low-crawled the last fifty yards until he made his way to the back of the first truck and took a moment to look at the building close up.

It was a large metal Quonset hut painted over with a sand-and-white camouflage pattern to help it blend in with either snow or the sparse earth that surrounded it. A tower on the back side of the building held some kind of electronic equipment; he could hear the faint hum of it, even from his position. Based on the fact that none of this had been picked up on any of the satellite imaging they'd done prior to the mission, he assumed that it was some sort of radar-jamming device.

He checked the two guns he was carrying and made sure the extra clips were still on his belt. He attached a small sound suppressor to the end of his Glock, and moved around the truck, looking for an easy entrance into the building. He paused and lifted the flap covering the truck's cargo area. As he suspected, it was filled with crates much like those he and Tina had recovered from the smugglers before.

He kept moving and peered around the end of the truck just as a man walked out of the building, lighting up a cigarette. As the man moved off to the other side, Jason pulled a knife from his boot and threw it into the ground, blocking the door from closing and locking. Moving on silent feet, he quickly assumed a position behind the smoker. Some tiny sound must have alerted him because he started to turn just as Jason reached him.

The man opened his mouth to shout a warning, when Jason's palm slammed into his throat with brutal force. The only sound that escaped was a dry wheeze as the man stumbled to his knees, gagging and trying to find enough air to breathe through his crushed larynx.

Spinning him around, Jason grabbed the man's head and neck in a lock and twisted it hard. The bones snapped like dry twigs. Jason dragged the deadweight around the corner of the building and back over to the far side of the truck as fast as he could.

No one seemed to have noticed the quick and dirty fight, so he ran to the door, peeked inside, then pulled the knife from the ground and slipped through, letting it shut softly behind him. The entry was barren. There was no sentry or front security except the lock on the door that clicked in place once the door shut. Jason was a little surprised at how it all looked, but he knew that looks could be deceiving and he wasn't about to let his guard down. Someone here had to have money, access and power to have that kind of equipment, and no one wanted that many weapons unless they had a dangerous agenda.

Jason walked down a narrow hallway. The first door on the right was an office. The door was locked. He heard footsteps heading his way and behind him, the front door was opening again. Damn! he thought. There must have been a second guard on the far side of the building.

He pulled his knife free again, slid it into the doorjamb and pried upward, popping the lock. He ducked inside the office as quickly and quietly as he could, then slid down against the wall, waiting to see if they were coming his way. The two sets of footsteps passed as the two men acknowledged each other briefly, and then they continued on to their original destinations. Jason knew it wouldn't be long until the missing man was noticed.

He moved to the desk against the far wall. The desk itself was clear—no phone, no computer. He opened the drawers—nothing there. The office was clean except for a map on the wall. Jason took an image of the map and then headed to the door.

The hallway was clear, and he kept moving. There were no other offices, but he found two other rooms, both of them situated as barracks-style sleeping quarters. One held two men snoring heavily, most likely the guards who worked the night shift. He left them alone.

What the hell was here that was important enough to require radar jamming? No receiving area, not even one for smuggled rifles, would be this well guarded, and it didn't make sense that the Asp was housed here. There was no cover for it outside.

The hall curved and then steps moved down and into the earth. The temperature increased and steam blew past him. He kept going, trying to make his large frame invisible against the wall. The stairs emptied into a large cavern that appeared to have direct access to the ocean. Packing crates along the side provided cover, and Jason was glad for the shadows and the chance to assess what he was seeing. It was going to take him a minute to recover from his surprise.

Three submersibles were docked along the underground waterway. One was being loaded by two men, at least one of whom must have been one of those who had passed him in the office upstairs. The cavern was massive, but the water was divided by sections of rock, and some sections of the water had steam pouring off, making the air stifling.

The submersibles were standard Russian Mir minisubs. Nothing looked particularly different except the extra length for the cargo that was being loaded. Jason pulled out his PDA. The scanning system showed that most of the weapons in the room were the same, but he was getting a nuclear signature from one of the crates. It was already on the sub farthest down the dock. Jason moved to the next set of crates, trying to get closer. The reading came back as enriched uranium. He wasn't sure what the exact device was, but he knew the product was bad. He waited another minute, but realized that he was too late as the sub began to sink into the depths.

A submarine with supercavitation capabilities and a nuclear weapon in the same area? The smugglers weren't just a small-time operation. They'd gone corporate or were being led by terrorists or Mother Russia was back and she was pissed.

Jason took as many readings as he was able from his position, then headed back out of the room. He needed to get out and get word to Denny that things were much worse than they'd feared.

He was almost at the front door when he was spotted. The guard pointed at Jason, but before he could sound the alarm, Jason was on him. He pulled a pen from his pocket, leaped forward and yanked the man to him, whipping him around and covering his mouth with his free hand. The man's dark eyes widened in surprise at the sudden attack.

This wasn't the time for a fight and even just snapping his neck might take too long. Jason pushed a tab on the pen and a needle extended from the tip. He jabbed it ruthlessly into the man's neck, and held him tightly as the poison raced through his system, killing him in seconds. Jason lowered him to the floor, noting how the guard's hands were still grasping for his heart even as it stopped.

Jason had picked up the poison during one of his first trips into South America. Some members of the indigenous tribes were experts in herbology. The poison was lethal and untraceable, and best of all, it came from a pretty flower that he could order online and was perfectly legal. So far as he knew, only a handful of people in the world knew the more esoteric uses for it.

He ran from the building, dodging behind the trucks, then made his way back to where he'd left the quad. He started it up and was heading back to the village when he noticed Tina waiting for him on the next rise.

"I thought I told you to go back to the village," he shouted as he pulled to a stop next to her.

"Well, I was worried you might need help," she said.

"Not this time. We need to get back and quickly. They'll be looking for whoever infiltrated their operation down there, and I need to get in touch with my superiors. This isn't just a small-time weapons-smuggling outfit."

"Okay, but could we plan these outings a little better? I felt like a sitting duck out here, and I absolutely hate feeling like that. If nothing else, I would rather have some different equipment with me, including some better cold-weather gear," Tina said.

"If you'll recall, I told you to go back to the village and wait. In fact, I told you not to come when we were down at the cove." Exasperated, Jason asked, "Do you ever listen to anything you're told? You must have driven your poor grandfather to the edge of insanity."

"You might as well accept the fact that *that* is never going to work."

"What's never going to work?" he asked.

"Trying to tell me what to do," she said matter-of-factly. Then she started up her quad, turned it around and left without him again, once more leaving him to play catch-up so he might have a shot at missing at least some of the boggy spots along the way.

"I hate complications," he muttered to himself as he followed behind her. "Why couldn't this have been a nice, simple assassination mission? Those were so much easier."

THEY GOT BACK to his cabin and Tina left to go check on her grandfather, with a warning from Jason to keep her eyes open. People knew that she'd brought him up here and they might decide to move against her on that basis alone. She assured him she could take care of herself and left while he went inside to contemplate the stubborn nature of the female half of the human species and log into Room 59. It was time to talk to the boss.

His avatar traveled down the hallway, but Denny wasn't online. Using the emergency-notice icon, Jason left an urgent message and waited. He didn't expect it to be long before Denny showed up and he was right. He only had to wait a few minutes before he received a notice and went back to Denny's online office.

"You must have found the sub," Denny said without preamble when Jason entered. "Good work."

"No, I haven't found the sub," Jason said.

"You used the emergency notice to pull me out of a meeting and you haven't found the sub?" Denny asked. "This better be good."

"It's not good," Jason replied. "Not good at all. That's why I used the emergency notice." He uploaded the images and the scanned data from his handheld onto Denny's system. "This is what I found. Most of the weapons are inconsequential, nothing that would really interest us, but then I found this…" His voice trailed off as he saw Denny's reaction to the data.

"A nuclear signature?" the older man said. "You have a gift for understatement. 'Not good' barely touches the surface of it."

"My equipment wasn't sufficient to determine the exact nature of the weapon, but I figured it was worth interrupting you for," he said. "It's not a huge leap to believe that if there's a nuclear weapon in this part of the world, the sub exists. Maybe it has supercavitation, maybe not. But it's here. It has to be."

"You're probably right," Denny muttered, studying the images in front of him.

"There's something else," Jason said.

"You mean it gets worse?"

"To be honest, yes," he replied. "This may be worse." He uploaded the next set of image files, which showed the Asp helicopter.

Denny didn't say anything initially, but stared at the image, stunned silent for a moment, before he whispered, "Aw, shit. How'd they get ahold of that?"

"I don't know," Jason said. "But I thought there were only a few people who even knew of its existence." He knew he didn't have to say anything else.

"Damn," his boss said. Jason could see him mentally running through scenarios and ways to address the problem. After a moment, he said, "Okay, I'll try to see what I can dig up on this end. Do you have any other information yet?"

"Just a name," Jason said. "Boris Ambros. I didn't find anything on him in our system, but he's involved on this end, so I figured you'd want to flag the name, see if anything turns up."

Denny made a quick note of the name. "It doesn't ring any bells for me, but I'll see what I can find. For now, I want you to stay focused on finding that sub and that warhead. Shut the whole thing down, Jason. I'd prefer to keep the midnight teams out of this if at all possible."

"Understood," Jason said. The very idea of having to have a midnight team called in for his first official mission made him squirm uncomfortably. They were the last-ditch resort of Room 59—ruthless killers who would eradicate anything and anyone to "clean" an operational area. It would also make him look pretty incompetent if they were needed his first time out.

"Do you have anything else for me at this time?" Denny asked.

"Just a thought," he said. "I'm not sure how an operation this big has been going on without our knowledge."

"What are you getting at?" Denny asked.

"Just that if we didn't know, it makes sense that someone did. Maybe you could reach out to our friends in the CIA and see what they know about this. Either they know about some of it and it's covered or…"

"Or someone way up in the food chain is on it and has been helping to cover it up," Denny finished.

"There is no way that this has gone completely unnoticed. It's too big. I know that the resources up here are limited, but this would just be crazy to miss. The FBI has information on the gunrunning that is going on, so it has to be being watched by somebody."

"I saw the access to the FBI file. You think that this guy…Jesse is your family?" Denny asked.

"Even if he is my brother by blood, he's a total stranger to me. I'll handle it."

"If I need to assign a different agent, I need to know it, and right now," Denny said. "This is too big to let it get personal."

"No, sir," Jason said. "It's not personal and there's no need for anyone else. An extra player in the field would only make things more complicated." He shrugged, remembering how Jesse had acted toward him. "Besides, right now this guy is a suspect, nothing more. An expendable asset, just like the rest."

He knew what Denny was nervous about, but this was the job and there was nothing that was going to get in the way even if this was his brother and he had to kill him. There was a long pregnant pause.

"Look," Jason continued, "I know you can run the new biometrics tools on this conversation, see if I'm telling the truth. Go ahead. Review the data. I'm here for the job, and that's it. If it could become a problem, you'll be the first to know."

"All right," Denny said. He paused once more, considering, then added, "I'm going to send in some new equipment for you. Send the Scorpion out again and I'll have the offshore team load it and return it tonight."

They said their goodbyes, and Jason logged off. He looked at the images on his computer again. About the only good side of all this he could see was that no one appeared to be in any hurry. If they had a plan, it didn't seem to involve an immediate launch.

There was a sharp series of raps on his door, and he picked up his Glock and peered outside through the window. Tina was standing on the porch in only a sweater, rubbing her arms to try to stay warm. He quickly pulled open the door and moved out of her way, knowing she would rush inside.

"Are you crazy?" he asked. "It's freezing out there!"

"You're…telling me," she said, teeth chattering. "But I left my coat at my grandfather's. I was halfway here before I realized I'd left it behind and the wind started picking up. So I ran." She shivered again. "That almost helped."

Jason pulled a blanket off the back of the sofa and wrapped it around her, rubbing his hands up and down her arms, trying to get her circulation going again. "Come here," he said.

He slid his arm around her shoulder and walked her closer to the fire, pulling a chair forward for her to sit. She eased herself down gratefully.

"Hang on a minute," he said. He went into the kitchen to pour her a cup of hot coffee mixed with a little brandy. It would warm her on the inside and help chase away the feeling of cold. He pulled a chair up next to hers and placed the drink in her hand, wrapping his hands on the outside of hers.

"That should help take care of some of that shivering."

Tina took a sip and cringed a little as the brandy seared its way down her throat.

"How much antifreeze did you put in that?" she rasped.

He chuckled. "Just enough to keep you from turning into a giant ice cube."

"Thanks," she said. "It feels wonderful."

She took another sip of the drink and set it aside. He reached forward and put her hands in his and rubbed them gently. He lifted her hand, trying to warm the backs with his breath. Her shivering started to subside. He stopped his ministrations and stared at her.

Jason could feel the room heating up and not from the fire. She didn't look away, but started chewing her lower lip. That was the last thing Jason could take. He wrapped his hand around the back of her neck and pulled her into a kiss. It was consuming and possessive, but there was nothing more that he wanted in the world than to be with this woman, this minute.

They stood and Jason gently pulled her into the bedroom. The room was dimly lit, the only illumination coming from the moonlight that slanted in through the one small window. He led her to the bed, keeping his silence, letting the anticipation build for them both by the simple touch of his hands on hers.

When they reached the bed, he moved to stand in front of her, then wrapped her in his arms, brushing her lips softly at first, then more urgently when a quiet moan escaped her lips. She pressed herself against him, and he could feel the length of her body through his clothes, the wanting pouring off her in heated waves.

His hands found her hair, and he eased her head backward, trailing kisses down her neck and then undoing one button of her shirt at a time, following each with another kiss.

He slid her shirt off her shoulders, kissing her soft skin and cupping her breast through the satin material, rubbing his thumb across her nipple, smiling to himself as it responded to his touch.

She pulled his head up and imitated his motions, first trailing kisses down his neck and then his chest as she undid the buttons. She paused only for a moment and undid the button of his jeans and zipper, nipping the tender flesh that was protected by the clothing.

Jason pulled her to him and they finished undressing with more urgency. Their clothes finally out of the way, he lifted her, one arm around her waist and the other supporting their weight as he laid her on the bed. He was so hot and intense, every muscle in his body ready to devour her, but wanted her need to be as intense as his.

He stroked her skin, kissed her lips and slowly moved his fingers to the soft wet folds that held his salvation and slid a finger inside of her. Her plea for more as her hips pressed up into his hand was more than he could take. His hand moved to her hip and guided her upward as he plunged inside.

Rocking forward, his head swooped downward, clenching her nipple in his teeth. Her cry of ecstasy along with her orgasm sent him over the edge.

Jason rolled to his side, pulling her into his arms as he did. Their labored breathing was the only sound filling the room. He rubbed his hand on her arm, not really certain what to say. He'd certainly had sexual encounters on other missions, but everything seemed to be different in this place. He began to wonder if he was looking for more than was really there because he was starting to find the connections to his family and that was triggering other things.

He tilted his head and kissed the top of hers. Her hair smelled like cinnamon, clean and sweet and exotic all at the same time.

Tina pushed away from him and sat up, a look of wonder and concern on her face. He tried the silent angle again, hoping to hear her thoughts first, but not certain he should let her mixed emotions come out with a statement first. He wanted to reassure her, but he wasn't sure what he was supposed to reassure her about. They both knew that he wasn't here to stay.

"I should go home," she said.

Her quiet tone was more of a question than a statement. She waited for his reply, but he wasn't sure what to say. She started to move off the bed, her head hanging a little low. All of a sudden Jason felt like a heel.

"No," he said, keeping his tone low and soft. "Stay."

"Stay?"

"You didn't bring your coat and it's freezing outside," he said.

She went from shy to furious in the span of two heartbeats. She started stomping around the room gathering her clothes. Jason knew he had done that wrong, but wasn't sure how to rectify it. His experiences with women weren't the kind that demanded the right words at the right time after sex. He'd successfully avoided real relationships his whole life.

He slid off the bed and put on his pants. Grabbing her arm as she stormed past him, he tried to pull her in for a kiss, but she stared at him as if he were a snake. He was beginning to feel like one and not quite certain why. "Tina, wait," he said. "I'm sorry. All of this has taken me by surprise. I don't know all the right words to say. Just stay and we can talk about it."

She left the bedroom with her clothes in hand and went to the bathroom. She came back out dressed and slipped on her shoes.

"Come on," he said, hating the pleading sound in his voice. "Don't leave like this."

She turned to look at him and before he could say anything else, grabbed his coat off the table and stormed out the door.

Jason sank into one of the chairs, running his hands through his hair. A sudden thought occurred to him. And he turned his gaze over to the table where his computer and other equipment were situated.

Tina had just walked out the door wearing his coat. The coat he'd put his handheld system in just before she'd arrived.

"Damn women and damn complications," he shouted.

11

Jason grabbed his shoes and a sweater from the bedroom. Throwing them on, he half ran to the front door and opened it. As the blast of freezing-cold air hit him full-force, he knew that this wasn't going to go well. He glanced at the thermometer as he ran out the door—thirty-five degrees before the windchill, and an icy rain was starting to fall.

He ran across town to Tina's house. No matter what, he needed to get his PDA back so that he could call in the Scorpion and get the other equipment that Denny thought he needed and maybe…maybe he could muddle through an explanation.

He wasn't good at this sort of thing, talking about what he was thinking or feeling, and he couldn't afford any more interference in this mission. Where Tina was concerned, it seemed that none of the lines that were supposed to work felt right. And besides that, she was different. Different than any other women he'd ever known, ever been with. She would see what he could say as the cheap platitudes they were. Sadly, they were all he could offer her. His mission had to come first.

By the time Jason made it to Tina's street, he was soaked and half-frozen. As he turned the corner, he stomped in a puddle that didn't look deep, but was actually a pothole in the road deep enough to slosh icy-cold water past the top of his boot.

"Damn it," he cursed, feeling his toes curl as his sock turned into a freezing sheath of wool.

Taking her porch steps in one big motion, he banged on her door, knowing that he could only stand there for a couple of minutes at most before he really needed to be inside and out of the cold. The wind shifted, and rain started slanting in sideways. The porch wasn't much protection and his foot was turning to a Popsicle with each passing second.

Tina pulled open the door a crack, and Jason didn't wait for an invitation. He pushed his way inside.

"What the hell are you doing?" she yelled.

"Freezing my ass off!" he snarled. "You took my coat."

He stepped farther into the room and came to an abrupt halt when he saw Chris Marley sitting on her sofa. Jason turned to stare at Tina, then back at him. The warmth that he had felt as he initially entered the house was replaced by a wave of ice that cut deeper than the storm brewing outside.

The evidence was damning. Chris must have been waiting here for her to report back to him.

Inside, all the confusion he'd been feeling since this mission started faded away. He knew who he was, what he did, what he had to do. He didn't need or want a family. He was an assassin, a spy, a professional—and he'd let his feelings for Tina get in the way.

Jason turned his gaze back to Tina, letting every ounce of cold he felt pour out toward her. "Not involved, huh?"

He grabbed his coat off the chair by the door and could tell from its weight that the handheld was still in the pocket. He pulled it on, turned and stormed out the door, slamming it behind him. Taking several deep breaths, he stood for a moment on the porch and wondered why he hadn't just killed them both, but he realized that no matter what, he needed time to process this new information.

Maybe there was a way to work all this to his advantage, to use them both. In all his years, he'd learned that wasting a local asset should always be reserved for a final option. They were all but impossible to replace quickly. And the simple fact was that he wanted to go back in the house and take them both out, but he knew that was his anger doing his thinking for him. He had to hold back a bit, to wait. They weren't direct threats, at least not yet.

He ran all of the way back to his cabin, cursing himself the entire way. How could he have missed it? How could he have been so blind? She was a better actress than he'd given her credit for, and he'd fallen for the entire show. He tore open the door to his cabin, the wood creaking in protest, and stomped inside.

The whole mission was compromised. His cover was totally blown. And now, in addition to everything else, he was going to have to kill Tina. There was no other choice.

"Damn!" he said.

He changed into dry clothes, making sure to put on several layers to keep the cold at bay. He checked his weapons and stepped out into the bitter night. He still had a lot to do. Checking his watch, he knew that the first order of business was to get to Blue Whale Bay and send out the Scorpion to get the next load of equipment. Once that was done, he could come back and do what needed to be done with Tina and Chris.

The only silver lining to having his cover blown was that he could use whatever means were necessary to extract information about the operation from Chris.

Considering the man's attitude and how he was feeling right now, he might actually enjoy that.

JASON SENT the Scorpion to the offshore team even before he reached the cove. The rain had eased its temperamental drumming, but it did nothing to change his mood as he waited for the machine to return. He waited nearly an hour, huddled on the rocks, before the Scorpion returned, climbing onto the beach like a giant insect. The new equipment in tow was easily removed, and he started entering the navigational coordinates he thought he would need to get into the underwater cavern. Then he'd follow one of the submersibles out into the ocean, and with any luck at all, it would lead him straight to the submarine. He could accomplish his primary and secondary missions, then handle the cleanup.

"I thought I'd find you here," he heard Tina say.

He almost smiled. The damn woman had done it to him again. He reached into the Scorpion once more and turned on the scanners, then pulled his Glock out and turned around to face her. A quick glance at the scanners showed that there was no one else in the area. She was either extremely confident or extremely foolish to come alone. He knew what he needed to do next, and the laser dot appeared on her chest.

In the darkness, she noticed the steady red point of light, then brought her gaze up to meet his.

"It's amazing how quickly we've gone from stay to go," she said. She took a hesitant step back. "At my house, you thought I'd betrayed you," she said.

"Don't move," Jason said, his voice calm. She knew he intended to kill her and would do so without hesitation. "So," he continued, "I suppose this is the part where you tell me it was all a coincidence. Chris just happened to be at your house."

"Yes," she said. "It was a coincidence. It's not like I invited him over." She sat down on his quad and waited for him to approach.

He moved closer, keeping his aim steady. "Well, at least you're following the script now," he said. "Next you'll beg me not to kill you or maybe offer me up some of your smuggler friends instead—isn't that right?"

She started to reply, but he cut her off.

"I knew that I shouldn't have trusted you," he continued. "Save the pleas for mercy and since I already know who the smugglers are, offering them up won't do you any good. I should have ended all of these complications the first day out of Nome."

He raised the weapon a little bit higher. "The mission comes first."

"You really do live an empty life, don't you?" she asked. The words hit him like a cold, hard slap on the face. "You don't have *anyone* in your life that you trust. No one you can count on. I almost feel sorry for you, having been there myself once."

His finger tightened on the trigger. He had to do it.

Tina kept talking. "You know, if I really believed that you would kill me outright, without giving me a chance to even explain, I wouldn't have come out here. I hope my grandfather is right and that I'm a good judge of people. I think if you were going to kill me, I wouldn't have gotten out word one."

"Perhaps," he whispered. "I've been doing this job a long time. It's the little amusements that carry one through the tougher times."

"I don't know who you really are, Jason. And I've told you the truth. I'm not involved and I don't have any friends that you would really be interested in. I can't imagine telling you that my grandfather smokes illegally imported Cuban cigars will win me many points." She held up her hands in defeat. "I guess you'll either have to listen and make your choice or kill me and have to go on living life just as you have in the past."

He shrugged. "My past isn't so bad. I've been living with it for a long time. But what the hell, I'll play along. Why was he there? And don't tell me he was just taking a walk around the block and you ran into him."

"I don't know," she said. "He was waiting at the house when I got back. He's been after me for some time to go out with him, but I've always turned him down. I sort of figured it was done, that he'd gotten the message. Suddenly he has a renewed interest and I don't know why. But I do know that after you barged in, he didn't seem all that excited to be talking with me. If I were to guess, I'd say that he and his smuggler friends suspect you of being onto them, of having been the one that broke into their facility earlier. They probably sent him to me to try to get some information."

Jason nodded. It made a certain amount of sense. How did she manage to cloud his judgment so easily? "Anything else?" he asked.

"That's all I've got," she said. "He took off right after you did, so at this point your guesses would be as good as mine."

He moved closer, watching her breathing patterns, studying her body language. If there was even a hint of a lie, he'd shoot her dead…but there wasn't. If she was lying, she deserved an award for her acting. Still, he had to know if he could really trust her. A wandering nuclear weapon and a submarine capable of delivering it were far more important to the safety of the world than one dead woman, whether he liked her or not.

There was one button he could push, and maybe find out where she really stood.

"And the sex," he asked. "Was that all a setup, too?"

Tina jumped off the quad, marched straight up to him and slapped him across the cheek. Hard. He didn't stop her. "You bastard," she hissed.

"So, that's a no," he said, holstering the Glock.

"So you're not going to kill me?"

"Not yet," he replied. "But the night is young. I'm either a trusting fool or a very lucky guy. I guess only time will tell."

"You've worked for the government for too long. It's made you too suspicious," she said.

"In my line of work, there's no such thing," he said quietly. "And it's what has kept me alive."

Tina moved to his side and rubbed his cheek, kissing the handprint that she left. Jason turned and kissed her deeply. "I wish you'd had a better life," she said when they came up for air. "Being alive isn't the same thing as living."

This was no time for emotional entanglements. "Maybe someday I'll get the chance to try it out, but right now, you need to get back to town and I need to get back to work," he said.

"When should I expect you?"

"Probably not until later tomorrow," he replied.

"I'll see you tomorrow, then. Don't make me come looking for you."

Tina got on her quad and left. Jason watched her drive off into the distance, then turned his attention back to the submersible. He watched the radar, making sure that her signature was well and truly headed back to town. Suddenly, he saw another one pop up on-screen. And another. They were approaching fast.

Acting on instinct, he ducked his head down just as a bullet whizzed through the air where his head had been a moment before, sounding like an angry bee. He dived out of the submersible and somersaulted on the ground, his gun ready as he came up. During the roll, he heard an odd cracking sound from inside his coat, but ignored it for the moment, knowing that the quad speeding down the hill toward him took precedence. He took aim at the driver, but had to move again as a second ATV crested the hill, the passenger firing repeated bursts with a MAC-10 submachine gun.

Jason fired as he rolled, taking out the driver of the first ATV. It spun out of control, throwing the driver and the shooter to the ground in a crumpled heap. Taking cover behind a cluster of rocks, Jason turned his attention to the second quad. Like the first, there were two people on board, one driving and one shooting.

The shooter opened up with the MAC-10 again as they sped toward him. Sharp shards of rock chips flew through the air, but he kept his profile low, waiting for an opening.

Just as they turned to get a better angle, Jason moved again, rolling to one side and yanking the gunman off the quad and to the ground. The momentum of the movement had both of them tumbling toward the beach.

Jason found his feet first and pounced on him, but the man was motionless. His neck had been broken in the fall. He spun around to take on the next threat, but realized that both the quads were gone. The survivors had left their dead companions and disappeared into the night.

He quickly checked the bodies, confirming what he already suspected. The men were from town. He hopped into the submersible and checked his radar. The two quads had made it into town, and there were also boats nearby in the water. They must have been planning another weapons drop and his timing had just been bad. He quickly programmed the Scorpion to retreat back into the water, then checked his coat. Damn, he thought, pulling the shattered remains of his shooting glasses free from the pocket. So much for that toy.

If possible, he needed to keep his cover if he could. Jumping on his quad, he raced back into town, cut down an alley and went straight to Tina's. This time he didn't bother knocking as he ran into the house. He slammed the door shut as she came out of her room.

"Jason, what—"

"No time." He grabbed her by the hand and pulled her to the bedroom, stripping off his shirt and tearing hers off over her head.

"Jason—"

"They're coming," he whispered. "Move fast."

She complied, pulling at his clothes, throwing them on the far side of the bed. Jason pulled her on top of him on the bed.

They could hear someone pounding on the outer door, but neither moved to answer it. Jason heard it slam open and the rush of footsteps, but tried to focus on keeping calm, knowing that he still held his Glock beneath the blankets in his other hand if the situation went south on them.

"Tina!" someone shouted from the living room.

"What the hell!" she yelled as three men burst into her bedroom.

The cop stopped short and fumbled for words, stammering and stuttering.

She didn't bother to cover up as she turned, exposing her breasts even more as she faced them. She climbed off Jason and yanked a robe down from the closet door. "Get out! Get out of here right now!" she shouted.

The three men retreated to the living room as Tina slammed the bedroom door, then turned to Jason and winked at him. She put on her robe while Jason slipped on his jeans and a shirt, tucking his Glock into his waistband and covering it with the long shirt. Together, they walked out into the living room.

"Which one of you is going to tell me what the hell is going on here?" Tina snarled. "Sheriff Giles? Do you have an explanation?"

Giles, Chris Marley and a man Jason hadn't met before all stood in the living room, staring at the floor and looking pretty sheepish. On a bet, he would guess that the third man was one of the drivers from the quads.

"Two men were killed tonight," Giles said. "These guys think that your friend there might have done it."

12

"Oh, my God," Tina said, her voice filled with alarm. "Who was killed?"

"Rod Omiak and Joseph Kuzruk."

"What happened?" she asked.

She gestured for the men to sit down on the sofa, and took her own seat in an overstuffed chair. Jason sat on the arm of her chair. If things turned ugly, he wanted to be close to her.

"I'm not sure yet," Giles said. "I haven't even seen the bodies. Chris and Troy here came over to the house and said there was a murderer in town and they thought you might be next." He shrugged, blushing furiously. "Then when we got here, we heard noises and… Well, you know we thought…and so we… Sorry, Tina," he finished.

"Did it look like I was being murdered to you?" she asked.

"No," Giles admitted, "but there are the bodies."

"Didn't you say you haven't even seen them yet?" she asked.

"Troy here thought he saw…"

Tina turned her attention to the other man. "I'm curious to know, Troy. What did you see?"

They all gave Troy their full attention. "Well, I'm not really sure. I was just out riding my new quad, getting a little fresh air, and I thought I heard gunshots and I saw people down on the beach."

"How scary for you," Tina said. Jason could detect the mocking tone in her voice, but he wasn't sure that the other men did. "And how very brave of you to drive straight into the middle of a gun battle. You must have seen the whole thing, then."

"No, no…" he stuttered.

Jason had to stifle a smile. She was good. She had him trapped and everyone in the room knew it.

"Sheriff," Tina suggested quietly, "maybe you should investigate a little more and then come back if you have any questions for us. Jason and I have…a lot yet to do."

She stood up and walked to the door, opening it as the men followed behind her without another word. "Sheriff Giles, I know that you have so much to do, but please let me know if there is anything I can do for the families," she said.

The men walked out and Tina shut the door. She leaned against it, doing her best to hold back her laughter, while Jason watched the men retreat through the window.

"That was close," she said. "We—"

Tina turned to see Jason pulling the gun from the waistband of his jeans and sitting back on the arm of the chair with the pistol in his hand.

"You're not starting to suspect me again, are you?" she asked.

"No," he said. "But I don't think that I can leave you here and expect to come back and find you alive. The fashionable route didn't work for Chris. Something tells me that he's not going to give up on this as simple as that." He thought for a moment, then added, "He and Giles and that other guy…what was his name?"

"Troy Keelut," she said. "He's a local."

"Those three seemed pretty tight. We already know Chris is involved in the smuggling operation."

"You think Giles and Troy are working for the smugglers, too?" she asked.

"Well, let me ask you this. What did you do with that crate of weapons we brought in?"

The light dawned in her eyes, and she gritted her teeth. "I took them…"

"To Giles," he finished for her. "And he said he'd look into it or take care of it. Am I right?"

She nodded in defeat. "You were right. We should have tossed them all in the ocean. So what are you suggesting we do?" she asked.

"To use the bad cliché, I think it's time for us to get the hell out of Dodge." He gestured vaguely. "More specifically, I mean you."

"What about the sub and all of the guns? You're not just going to let them get away with what they're doing, are you?"

He shook his head. "Look, Tina, this mission is turning into a disaster, and if things keep going like they are, you're going to wind up dead!"

"You're telling me you never had a civilian die when you were working before?" she asked.

"Sure, I have," he said. "Casualties happen, but only a fool continues an operation when there has been so much exposure."

"Let me ask you this, then," she said. "If you leave now, what are the odds that you'll get the information you need about either the sub or the weapons?"

Jason stood staring at his feet for a moment, then he looked at her and said, "Slim, but that has nothing to do with it."

"I'd say it has everything to do with it. You're the one who keeps talking about the mission. Plus, I think you're forgetting something. Sure, I could leave and go with you now, but I'd never be able to come back. This is my home and I would always be in danger here. Unlike you, I happen to give a damn about whether or not I see my family and friends again."

Tina clenched her hands at her side. Jason wasn't sure if he should hit her or kiss her.

"What are you suggesting?" he asked.

"I'm suggesting that I stick with you until this is—"

"Impossible," he said flatly.

"Why?"

"You could get hurt."

"That's different because…" Her voice trailed off.

"It's different because then *I'm* putting you in harm's way."

"You've threatened to kill me yourself," she said, chuckling. "Besides, I have great faith in your ability to keep me safe."

"You're not getting it, Tina," he said, once more finding himself caught between exasperation and fondness for her stubborn streak. "I can keep me alive just fine. That's what I've been doing my whole life. But when bullets start flying, I can't make you do what you need to do in order to stay alive."

"Well, I don't see a whole hell of a lot of other options. You leave and I'm in danger. You stay and I'm in danger. I leave with you and I can't come back. At least if we stick together we have a shot at making it out of all of this alive and getting the information that you need."

Tina stuck her hand out. Jason raised an eyebrow.

"Let's meet again," she said, smiling. "Supersecret spy Tina, at your service."

Jason shook his head, laughing ruefully, then reached out and shook her hand.

"Apparently not so super or secret spy Jason, at yours," he said. "You know, you may not live to regret this."

"You won't get rid of me that easily. I'm tougher than I look," she said.

TINA RAN AROUND her cabin gathering a few items. Jason watched her, feeling more uncertain about a mission than he ever had in his life. It was just before dawn, but she didn't seem tired. He knew she hadn't really slept, but it was something that he was used to.

Most people wouldn't have been at their best this early in the morning, especially on little to no sleep.

Jason watched her struggle with pulling open a drawer. His curiosity got the better of him and he stepped forward and pulled it open for her. She reached in and stunned him silent as she removed a Russian GSh-18 model handgun and a box of 9x19 mm armor-piercing rounds.

"Not involved?" he said.

She laughed. "I told you I'm not involved in the smuggling, but I also told you we are kind of on our own up here. I bought this back before I went to New York, and I didn't ask a lot of questions."

"Mind if I take a look?" he asked.

She handed him the weapon and he checked it over. "It's a little dated," he said, "but a perfectly functional weapon." He loaded the clip, checked the action, then handed it back to her.

"Dated?" she asked.

He nodded. "This model came out in the late nineties," he said. "It received mixed reviews, but overall, it's a solid piece. Have you fired it much?"

"Just a couple of times, back when I bought it," she admitted.

"Well, the trigger pull is a little stiff, but it's consistent. The sights are okay. If you have to use it, just take your time when you fire. The feel will come back to you quickly."

"Got it," she said.

"Oh," he added, "and one other thing." He pointed to the box of shells. "Those are armor-piercing rounds, but don't count on them being able to do the job against the body armor in use today. They might, they might not, depending on the distance and the armor. Make sure before you get too close to someone you *think* is dead, okay?"

She nodded.

"Good," he said. "Now, let's go over this one more time."

"I do exactly as you say, when you say, and I never go anywhere you haven't told me to go, and if the shooting starts I keep my head down until it's over," she recited by rote. "And—I'm guessing here—I'm not to use this weapon unless I have no other choice."

"Right on all counts," he said. "And if something should happen to me?"

"I take any information that we've got and call this number—" she held up a slip of paper, then slipped it into her jewelry box "—and tell them you sent me and wait for instructions."

"Good. Let's go."

Jason looked out the window, and then headed for the door. The coast was clear as they headed for where the quads were parked. Jason climbed onto his quad, and Tina got on behind him. They drove out to a different waiting spot for the Scorpion, on the other side of the cove. The ride on the ATV was becoming commonplace, and the terrain familiar, but he was still careful to watch for spotters as they moved along the shore.

He climbed off his quad and pulled out his handheld, then quickly typed in a code, summoning the Scorpion to their location.

"How does it know where to find you?" Tina asked.

"I've mapped this entire area with grid coordinates," he said. "My handheld sends out a homing beacon of sorts—a signal, with the grid coordinates encoded. It will automatically follow the signal that it receives, so long as the coding is correct."

A small ripple of water was the only indicator that there was anything beneath the shimmering black. Jason smiled as she peered into the depths trying to discern when it had arrived. Tina jumped back as the machine made its way up the shore. Jason typed in the code on the door and waited for it to open. Tina looked inside and then at him.

"There isn't room for both of us," she said.

"Not yet."

Jason typed a new command onto his PDA and he could see the astonishment on her face when the interior adjusted to hold another person, shifting the cargo it was carrying.

"That's amazing," she whispered.

Jason was a little impressed himself. "Yeah, us superspies get all the cool toys," he said, helping Tina climb in, and then following.

"It's a little rocky until we get in the water," he warned.

Jason closed the hatch, cycled the air exchanger, then took the controls. The Scorpion propelled into motion, throwing Tina into his lap.

"Did I forget to mention that you should always wear your seat belt?" he asked, grinning.

"If that's the worst of it I should be—"

Just then Jason plunged the stick forward and commanded the Scorpion into the water.

"Fine!" Tina shrieked.

They sank into the water and the awkward motions that plagued them on land turned into graceful movements. The Scorpion moved like a dancer, pushing off any obstacles to give it extra momentum as they moved through the water. Jason decided to show it off a little as they sped along the ocean floor. The infrared radar showed their path. They slipped through the water like a fish, and the resistance seemed to disappear as they crept ever closer to the cave.

"How is it that I couldn't see something this big moving through the water?" Tina asked.

"The same reason they won't pick us up on radar," he replied. "It has a protective shield that bends light around it, making it practically invisible. It's a little like the stealth system used by Air Force planes, but better."

"Like a cloaking device," she said. "Like on *Star Trek?*"

"Never figured you for a Trekkie, but something similar, yes."

They continued to travel until they reached the mouth of the underwater cave. The luminous glow from the lights on the Scorpion dissipated as they got closer, leaving only instrument navigation. Jason watched the small blips on his screen.

"So now what?" Tina's voice was tight with anticipation.

"This is where we wait."

"Wait," she said.

Tina sat back a little stunned. The tour of the under-water wonderland had her jazzed to find out the rest. Jason knew the thrill of anticipation that knotted up in your stomach as the trap was laid, ready to move into action.

"Yes, we wait. We need to find out who these guys are reporting to or how the trade is structured. If it's just a local matter, then I'll leave it to the locals. I'm not here to divert that plan unless it coincides with mine."

"I know that you're right, but I'd rather not get involved unless we have to. I still think that I'm right. I can't believe anyone in the village would willingly do some of this stuff. I know that there are already a few that are guilty of the guns, but the other stuff…I don't want to believe that," Tina said.

"I know you don't, but we're looking for facts here. If it's any consolation, what I really want are the people involved with the sub. I don't think there are a whole lot of people in the village who know about that. A sub docking off your shores wouldn't be beneficial for the village, and I think people realize that. Plus, if it was that open of a secret the information would have gotten back to my bosses by now."

Jason punched in a few keys, and a new screen came up with 3-D images of the caves. Three submersibles looked suspended in air as the screen began to fill in.

"How are you doing that?" Tina asked.

"I put sensors in the water when I first arrived. They are tracking to the cave and bouncing information off each other and then feeding information back to the Scorpion. The program takes all of the information and compiles it into the images on-screen. It should give us a pretty good read of what is going on in the cave."

"Why not use the sensors to find the submarine?"

"If it were that easy, they wouldn't have sent me in the first place. The sub must have a pretty good hiding mechanism, or one of our satellites would have picked it up by now. If it were right in front of the sensors they might have a chance to pick it up, but it's a big ocean and so far they haven't picked up anything that large. The cave has some of the same antidetection mechanisms in place, but I know exactly where to send them so they are slipping through their sensor nets for the moment."

The three submersibles sat at their docking stations. Infrared figures were walking back and forth from each of the vehicles, loading boxes. Jason used the trackers and locked on to the boxes. Most had weapons signatures but were relatively benign. He clicked on the boxes being loaded into the third submersible, and the weapons signatures came up as nuclear. Someone very big had to be behind this, he knew. None of the locals had the resources to get the plans for the Asp, build it, plus get their hands on nuclear weapons to sell to the Russians.

Jason locked the sensors on to the third submersible. Whether or not it took him to the sub, he wanted to know where those nuclear materials were going. The three craft began to submerge and move closer to the Scorpion. Jason guided his craft farther back into the cave and waited for the cruisers to move past so he could follow.

"Did that say nuclear?" Tina asked.

"Yes," he said. "So that's the guy we're going to follow. I want to know where that's going."

The first craft glided by so close they could have reached out and touched it, but it showed no signs of detecting them. The second glided closer to them and came to a stop hovering outside of the cave. There was still no sign that they had been detected, but the second submersible held its position. Jason stared at the monitor and watched the third, his prey gliding farther and farther from him.

"They're getting away," Tina said.

"Not for long."

Jason punched up the sonar pulse.

"What does that do?"

"Hopefully, it will just seem like a strong ocean current that pushes them out of the way a little bit."

Jason hit the button and watched as the submersible moved back and up just enough for him to glide the Scorpion underneath it. He used the arms of the Scorpion to hug the seafloor until he was far enough away to move undetected. Jason maneuvered the controls and started pushing off the seafloor to get them closer to the third submersible, which was quickly moving out of tracking range.

"Damn, it's outrunning my sensors!" he said.

"Can't this thing go any faster?" Tina asked.

"The faster I move the more likely it is that we can be detected, but maybe we can push it just a little bit more," he said.

Trusting that the Scorpion would be safe, he accelerated and closed in on the third submersible.

The hum of the Scorpion's engines filled the cabin as they moved through the water. The screen began to short out, blinking out of existence as the power was drawn away from the controls and to the engine.

"We have to slow down before we lose all of our systems," Jason said.

He throttled back and tried to reboot his computer systems. The emergency system was still operational with minimal navigation and life support, but nothing else was responsive. Jason shut down the overhead switches and tried to restart it all from scratch.

"I'm not going to be happy if you kill me off in the middle of the ocean," Tina said.

"I could get us back to shore with what we have operational now. I don't want to give up the pursuit when we are so close."

Jason booted the system again, and the lights started to flicker on the screens. He turned his attention to the propulsion system to see if there was any part that was overloaded or needed some help before they took off again. He heard Tina laugh.

"What's so funny?"

"You computer must have put those submersibles in its memory. It's showing all three of them on-screen."

"What!"

He barely had the word out before the second sub crashed into the Scorpion. Tina and Jason were knocked back in their seats as the Scorpion was tossed between the three submersibles like a volleyball. Propulsion controls in hand, Jason punched in a boost command, and it rocketed them forward and out of the grasp of the underwater bullies that were pushing them around.

Jason looked at the three lights that indicated various damage points on the Scorpion.

"Now *that* pisses me off," he muttered.

He swung it around and charged at the back of the second submersible. They were bigger than the Scorpion, but not as agile. He used one control arm to grab hold of the back and the other to slash at the oxygen system. He spotted his target and took the shot, launching the arm forward and puncturing the air tank. The pressure separated the two vehicles and sent the Scorpion spiraling backward. The damaged submersible took little time in getting away and heading toward the surface for air.

The third craft charged forward into the Scorpion. Jason saw it coming and dodged at the last second, pushing off the side of the vehicle.

"Hang on!" he yelled to Tina.

Jason hit the booster again and charged toward the first submersible. He locked in and shot a harpoon into its side from the arm of the Scorpion. The submersible lurched backward and tugged at the Scorpion as it went. They plunged toward the bottom of the ocean, pulling the submersible behind them. The pressure increased around the Scorpion, but the strong shell held up against the force of the water.

The submersible pulled away from the Scorpion, but Jason was relentless. He pushed the engines to their limit trying to drag the vehicle farther under.

The towline broke and the submersible took off like

a shot. Jason looked at his radar, but they weren't on-screen.

"Where did they go?" Tina asked.

"They're here somewhere. They must be jamming our radar."

They both looked intently into the black, trying to catch a hint of the other vehicles. Small fish swam by, but the water looked undisturbed otherwise. Jason maneuvered the vehicle in a circle.

"There!" Tina cried, pointing up.

The two submersibles were descending on them, and Jason didn't have time to move as they crashed on top of the Scorpion. Jason guided the Scorpion lower, trying to get out of their range. The third submersible came around and Jason could see the pilot, and felt his jaw go slack.

It was his brother.

"No," he heard Tina gasp.

Jason moved the controls forward and rammed into the cab of the submersible. A chunk of the Scorpion's armor broke as they collided. He pulled back and was about to ram again when he realized that his anger was making him a sitting duck for the other pod. He changed course and the Scorpion dived. Looking at his radar, he saw what he was really looking for and turned toward the first pod.

"What are you doing?" Tina asked.

"I'm drawing him in closer."

"Why?"

"I have an idea."

Tina braced her hands on the frame of the cockpit and said, "I hope it's a good one."

The first submersible hit and Jason punched one of the keys. A small explosion rocked the outside of the Scorpion and small pieces of it began falling away along with a small oil slick. Jason turned the pod and pulled away from the other two. Adjusting the variable on the shield, he moved the Scorpion off to a rocky outcropping and shut everything down but the radar and the life support.

"Some idea! Now we're sitting ducks," Tina said.

"That's the idea."

"This was your clever idea? To disable us in the middle of the ocean!"

Jason smiled and looked at Tina.

"No, that was just the idea I wanted them to believe."

"I don't understand."

Jason pointed at a radar image as a large submarine came on-screen. "I wanted them to think we were out of the way so I can follow that."

13

Jason and Tina sat in awe as the submarine passed in front of them. He would have given anything to snap pictures of the exterior because he had never seen anything like it. To say it was large would have been an understatement. Jason estimated that it was at least as big as the largest sub in the American fleet. The Scorpion's cloaking device kept them hidden, but they sat in silence, afraid that the submarine's sonar might pick up them up. Jason tried to memorize every detail and let his instruments record as much data as possible.

The submarine continued to move forward and far enough out of range that it was safe to talk.

"I need to go after it," he said. "The scoop on the front is proof that they're using some form of cavitation, but it's not what I need—I need the design."

"Proof of what?" she asked. "Cavi-what?"

"They've developed a nuclear sub with supercavitation capabilities."

"Super-what?" she said. "Would you mind speaking a language I happen to know?"

"Supercavitation," he repeated. "I won't bore you with the science, but the easiest way to explain it is that they have a sub that can travel twice as fast as anything we have in the water."

"That can't be good," she said. "Okay, let's go."

"There is no way to get the Scorpion close enough without being detected. I have a dry suit on under my clothes and there is dive gear on the Scorpion."

"I'm not really keen on the idea of you just popping the hatch. I'm not the Boy Scout that you are, and I left my dry suit in my other pants," Tina said.

"You won't be getting wet, I promise," he said. "This thing comes complete with an escape hatch."

"You're not going to leave me here, are you?" she asked. "Alone?"

"It's the only choice I've got," he said. "You'll be fine."

"What if something happens?" she asked, panic filling her voice.

"Calm down," he said, soothingly. "Nothing is going to happen."

At least, that's what he hoped.

Jason typed in his wish list of dive gear on his computer. Room 59 had been very thorough in giving him the equipment that he wanted. The only thing missing was a particular regulator that he liked, but the one in inventory would work fine.

He slipped into his equipment and dialed in the escape hatch. The floor beneath his feet became translucent, and he could feel the power shield surge as he placed his feet along the edges.

"I see water, but we're not sinking," Tina said. "That's a good sign."

"The portal actually retracts and is covered by a thin layer of positively charged energy, kind of like static electricity. It tells the water to stay out, but isn't dense enough to cause me harm. Plus, the oxygen exchangers keep the compartment filled with fresh air—in other words, it keeps everything afloat. As soon as I'm through, I'll close the hatch. I have a remote to open it when I return."

"So you're really going to just leave me here. What if something happens to you?" Tina asked.

He pointed to the control panel. "See that red button on the center of the console? If you think I've gone to the great beyond, then just press that. It's preprogrammed to go to the last beacon point, which is up on the shoreline. Just be quick getting out—you'll only have a minute. A secondary protocol will go into effect, and it will return to its primary base of operations. In this particular case, that's not a place you want to visit."

"Good to know," she said. "How long—"

"Should you wait?" he asked. "I don't know, but if I'm not back in two hours, hit the button. If I'm still alive, I'll get back to shore on my own."

She was silent for a moment, then said, "You're the real thing, aren't you?"

"The real what?" he asked, confused.

"Superspy," she said. "It's not like a desk job, that's for sure."

"You don't strike me as the kind of person who'd be very happy sitting at a desk yourself," he said.

"I wasn't," she replied, maneuvering herself around to face him more directly. She kissed him lightly on the lips. "Be careful."

"It's practically my motto," he said.

Jason sealed his face mask and slipped through the portal into the cold ocean depths. The water enveloped him and he adjusted his gauges to the current depth, pressure and temperature. The dive suit itself was another Room 59 marvel—a flexible skin that would keep him warm in the extreme environment, but was strong enough to repel small-arms fire. His dive equipment included a suite of modified tracking sensors and a radar-distortion device that would make him look like nothing more than another sea creature to the sonar on a submarine or other seagoing vessel. He detached the personal propulsion system from the hull of the Scorpion and made some quick adjustments, then tapped a few buttons and he was off, headed after the submarine.

The propulsion system pulled him through the water. He hadn't traveled with this particular system before and was surprised at the speed he was able to travel. The submarine was holding a position about four miles offshore. Jason slowed his approach, not wanting his speed to give away his presence. Few sea creatures would swim as fast as he was moving, and being detected now would make getting to the sub impossible.

The massive vessel floated still and silent in the

water. Jason was amazed at the lack of distortion in the water surrounding it. Even though it was holding position, he still expected to feel the suction of the engines as he approached it, but the water was absolutely still. Either the engines were off-line, or this was the kind of technology that the bad guys should never be allowed to have.

All around him, tracking beacons floated in the water—some were his, some were not. So far, his hadn't been able to transmit the information that the submarine was in the area, so they were either jamming or ghosting on top of the signal or it was just invisible to them. From the pack he'd attached to his back, Jason removed a different type of beacon and made several adjustments to it, spreading the signal out over a larger bandwidth and on several different frequencies, including radio and ultraviolet pulse.

Shutting down the propulsion system entirely, he swam in closer to the hull of the boat. He was careful not to bump any of his equipment on the hull of the vessel, knowing the sound would travel easily through the metal skin and might alert the crew to his presence.

He attached the sensor to the underside of the sub, marveling at the smooth metal skin that was so unlike any sub he'd ever seen before. At least with the sensor placed where it was, even if it surfaced, someone would have to go beneath it to find and remove it. He began to swim along the hull, noting the location of the torpedo tubes and which one might give him the best chance for access. Using a handheld sensor, he scanned the tubes carefully, looking for anything out of the ordinary. By all indications, they were fairly standard launch tubes.

Each one had two openings. One was on the inside of the sub, where a torpedo or—in his worst nightmare—a nuclear warhead was loaded. The second was on the outside of the sub, which opened during the launch sequence, and was controlled by a computer system. He positioned a set of locking magnets around one of the tube doors.

The easy part was done. Now all he had to do was somehow access the computer system from the outside and tell it not to go crazy when he disengaged the locking mechanism and opened the tube from the outside.

He continued moving farther down the sleek hull of the sub, taking readings as he went. Finally, he found what he was searching for—a watertight access panel that had one of the main computer lines running through it. In an emergency, a crewman could open the panel and work on the system from the outside. Still, if he opened it, alarms would go off on the bridge and his mission would be doomed to failure.

Sometimes, what was needed was a subtle touch rather than brute force. He reached into his pack again, this time taking out a small transmitter with a magnetized backing and a shield much like the one that operated around his dive suit. Visually, it looked like nothing more than a sea barnacle, but if one looked closer, tiny metal tendrils could be seen floating from its surface.

He attached it to the access panel and activated the

tendrils. Much like the antenna of an ant or the tongue of a snake could read the environment, the tendrils from this device would tap into the submarine's computer system line by extending into the line itself. In some ways, it was like a computer parasite. Once it was in place, he could use his handheld in sync with his computer and tap into the sub's system. With any luck, it would be fully online within eight hours—and totally undetected.

Jason turned and began making his way back to the front end of the sub where he'd left the propulsion unit. Preoccupied with thoughts of everything he needed to accomplish, he was slow to notice the two Russian minisubs headed straight for him. He did a double take, then put on a burst of speed, barely avoiding a harpoon fired from the nearest one.

It clanked off the metal hull of the sub behind him with a sharp *pang* that echoed through the water. He knew that even a dry suit as advanced as his would have a hard time fending off gas-fired harpoons. He reached the propulsion unit just as they closed in.

Fortunately, he'd left the machine on standby mode, and it launched itself forward with barely a touch of a button. The timer on the console showed that he'd been in the water for the better part of an hour, which meant that Tina should still be waiting in the Scorpion where he'd left her. If he could somehow survive long enough to make it back, he might have a chance at escape. Out in the open water, however, he was as good as dead. Sooner or later, if nothing else, they'd simply run him over.

He pushed the unit to its top speed, then dived for the

shelter of a rocky outcropping, zipping around it just as the minisubs closed the distance once more. They would expect him to try to hide, so he did the opposite, careening around the far side and heading straight for the surface.

On the map display, he could see his location and the location of the Scorpion, but he didn't want them too close when he got there. That would be almost as bad as having them catch up to him in the open water.

He risked a glance behind and saw that the minisubs had slowed and were carefully searching for him around the rocks. The light-bending technology was working and he wasn't showing up on their sonar; they had to spot him visually in order to find him.

Jason took an indirect route back toward the Scorpion, zigzagging in different directions and varying his depth, just to be on the safe side. At one point, running without lights, he nearly collided with the bottom of one of the minisubs, but fortunately, he saw it in time to swerve away. He breathed a sigh of relief that it had been the bottom side, rather than the front where the operator would have had him dead to rights.

It took the better part of his second hour, but he finally made it back to the Scorpion and came to a stop beneath it. He knew that he had a few minutes, maybe five at the most, before they'd find him again. They'd adopted a grid search pattern and were likely using their own sonar, as well as the sub's, to track anything remotely suspicious in the water. He attached the propulsion unit to the underside of the Scorpion, grabbed his pack and used the remote to open the hatch.

He stuck his hands through the opening and pulled himself inside.

Tina was watching him, her eyes filled with fear and anxiety. As soon as he had his faceplate off, she said, "Oh, my God, are you okay? I was just about ready to push the button and give you up for dead!"

"I'm fine," he said, peeling off the dry suit as quickly as possible. "But we've got to get out of here in a hurry."

"Did you find the sub?" she asked.

"Lots of them," he said. "Including the one I was looking for."

He slipped back into the seat for the controls. "I'll bring you up to speed later, but right now, time is not our friend."

"Why not?" she asked.

"Because of the other subs I found," he said. "Or, rather, the ones that found me."

"You mean those subs?" she asked, pointing through the view screen.

"That's them," he said, punching at the controls.

The Scorpion leaped off the rock perch he'd parked it on and shot between the two oncoming minisubs like a missile. The sharp clank of another harpoon hit the side, but bounced away harmlessly. They would have to do better than that to stop him now.

"Where are we going?" she asked, watching the sonar as the subs gave chase.

"Anywhere but here," he said, trying to focus on maneuvering the vessel around rock clusters and large chunks of floating ice. The tide must have come in, bringing the ice with it. "For now, we just need a place to hide, but before we can do that—"

He veered sharply to the left, dodging a massive piece of ice and one of the other subs that had somehow managed to pull even with them.

"We've got to get away from these guys," he said.

Tina had been smart enough, he noted, to buckle herself in, and she'd quickly learned how to move with the craft, rather than fight against it. "If you can lose them, I think I know of a place we can hide," she said.

He was about to reply when she shouted, "Look out!"

But the warning came too late. The Scorpion clipped one of the larger pieces of floating ice, spun in the water and came nose to nose with one of the minisubs.

"Damn it!" Jason yelled. "Hang on!"

He slammed the craft into full reverse, but it was almost impossible to maneuver. His collision with the ice had damaged something, and the other sub stayed with him. Taking a risk, he extended the arms of the Scorpion to their full length, then slammed on the brakes. "Brace yourself!" he shouted.

The other sub smashed into the arms at nearly full speed. They pierced the main window of the craft, shattering it and allowing the sea to pour mercilessly inside. He could see the horror and surprise on the faces of the two men inside. Their mouths were open in screams of panic that he was grateful he couldn't hear. At least their deaths would be quick, Jason thought. That was more than they would have likely offered him if he'd been captured.

Engaging the engines once more, Jason began to back off, using the extended arms to shake the other sub free. One of them broke off completely, lodged in the metal frame of the craft. The other came free and he retracted it back to the body of the Scorpion.

He got them turned around, and dived lower, hoping that the other sub would be too busy trying to figure out what had happened to keep tracking them for at least a few minutes. Glancing at Tina, he saw that her eyes were filled with tears and her lips were moving silently.

"I didn't have a choice," he said softly. "They would have tried to sink us."

She shook her head. "I'm not…I'm not upset at you. All of this is just…it's so real…I don't know if that makes any sense or not."

"I'm not sure," he said. "What do you mean?"

Tina wiped her eyes. "Ever since we met, it's been like one long video game, you know? People shooting and dying and danger and thinking about those things, even playing games or watching movies, it's…it's not the same, is it?"

He shook his head. "No, I suppose it's not. Especially when you're not used to it."

"Trust me," she said, "I'm way beyond my depth here—no pun intended." She gestured at the murky water all around them.

He chuckled. "Fair enough," he said. "But I need you to hang in there for a bit longer, okay? There's at least one more sub out there looking for us, so if you know of a safe harbor where we can hide for a while, I'd sure like to know about it."

"I do," she said. "Can you bring up the map again?"

He tapped the controls and checked the sonar again for the other sub. He didn't want any more surprises at this point. He could handle it, but the Scorpion wasn't in great shape and Tina surely couldn't handle much more. She wasn't cut out for the life of a supersecret spy. But then again, not many people were.

"There," she said, pointing to a little inlet not far away.

"Why there?" he asked.

"Because there's nothing there," she said. "The ocean has eroded all the soil beneath the grasses, but they still float on the top of the water most of the year, except when it completely freezes. There should be plenty of hiding room beneath them."

"Good idea," he said, steering the craft toward the coordinates she'd pointed out.

Maybe she wasn't cut out to be a spy, but she was smart enough to think like one. He decided that no matter what, he did like that in a woman.

In fact, he liked her more than he wanted to admit. And that, he realized ruefully, made it personal.

He had to get her out of the way or abort, because once it got personal, almost every mission failed. Denny was right about that much, anyway.

14

"I think we lost them," Jason said, alternating his gaze between the view screen, which showed little but dark, muddy water and the hanging roots of the grasses above them, and the various scanners and sonar the computer was running.

"Good," Tina said, breathing a sigh of relief. "Now what?"

"We need to find a place to dock," he said, engaging the engines and easing the damaged Scorpion through the water. It lacked much of its normal grace and was running on about half its usual power. The currents that would normally be of little consequences buffeted the craft with disturbing force. Jason looked over the damage report again, and knew he needed time to do some repairs on the craft and to try to get it in a position where he had more power and control.

"We'll make port in Blue Whale Bay," he said. "I can

try to make some repairs there. While I'm doing that, you need to get to the village, pick up your grandfather and get out of here."

"I think we've had this conversation before," she said.

"The last time we had this conversation, it was a discussion. This time, it's an order. I need to get you to safety."

Tina didn't protest any further, which made him automatically suspicious. He knew he was going to have difficulty getting her to comply. His only ace in the hole was that he knew she would want to keep her grandfather safe and unharmed.

They slowly glided to shallow water, and the Scorpion's legs found land. He guided the machine behind a large rock formation that jutted out into the water. The jostling was made even worse by the damage they had taken in battle. He looked at his maintenance monitor again and realized that he was leaking fluid from one of the legs and it was barely supporting any weight. Jason didn't wait for the shutdown, but ordered the internal repairs that the system could do on its own. All of the damage couldn't be righted with the repair, but he thought it should be enough to stabilize the machine.

Jason tried to scan the area for life before they left the Scorpion, but was unable to get that sensor array up and running. They'd just have to take their chances. He popped the door and he and Tina slid down to the ground. Cramped legs and freezing temperatures made them both move a little more slowly than normal. Jason scanned the water's edge, but couldn't even detect a small ripple.

"Looks like we—"

The words weren't completely out of his mouth before Tina's scream rent the air. Jason turned, poised to shoot, but paused when he saw Sheriff Giles holding a gun under her chin. Tina's struggling stopped when he cocked the pistol.

"Giles, what the hell are you doing?" she yelled.

"Let her go, Sheriff," Jason said. "She isn't a threat to you."

"Oh, I beg to differ," Chris said, stepping out of the shadows, flanked by his friend Troy. "Ever since you showed up, our little Tina has become quite the nuisance." They moved to stand next to the sheriff, both of them with guns drawn and pointed at Jason.

He didn't blink.

Jason took each breath carefully, waiting for the opportune moment. He inched forward, pressing his body weight onto the balls of his feet, seeking that minute second when he could strike.

"I wouldn't do that if I were you," a voice said from behind him.

Jason glanced and saw his brother moving closer, aiming a nice new Russian assault rifle at his midsection. He turned more fully to stare past the rifle and into Jesse's eyes. He had already made the decision that he was going to have to kill him, but if they hurt Tina, he mentally promised a slow death. Surprised at the intensity of his own feelings, he pushed them aside.

"So," Jason sneered, "are you actually going to

shoot me with the rifle or just hold it and keep on playing soldier?"

Jesse shrugged, indifferent. "You or your girlfriend, *bro*. It makes zero difference to me. I get paid either way."

"How nice for you," Jason said.

Chris moved away from the group and walked around the Scorpion, then tried to take a look inside. Jason had already set the vehicle to automatically lock if unoccupied for more than two minutes. Chris pried at the door, but it wouldn't budge. He jogged away then returned with a crowbar. Jason couldn't help but laugh.

"You think it's funny to have your little toy smashed?" Chris said.

"No," Jason said. "I think it's funny that you're going to try. The shell is a modified titanium skin, and it's been positively charged."

"What the hell does that mean?" Chris demanded.

"It means that the locking mechanisms have been engaged," Jason replied, "and there's no way in hell you're getting in without a key."

"Yeah, well, I have my skeleton key right here."

Chris took a swing at the Scorpion. The crowbar connected with the hull, and the ion field immediately reacted to the negatively charged magnetic particles in the crowbar. Twenty-five thousand volts of electricity arced through the metal with the tangy smell of ozone and a buzzing noise, tossing Chris to the ground in a jerking heap.

"That's a pretty lousy key you've got there, Chris,"

Jason said. "And as for what a positively charged field does, I think you probably understand it better now than I could ever explain it to you. Am I right?"

"That's enough!" Giles barked. "Chris, get up, damn it."

Troy moved to help Chris up, and Jason thought about using that moment to launch an assault, but even as he tensed his muscles, he saw that Jesse's gaze wasn't the least bit distracted. "You're not that fast," he said.

Jason felt the muscles along his jawline clench in frustration, but he knew that his brother was speaking the truth. No one was that fast.

"All right," Giles said. "Let's get back to base. Troy, you and Chris in the first truck, with Jesse and Jason in the back. Tina can ride with me. That way, the hero won't get any funny notions about a rescue attempt."

"Fine," Chris snapped. "Let's do it. I know there are a few questions that I would like some answers to."

"What about the machine?" Troy asked.

"Leave it," Chris said. "We don't need it right away and it's not going anywhere. Besides, there are other things that I'd like to focus my attention on right now. There's some information that I need, and Tina and I are way overdue for our heart-to-heart conversation." He turned a leering grin in her direction. "Isn't that right, my dear?"

He leaned in closer to Tina and ran a finger along her cheek. She tilted her head invitingly and he dropped his head closer to hers. Jason saw her muscles tense and knew what she had planned. She launched forward, slamming her head into his nose with a resounding crunch.

Chris screamed in agony, and it was enough of a distraction, moving Jesse's eyes just a fraction of an inch. Jason spun and grabbed the barrel of the rifle, yanking it forward and out of Jesse's hands.

"Wha—" Chris managed to get out before Jason spun the rifle like a baton and drove the stock into his brother's chin with a crack.

Tina jumped away from Giles and Chris, moving to his side, and they began to run when Giles shouted, "Don't!" A shot from his pistol ricocheted off the rocks. They slammed to a halt.

As Jesse grabbed the rifle from Jason's hands, Chris got to his feet, blood pouring from his shattered nose. "Oh, you fucking bitch," he said. "I knew you wouldn't come quietly."

"She isn't the one that's going to have the information your boss wants," Giles said. "We should kill her and be done with it. We've wasted enough time."

"No," Chris grated between his teeth. "We'll bring her. We don't know what she knows. And besides, I know exactly how we can get her to cooperate. Send a couple of deputies over to pick up her grandfather in the village," he said.

"No!" she shouted. "Leave him alone!"

Chris walked up and grabbed her hair, wrenching her head backward. "You want him left alone? Then I suggest you learn to cooperate, starting right now, or by the time I'm through with you and your pathetic grandfather, they won't be able to identify enough of your remains to even conduct a ceremony to get you into the next world." He shook her roughly and a small cry escaped her lips. "Got me?"

She nodded, mute, and Jason knew she was finished. There was little she could tell them, though, and it would go easier for her if she broke sooner. He thought of what they might do to her to make her talk.

Chris turned his cold stare at him. "As for you, hero, I can't wait to see what my boss and I find tucked away in that brain of yours. I bet you know all sorts of things we'll find interesting."

Jason laughed softly. "You aren't smart enough to figure out that an iron crowbar and a charged field don't mix, and you think you can get me to tell you things I don't want you to know?" He laughed again, the sound mocking. "You're the most ridiculous bad guy I've ever met."

"Oh, you'll talk, tough guy," Chris said. "After a few hours or days with me and my boss, you'll tell us everything we want to know and more."

"I don't know anything," Jason said, deadpan. "And my name is Doe. John Doe." He knew talking his way out of this one was impossible, but he also knew that anyone could be broken. He would have to come up with a plan to get both himself and Tina out of this mess and he needed do it fast.

"Get moving," Giles barked. "Save the talk for when we're back at the base."

Chris tied Tina's hands in front of her while Giles continued to hold her at gunpoint, then the sheriff shoved her toward his truck.

The others took far more precautions with Jason.

Jesse, his chin dripping blood, held the rifle steadily aimed at his heart and he looked more than ready to pull the trigger. Troy and Chris tied his hands behind him and his feet together, then picked him up and tossed him into the back of the second truck.

Jesse climbed in, holding the rifle firmly. "I should shoot you now for hitting me like that," he said.

Jason kept silent, thinking furiously. There had to be a way to escape and salvage the mission, but he was drawing a blank.

All he could think about was Tina.

THE RIDE WAS COLD and uncomfortable, and the bed of the truck provided little protection from the rough ground they traveled over, so by the time they'd arrived back at the Quonset building, Jason felt bruised from head to toe. Jesse had remained silent the entire way, which suited him fine.

They might be brothers in name, looks and even blood, but Jason held no illusions about their relationship. He would kill Jesse the moment the opportunity presented itself.

When the truck came to a halt, Chris and Troy jumped out and yanked him to his feet, tossing him onto the ground with enough force to rattle his teeth. They picked him up again just as Giles got there, angry, red faced and shoving Tina in front of him. "Don't say I didn't try to help you, girl," he snapped. "Take them inside to the holding cells. I've got to get back to the village."

"What for?" Chris asked. "Don't you want to see them questioned?"

Giles grunted. "You won't get anything out of her short of torture, and he'll be even worse. Besides, your boss called and wants me to search Siku's cabin."

"What, no warrant?" Jason quipped. "I'm really beginning to think that due process hasn't come very far up here." His comments earned him another shove and he almost fell again.

"Shut up," Troy said.

"Come on," Chris said, grabbing one of Jason's arms and gesturing for Troy to take the other. "Jesse, you cover Tina. Let's get them inside. The boss will be here soon enough."

"Who's the boss?" Jason asked.

"You'll find out, and then wish you hadn't," Chris said. He and Troy lifted him and began carrying him to the building.

"You don't mean Boris, do you?" he asked. "Boris Ambros?"

They stopped suddenly. "How'd you know—" Troy demanded.

"He's a spy, you dumb-ass," Chris snarled. "How do you think he knows?"

"Oh," Troy said, then they kept moving.

The guards let them pass into the building without saying a word, and they entered the building through the same door that Jason had used before. "Say, this looks familiar," he said.

"I don't think the problem is going to be getting him to talk," Jesse said. "The problem will be getting him to shut up."

"This is what family means to you, huh, Jesse?" Tina

asked. "You and Giles have a lot in common. He seems to think that his only family is money. That how you feel?"

"That how you got him so riled, Tina?" he replied. "Talk to him about his family? Do you know his mother has cancer and no insurance? He's doing what he's doing *for* his family."

"You don't hurt other people for your family, you idiot," she said. "Not for money and not for anything else. A real family doesn't expect it from you and wouldn't want blood money, anyway. The ties that bind a real family together are more tightly wound than any packet of cash you'll be earning for your work today."

"Maybe," he said, shoving her along. "But I don't have a family, remember?"

"You could have," she whispered. "But you were too selfish to see it."

"Just shut it, Tina," he said.

Instead of going down into the cavern below, they went to the far side of the building, an area Jason hadn't explored before. Along the wall, six heavy metal doors were set at even intervals. Each door had a small slot at the bottom where a tray could slide through, but no windows. The lock was electronic and Jason studied it carefully as Chris opened the first door and shoved him into an empty eight-by-eight room. The floors and the walls were made of poured concrete.

"Enjoy your stay." He laughed. "I'll be seeing you real soon, hero."

Troy stepped forward and cut the ropes binding his

feet together, but left his hands tied. "Don't try to escape—" he said, but Jason cut him off.

"Wouldn't dream of it," he said. "I wouldn't want to miss the chance to visit with old Boris in person."

"Yeah, whatever," Troy said. "It's your death."

They slammed the door, and Jason could hear a series of clicks as the lock was reengaged.

He listened carefully, worried that Chris might try to force himself on Tina, but from the sounds of it, they put her in the next cell over and locked her in. The lock was the same electronic model as the one on his door, and the tones were the same, too. He heard the three men leaving, but they didn't speak other than to taunt them both with a final call of, "See you soon!"

Silence descended and Jason studied the room once more. Pounding on the walls would be useless and there were no windows.

He lay down on the cold floor and pushed open the tiny slot for the tray. "Tina?" he said. "Can you hear me?"

He heard the squeak of metal and then her reply. "Yes, I can hear you," she said.

"Are you okay?" he asked. "Giles didn't hurt you, did he?"

"I'm all right," she said. "Scared witless, but physically okay."

"Good," he said.

"Jason?"

"Yes?" he replied. "What is it?"

"We're in serious trouble, aren't we?"

He tried to think of something clever to say, some

lie that might soften what was coming, and knew that nothing he could say would make the situation any better. She was strong enough to know the truth, probably knew it already.

"Jason?" she repeated.

"Yes," he admitted. "We're in trouble. Big trouble."

"That's what I thought," she said. "Do you have a plan?"

"Just one for the moment," he said, sighing. He was bone tired and things weren't going to get any better in that regard anytime soon.

"Great!" she said. "What is it?"

"Pray," he replied, his voice grim. "It's pretty much all we've got left."

15

Several hours passed in the cold cells and they spoke very little. There wasn't much to say, despite the thoughts racing through Jason's mind. Finally, they heard the sound of boots approaching, and Jason risked one last bit of conversation.

"Remember what I've told you," he said. "Let them focus on me and answer anything they want to know. Don't make them hurt you. With any luck, they're more interested in what I know than what you know."

"With any luck," she said. "Since when have we been lucky on this trip?"

"Well," he said, "just the once."

They both laughed and it felt good to be able to do so, regardless of their circumstances. Jason got to his feet and stood waiting for them to open the door. The electronic lock was once again keyed and his door opened, revealing Troy, along with two of the uniformed guards he'd seen before.

"Come on," Troy said. He held Tina's 9 mm Russian pistol in his hand and gestured with it. "It's time to go see Boris."

Jason shrugged and stepped out of the cell. "They left you in charge?" he asked. "Desperate for help, are they?"

Troy sighed heavily. "Just please shut up, man." He glanced at the guards and they took up a position on either side of him. Both of them were armed with the Russian assault rifles, as well as handguns. Once he felt that Jason was secure, Troy unlocked Tina's cell and motioned for her to step out.

She did and he fell in behind her, telling the guards, "We're taking them to see Boris."

Both guards sniggered under their breath. Boris, Jason thought, must be a real charmer.

Their trip didn't take very long, and soon the guards led them into another concrete room. This one was decorated, however, in the tasteful style of the Spanish Inquisition. It was going to be an interesting meeting, involving no small amount of screaming and bloodshed if the tools displayed on the stainless-steel surgeon's tray were any indication.

Seated on a folding chair in the middle of the room was a massive man. His eyes barely flickered when they entered, and in Russian he instructed the guards to handcuff Tina to the manacles on the wall. They did so, hoisting her up so that her feet were dangling off the ground. It was fortunate she didn't weigh very much or her own body weight might well have dislocated her shoulders. As it was, Jason knew the pain must have been considerable. She kept her lips pressed tightly together.

"What about him, boss?" Troy asked, shoving Jason forward a step. "Where do you want him?"

"I hate speaking English to you, peasant," the man rumbled, "but you would not understand me if I spoke Russian, which is a beautiful language." He got to his feet and Troy involuntarily took a step backward.

Jason followed suit, trying to gauge their interrogator. Aside from his massive size, which was all muscle, he was completely bald, with hard eyes so dark brown they were almost black. Thin eyebrows rode over the top of them and he had a hawk nose that had clearly been broken more than once. Several scars were visible on his arms, but the real eye-catcher was the grapevine scar that ran from behind his right ear, over his throat and down beneath his shirt. Must have missed his jugular by less than an inch, Jason thought. Too bad for us.

The man wore BDU-style pants, and a black T-shirt that was stretched over his body so tightly that every movement probably came close to rendering it useless. "I will handle him myself," he said. "You may go."

Troy and the guards didn't need much more encouragement and beat a hasty exit out the door.

In Russian, Jason said, "I was hoping we could spend some time alone together."

The giant laughed, his tone cruel. "No doubt we will, Mr. Siku, in due time." He gestured to the chair. "Please, sit down."

"I'd rather stand, if it's okay with you," Jason said.

"Not really," the Russian replied. He lashed out with one fist, and in spite of his size, the man was also gifted with surprising speed. Jason didn't have time to duck as the fist crashed into the side of his head, dropping him to his knees and filling his skull with a faint buzzing sound.

He felt himself lifted into the air and set on the metal folding chair. He shook his head to clear it. "Wow," he said. "You don't play light, do you?"

"I am Boris Ambros," the Russian said. "In Moscow, I am called the Siberian Bear."

"If the shoe fits…" Jason muttered.

"Yes, indeed," Boris said. "So, Mr. Siku, I want to reach an understanding with you. You are fluent in my language, so we will speak in the mother tongue. If you speak in English, I will break one of your fingers. Do it a second time—" he nodded in Tina's direction "—and I will break one of hers. Do we have an understanding?"

"Yes," Jason replied in Russian. "We have an understanding."

"Good," he said. "Now we can begin." He moved to stand closer to Jason, a slight smile on his face.

"I'm breathless with anticipation," Jason said.

The Russian laughed once more. "It is good that you have a sense of humor. We shall see if you still have it when we are finished here." He didn't wait for a reply, but dived right in. "You are Jason Siku, and you are a spy, sent here by your government. There is no question about this."

"I already told your men, my name is Doe. John Doe. I am not a spy, but a traveling salesman. I sell high-end personal submarines to the wealthy Inuit people along the coast here. Don't you know they're actually loaded with cash?" Conjuring up some saliva, he spit on the floor, barely missing the toe of the Russian's boots. "Can I get a drink of water? The standard of care in your cells is horrible."

Once more, the meaty fist lashed out, this time slamming into his jaw. Jason felt himself come out of the chair for a moment before he crashed to the floor in a crumpled heap. A groan escaped him as Boris picked him up again and set him back in the chair. It took all of his strength to not fall out of it again.

"You are Jason Siku, and you are a spy, sent here by your government. There is no question about this," Boris stated again. "They will not come for you. They never do."

Since he hadn't asked a question, Jason didn't bother with a reply. He knew what was coming and that he'd better start conserving his strength. When the silence stretched on for another minute or so, Boris said, "Good, you are learning."

He turned to Tina. "Your man is strong," he said to her. "And smart. See how he saves his energy? In time, I will break him. Then…I will break you."

That snapped Jason out of his stupor. "She doesn't know a damn thing," he said. "Why not stay where the action is?"

"I am already aware that she knows more than she has told you," Boris said. "I had one of my men run her fingerprints. It is interesting to me how a woman so young can have two identities. We will explore that later, I assure you."

Stunned, Jason said nothing. Had he been wrong about her all along? Who was she really?

Boris repeated his stock phrase once more. "You are Jason Siku, and you are a spy, sent here by your government. There is no question about this." He stretched his hands, cracking his knuckles. "You will tell me which agency you work for and you will tell me everything you have learned, and when we are done, you will tell me anything else I want to know."

Glaring into the man's eyes, Jason said, "Why don't you untie me? If you can beat me in a fair fight, I'll tell you everything you've ever wanted to know and more."

"Why should I?" Boris asked. "You will tell me anyway, and this way, the only blood on my clothes is yours."

"You're sure about that?" Jason asked. Even as the words left his lips, he lunged forward, snapping a kick at the man's knee. He felt it connect and Boris actually rocked slightly as the knee started to give.

But the angle was wrong and Jason didn't have enough momentum to break it or dislocate it. Before he could try another move, from his half-kneeling position, Boris sucker punched him in the solar plexus, and the air whooshed out of his lungs in a rush. Coming upright, the Russian followed up with an uppercut that took Jason directly under the chin, knocking him backward and half-senseless.

This time, the groan that escaped his lips was louder.

"Playtime is now over," Boris said, lifting him once more. "Now we do it slow, instead of nice and fast."

Before Jason could respond, the Russian slammed him down hard onto a steel table. From far away, he heard Tina gasp in shared pain. Boris quickly used leather straps on his ankles, then cut the rope tying his hands and strapped them down tightly, too.

His air was finally coming back and Jason said, "Normally, I prefer to do it slow, but are you sure we can't go back to the nice and fast way?" Even as the words left his mouth, he realized his mistake. He'd spoken in English.

Boris didn't bother with a reply, but simply reached out and snatched the pinky finger of his left hand and broke it like a winter-dry twig. Jason hissed in pain.

"That is the first time," Boris said. "You have lots of fingers left. So does she."

Jason knew it was useless. The mission was toast and sooner or later, he'd break. "Fuck you, Bear Boy," he snarled, returning to Russian. "You look more like a cub to me."

That did the trick. The Russian roared in anger and drove his massive fist into Jason's rib cage. Bracing for the impact did little to make it better, and he felt at least one rib, maybe two, crack beneath the onslaught.

Wheezing, he said, "Are you just going to beat me up? When are you going to start asking questions, maybe using all those tools you've got there?"

Boris took a deep breath. "Those tools are for someone else," he said, calm once more. "First question. What agency do you work for?"

"Several," Jason said, trying to make it sound like an admission.

"Which ones, then?"

"Let's see…there's P.E.T.A.," he said. "I just hate seeing animals mistreated or eaten. And there's the V.H.F.T.S., that's the Vegetables Have Feelings, Too, Society, and then—"

He didn't manage to get the last one out as Boris once again punched him in the ribs. Nothing broke this time, but once more he was without air.

"Which agency do you work for?" Boris said again.

Trying to somehow swallow enough air, Jason tried to reply and found he couldn't.

From across the room, Tina said, "I can tell you that." Her Russian was flawless, he noticed.

She was trying to buy him time to rest, and get his wind back, he hoped, and she was also wrecking what little plan he had. If he made Boris angry enough to beat him unconscious, they might just toss them back in their cells and try again later.

"Tina, no," he said. "Don't."

"Please continue," Boris said, moving to stand before her. "You do not like to see your man mistreated."

"You're right, I don't," she said. "He told me who he works for. I don't work for them. Never have. Can't stand the government, you know?" Her voice tone and pitch had suddenly changed into full-on, idiot-blonde mode. "I'd rather be shopping or going to the mall or—"

The slap sounded like a rifle shot in the small room and Tina's voice was immediately silent.

"I prefer not to hurt women," Boris said, his voice

low and deep. "But for you, I make a special exception." He slapped her again, and Jason almost felt it himself.

"You are Tina Kanut," Boris said. "At least, that is one of your identities. We do not think you work for anyone anymore. Who does your man work for?"

By craning his neck, Jason could see her hanging on the wall. Her head was lolling and blood trickled from where her lip had been split. Boris moved to the table and picked up a glass of water, then crossed back to Tina. "Here, drink this," he said. "It will help clear your head."

Tina gratefully took a long gulp of the water and her eyes regained some of their focus.

"I have been kind to you, see? Now, you be kind to me and tell me who he works for."

"He told me he worked for the CIA," she said, after a moment's hesitation. "Black ops or something silly like that."

"It is good work, if you can get it," Boris rumbled.

Wondering how a woman with Tina's background would even think to say "CIA black ops," Jason watched as Boris returned to where he lay.

"I have met several of your comrades, Mr. Siku, under similar circumstances. They were weak."

"I was pretty sure you had," Jason said. "You seem very practiced at this."

"I will accept your words as a compliment," Boris said. "Second question. What interest does the CIA have in this region? Why did they send you?"

"That's two questions," he said. "You only get one at a time."

Things got kind of hazy for a time after that. When Boris wasn't asking him questions or hitting him, he would move back to Tina and slap her around some. After a time, Jason had revealed that, yes, he worked for the CIA. Yes, he worked in the black ops division. Yes, they knew all about the submarine and he'd been sent here to confirm it. It was nothing they didn't already suspect or know.

Once, he asked for his phone call and a lawyer, which earned him another good pounding.

As he came to from that one, the first sound that registered was the very nearby whirling of helicopter blades. In fact, they sounded as if they were right on top of him. He opened his eyes and realized that the sound had stopped. The chopper was either shut down or gone.

"Ah, that is sad," Boris said. "Our time is at an end. Soon, you will meet the man I work for."

"I thought you were the boss," Jason said, his voice a croak. "That's what all the boys kept saying."

"No," the Russian replied. "I am his second-in-command, a lieutenant, if you will."

"So, who's the big boss?" he asked. "When can I meet him?"

"You will meet Feng Li soon enough," Boris said. "And you will not have as much fun with him as you have with me."

"Oh? Why's that?" he asked.

"Because Feng Li is the man who owns the tools on

the tray. He will peel back your skin one layer at a time until you tell him anything he wants to know, Mr. Siku. I have seen this many times before."

"Everyone needs a hobby. Besides, what else can I tell him that I haven't told you?"

"The truth," Boris said. "You have not told me anything I did not already know and you have told me lies, as well." He moved to the door and opened it, gesturing for the guards to step inside. "Take them back to their cells. Mr. Li will want to see them soon, but not just yet."

"Yes, sir," they said.

Neither prisoner could walk back to the cells, so the guards dragged them instead. There was no point in resisting. Tina probably couldn't feel her legs and had been knocked around pretty good. And Jason had taken worse beatings, but not many that he could remember.

He glanced at Tina and saw that she was looking at him.

"Who are you?" he mouthed, but she shook her head.

The guards returned them to their cells and tossed them inside, locking the doors once more. Lying on the cold concrete floor actually felt soothing to Jason's battered body. He crawled closer to the slot in the door.

"Tina," he said. "Can you hear me?"

"Yes," she replied, her voice barely a whisper.

"Who are you?" he asked. "Really?"

"Tina Kanut," she said. She sounded tired. "I've told you that already."

"Your Russian is flawless," he said.

"Thanks," she muttered. "I practiced hard to learn it."

They were both silent for a few minutes, the exhaustion setting in.

"I know that name," Tina finally said. "Feng Li. I know that name."

"How?" he asked. "From where?"

"I'm too tired, Jason," she said. "I can't think right now. I can't place it, but I know it."

"You need to tell me who you really are, why Boris said you have two identities," he said.

"Ask me again," she replied, "but after I've rested."

Then she went silent and while he was waiting for her to say something more, he fell into sleep himself.

The dreams were not good.

16

Consciousness returned slowly. The first thing Jason was aware of was the icy cold of the concrete floor, but the idea of getting to his feet seemed out of reach. A frustrated groan passed his lips and he struggled to his knees, trying to ignore the various pains the pounding Boris had given him.

He wondered how long he could hold out, how long Tina could hold out, but the answer was moot. The truth was that he'd hold out as long as *they* wanted him to.

"Tina," he called. "You awake?"

"Jason!" she said. "I've been calling your name for a half hour. I thought…I thought maybe you were dead."

"Not yet," he said. "But I've felt better."

"I was thinking maybe they came for you while I was asleep, and they'd killed you."

"Ha!" he managed to say. "Like they could."

"You still have the strength to be a smart-ass?" she said. "That sure helped you with Boris."

"Well, if you can't laugh when you're being tortured, when can you laugh?"

He could hear her pained giggle, followed by a few groans.

"How are you holding up?" he asked.

"I've been better myself," she said, "but it's nothing that I can't handle so far. I think they are playing with me for fun. Boris and Chris both know I don't have the information they're looking for, and the Russian found me a dull playmate." She paused, then laughed again. "You know, I think Chris is just pissed that I turned him down for a date. I knew that some people didn't take rejection well, but this does seem a little extreme."

Jason laughed and felt some of his tension ease away. If she could hold up just a little longer—he knew he could—then perhaps they'd figure a way out of this mess yet.

A slow scraping sound was followed by a loud crash in the hallway, and Jason dragged himself to his feet.

"Sounds like our boys are getting a bit rowdy out there," Tina said. "Is that a good sign or a bad one?"

"I don't know," he said. "Stay on your toes."

Heavy footsteps sounded outside their cell doors, and Jason knew it was a sound that he wasn't likely to forget in this lifetime. He stepped back and crossed his arms over his chest. Boris had already had his go at him, which meant they were probably coming to get him for Feng Li.

Boris didn't seem like the kind of man to lie. Feng Li would undoubtedly be worse. It was likely he wouldn't survive an interrogation with whoever the mystery man was. He was going to have to make his move now, before it was too late. Strapped down to a table, he wouldn't accomplish anything.

Jason stretched his arms and legs, trying to ease the cramped muscles. Despite his injuries, he could still fight and he felt a tight grin pass his lips.

Outside his door, he heard a familiar voice say, "How do we get them out of those?"

"I don't know," a second voice replied. "I thought you would know. Don't you work for these guys?"

Jason cocked his head. That last blow from Boris must have done more damage than he thought, because it sounded like Jesse.

"Grandfather?" Tina whispered.

Jason heard steps scurry to her cell.

"Grandfather, what are you doing here?" she demanded.

"Getting you out," he said, his voice gruff. "We just have to figure out how to get these doors open."

"Hey, guys," Jason called.

"Maybe if we smash the keypad the door will unlock," Jesse said.

"No," her grandfather argued, "that will keep them in there forever."

Jason couldn't believe that they were ignoring him. "Jesse!" he yelled.

"What?"

"The door code for Tina's cell is 1142658."

"How do you know that?" Tanuk asked.

"Trust me," he said, sighing. "I just know."

Jason heard the tones of the keys and her door springing open from its lock.

"What's the code for your door?" Tina asked as she ran to open it.

He gave it to her.

She punched in the code and the door swung free.

"So was that you guys making the ruckus in the hallway?" he asked.

"Yeah, but it should be clear for a little bit," Jesse said.

"Let's not count on that," Jason replied. "If it weren't for bad luck lately, I'd have no luck at all."

They moved to the long hallway, but had only taken a few steps when the first guard stepped into their path. Jason wasn't about to get stuck in that cell again, but as he tensed for action, Jesse reached forward, placed a firm hand on his shoulder and stepped in front of him.

"Hey, Paul," he said.

"Christ, Jesse! You scared the hell out of me. I thought those guys were loose for a minute," he said.

"I've got it under control," Jesse replied. He stepped forward and placed a hand on the Mini MAC-10 the guard had pointed at them. Paul started to lower the weapon and Jesse yanked the gun out of his hand and in one quick move, smashed it against the side of Paul's head.

The man dropped, hitting the floor with a thud.

"Will that do?" Jesse asked.

"Not all that subtle, but I like it," Jason said.

They made it to the front door and Jesse stuck his head out, then signaled for the others to follow. A small group of guards was approaching the building. Jesse raised his hand to wave, but they opened fire.

"I don't think they believe that you are taking us to see Boris again," Jason said. "Find cover!"

They ran for the other side of the building as Jesse laid down a burst of covering fire while they moved. A moment later, he was crouched next to them. In his shoulder holster, Jason saw that Jesse had his Glock.

"Hey, that's mine!" he said.

"I thought brothers were supposed to share," Jesse said.

Jason reached forward and pulled the pistol from the holster. "Mine!"

He leaped forward, moving into view and drawing the fire of the guards. Adrenaline and anger surged through his veins, and four well-placed shots later, the rain of gunfire dissipated. He took cover on the other side of a truck and waved for the others to join him. Jason and Jesse covered their movements, using any guard foolish enough to pop his head up as target practice.

He felt a tugging on the back of his shirt and glanced to see Tina behind him. "Time to go," she said. "Better to run and live to fight another day and all that."

He nodded. "All right." He fired one last burst, then turned to run and almost tripped over Tina, who he'd expected to already be moving. She was staring wide-eyed at the new group of men running at them from the Quonset building.

"Holy shit! That's it!" she exclaimed. "We've got to move."

"That's kind of what I'm trying to do," Jason said, promising himself that if they got out of this, Tina was going to be answering a lot of questions. "Get going!"

Startled into action, she ran for the SUV where everyone else was already seated. It started moving and they ran alongside and jumped in. The engines revved and the whine and ping of bullets could be heard as the guards opened up completely.

Jason was barely in his seat when Jesse tossed a grenade into his lap. He looked at his brother.

"Well," Jesse said, "you do know how to use the damn thing, don't you?"

Jason waited until the gang that was following got a little closer, then popped the pin and counted off a few seconds. Leaning out the window, he threw the grenade, which landed directly beneath the pickup that was in pursuit. It detonated, tossing the truck into the air. It landed on its tailgate, spilling out the guards in a heap on the ground.

Jason laughed and sat back down as Tina's grandfather drove into the frozen wilderness.

A few miles later, Jason said, "We've got to stop. I need to find where they're keeping my stuff. There are things I'm going to need."

"It's not a problem, little brother," Jesse said. "I've got it all here." He jabbed a thumb in the direction of the SUV's cargo area.

"What the hell is going on here?" Jason asked. "I didn't see you being all helpful when the bald beauty was kicking my ass. Could have used a little support then, *bro*. What's with the sudden change of heart?"

"Look, Jason, I told you the first time we met that I wasn't looking for family, and I meant it. But I suddenly realized I have no choice in the matter. Like it or not, you're family and that's it."

"Bullshit," Jason said. He could tell from Jesse's body language that his brother wasn't exactly lying, but he wasn't saying everything, either. "That's not what changed your mind. I want the truth."

"What are you, some kind of fucking psychic?" Jesse asked. "Fine, you're right. That's not what changed my mind. I didn't like what they were doing, but I needed to make a living and the pay was better than good. I didn't see a whole lot of other options."

"There are always other choices," Tina said.

"Yeah, well, I didn't see one. At least not until I got to Jason's cabin in town. Sheriff Giles was dead on the floor and Chris was there, getting ready to do a little inventory on your stuff. He told me to gather it all up and bring it to base and then he kicked Giles's body and told me to be sure and take out the trash before I left. That's when I realized it wouldn't be too long before he decided I wasn't worth any more than Giles had been."

"So you're bailing out?" Jason asked.

Jesse offered him a hard stare. "Listen to me. If I'd wanted to leave you in that cell to rot and taken off, maybe left the country, I would have. But sooner or later, they'd find me. Boris and his boss have a very long reach. I'd be a dead man walking." He broke the eye contact and stared out the window. "Guess I figured that if I'm going to die, it may as well be for doing something right for once in my life."

"We're here," Tina said as the SUV rolled to a stop.

"Where is here?" Jason asked. He looked around and couldn't see anything but the brown tundra grass and a few small birds in the distance.

"Things are not always what they seem," Tina said.

She marched forward and walked around in an area that was covered with grass. Then she came to sudden stop and pulled on a chain that was attached to a sliding door in the ground.

Peering into the darkness inside, Jason momentarily hesitated, but Tina scampered down the ladder, and the others followed behind. They all stood in one corner while Jesse lit several oil lamps to give them light. He went to work getting the generator cranked up.

Jason looked around at the crates that were scattered throughout the room. The labels were in several different languages, most of which he knew. Munitions, guns and other items were being stored underground.

"This one of your warehouses?" Jason asked Jesse.

"Not mine," he said. "This one belongs to Tanuk."

"Grandfather!" Tina gasped. "How could you? You told me you were out of the smuggling years ago!"

"All due respect to your grandfather, but, Jesse, you're using a guy that is like nine hundred years old in your smuggling operation?" Jason asked. "It can't be that tough to get good help out here."

Tanuk chuckled quietly. "No one looks twice at me. I am a very old man and I make a good cover for the operation."

Jason looked at Tina and raised an eyebrow. "Let me guess," he said. "You didn't know. Are you sure about that, Tina? Or is there some other name I should be calling you instead?"

She grabbed him firmly by the arm. "Come with me," she said. "We need to talk."

He allowed her to guide him farther back into the cavern. The crates made for crude hallways and seemed to go on almost endlessly until the space opened up into a much larger space the size of a basketball court.

"Okay," she said. "I know you have questions. And I'll answer them, but the important thing is that I know the man behind all this. Feng Li. I know who he is."

"You're kidding!" Jason exclaimed. "You mean that being here among your family and friends, who happen to be *working* for the man, has suddenly filled in the gaps in your memory? Color me amazed."

"It's not the way it looks, Jason," she said. "And sarcasm isn't going to help us. It's not what we need right now."

"I'm sorry, Tina," he said, his tone mocking. "I'm just a little cranky after having my entire mission blow up in my face, being captured and tortured, only to find out that the one person I've been trusting has been lying her cute little ass off to me."

She lowered her head. "You're right," she admitted. "I have…lied. But they were lies of omission, not lies of fact."

"That will make a big difference when my boss has me killed," he said.

"Denny?" she asked. "I'll take care of it."

"What do you mean you'll take…" Jason's voice faltered. "Denny? How do you know that name?"

"Jason," she said quietly, "I know who you are."

"You've known that since the day we met," he said.

"Not your name," she replied, "but God only knows if that is your name. I mean I know who you work for. Room 59. Ring any bells for you?"

"How do you—" he began.

She shrugged. "I know because I work for them, too."

"What?" he asked, her words not registering as real. "You're not a…you don't act like a field agent. I don't understand."

"I'm not a field agent," she said. "I went through the basic training, but most of my work is doing intercepted-Russian-communication translations. When I worked in New York, I did some intelligence analysis, too. I used a different name, but when I came home, I started using my birth name again." She looked up at him. "I haven't kept any secrets from you that you haven't been keeping from me."

Still stunned, Jason said, "You work for Room 59?"

"Yeah," she said. "I came up here when I realized that city life just wasn't for me. They found a way to keep me on up here, and the work I do is valuable. We both had the same secret, the only difference being that I knew who you were working for and you didn't know that I work for them myself."

"But if you knew who I was…" he said, then his voice trailed off. "They told you I was coming, didn't they?"

She nodded. "Yes. I was supposed to keep an eye on you, lend you a hand if you needed one. This is your first mission, after all."

"Keep an eye on me?" he snarled. "Is that what… what all of this was? You keeping an eye on me?"

"No!" she said. "Yes." She sighed heavily. "At first, yes. You were just an assignment, but…I do care about you. I don't know what that really means yet or how you feel or even what I'll feel when all this is over. I was doing my job, damn it, the same as you."

Running his hands through his hair, Jason tried to wrap his mind around the fact that she worked for Room 59, that she'd been playing him as well or better than he'd played her. "I guess you'd make a hell of a field agent, if you ever set your mind to it," he said. "You sure had me fooled."

"I wasn't trying to trick you, Jason. You've said it yourself—the mission comes first. I decided that it was time you knew the truth. We're coming down to the end here and you're going to need all the resources you've got—including me."

"True enough," he admitted.

"Look," she said, "I've been trying to help you, but I'm not a field agent, and really…I'm better at doing translations than analysis anyway. It's been great to have a steady paycheck while doing something that came easily to me, but I'm not a big part of the Room 59 machine. I'm a little, tiny cog and other than filing my reports, I have almost no contact with them. When I was there, I just figured out that it wasn't my world. It was me trying to be someone I wasn't."

Jason sat down on a nearby crate, trying to take it all in, then he sighed. "I can't think of any reason for you to lie," he finally said. "So, you work for Room 59. That *might* be enough to save me, if I can get this mission salvaged."

"And that," she said, "is what I've been trying to get at. Feng Li. I know who he is."

"I don't get it," he said. "How do you know him?"

"I want to be sure," she said. "Let's get your stuff set up and get online with Denny. All my gear is back in the village. We can pull up the databases we'll need at the same time."

Jason stood up abruptly and crossed his arms. "No way," he said. "You think I'm just going to take your word for all this? Your grandfather works for them!"

"So does your brother," she snapped back. "You're going to have to choose whether or not you trust me."

"I don't have any reason to trust you, do I?" he said. "You could have been straight with me from the beginning. You could have said you worked for the CIA, the FBI or the NSA. Why play the native guide?"

"It's my cover," she snapped. "And I happen to be a very good guide!"

"You could have said you worked for—"

"P.E.T.A.?" she interrupted.

He stopped suddenly, realizing that he was yelling and waving his arms like a madman. This woman was going to drive him completely insane before this mission was through. They both laughed, and once again the tension eased between them.

"That was a pretty good one, wasn't it?" he said.

"Considering the circumstances, I'd say it was comedic genius," she replied.

In two strides, he had her in his arms. "I thought…I thought they'd hurt you," he said, holding her tightly. "You get me all turned around, you know?"

Laying her head on his chest, she nodded. "I know. You do the same to me. There's a reason why they preach the Don't Let It Get Personal motto to every agent. It messes with your thinking."

"You weren't an agent," he said. "So how do I get you turned around?"

"I care about you," she said. "More than I wanted to admit."

"Are you two about done in there?" Jesse's voice echoed loudly through the cavern. "Or should we book you a nice room at the village motel?"

Kissing him softly on the lips, she said, "We're about done in here. Did you bring Jason's equipment in?"

"Yeah, and I hid the truck on the back side of those scrub trees and covered it up pretty well."

"They'll be looking for us," Jason said. "And when they find us, they'll bring everything they've got, including the Asp."

"I know," she said. "That's why it's time for us to report in to Denny and give him an update. Once he knows the situation on the ground and I can tell him about Feng Li, we'll have a better idea of what to do next."

"Who is Feng Li?" Jason asked as he followed her back to the other room. "You sound almost scared of him."

"There's no 'almost' to it," she said. "I'm terrified of him."

"Why?"

"Because he used to work for Room 59, too," she said. "He started out as a field agent, and worked his way up to running one of the midnight teams until he went to the other side."

Jason stopped suddenly in his tracks. "He's an ex-agent?"

"Yes," she said. "And he's supposed to be dead."

17

"You are well, granddaughter?" Tanuk asked when they entered the main room. "You told him the truth?"

"Yes, on both counts," Tina said, leaning down to kiss the old man's cheek. "Though at some point, you and I are going to have a talk about all of this. I knew of this place, but you'd promised me that you weren't involved in the smuggling anymore."

She knelt down next to him and took his hand. "I don't understand," she said. "It's not like we really needed the money."

"I am sorry," Tanuk said. "I did not do it for the money. I just wanted to feel alive again, Tina. The years have crept up on me and I wanted one more adventure. Had I known what I was getting into…" The old man shrugged. "Wisdom can come from anywhere, at any age. This turned out to be a little more adventure than I had in mind."

Jason chuckled. "That makes two of us, at any rate." He turned to Jesse. "You've got my stuff?"

"Over on the table there," he said. "And the generator is up, so we've got full power."

Jason pulled a rickety wooden chair over to the table and sat down. "The question is whether or not I can get a good linkup from belowground. That can be sketchy sometimes, but maybe today we'll be lucky."

"I thought you didn't believe in luck on this mission," Tina said.

"The tide's got to turn sooner or later," he said, booting up his computer. He quickly looked his system over, but it appeared that Chris hadn't had time to explore anything before Jesse arrived.

"All right," he said, launching the software that would connect him to Room 59 via a virtual private network, routed through a satellite. "Let's see if we can get a tune out of this trombone."

He listened as the computer clicked and whirred through its task. It took slightly longer than usual, but the log-on screen eventually came on and he went through the security protocols. Once confirmed, he sent his avatar down the hallway and into the virtual offices of Room 59.

As usual, he didn't pause to greet anyone else, but made a beeline for Denny's office. He tapped urgently on the door, and his boss's smooth voice said, "Come in, Jason."

Jason entered Denny's virtual office, while in the real world, he motioned for Tina to move closer. In the shadows under the table, he held his Glock in one hand. All he had to do was pull the trigger.

"I've been expecting a status report from you, Jason," Denny said, gesturing for him to sit down. "What's your mission status?"

"Complicated, sir," Jason said. "Before we go any further, I need you to do something for me."

Denny didn't reply, just lifted one eyebrow.

"I need you to pull up the personnel files database and confirm an identity."

"That's an unusual request," Denny said.

"I'm in an unusual situation," Jason replied. "Please."

"Very well." Denny tapped at some icons floating on his desktop and a modulated voice said, "Personnel database online."

"Tina Kanut," Jason said.

Denny chuckled quietly. "There's no need to search that name. I can confirm her identity. She's one of ours. You found her out, did you?"

"No," Jason admitted. "She told me that she worked for the agency a short time ago. She played her cover perfectly…though it does explain her uncanny ability to sneak up on me."

"I'm glad to know that all her skills haven't rusted away up there in the frozen north. She's mostly a translator."

"So she told me," he replied.

"What's going on that she needed to break cover?" Denny asked.

"The situation here has gotten extremely complicated," Jason said.

"All right," Denny said. "Break it down for me and don't leave anything out."

As succinctly as he could, Jason explained to Denny what had happened so far, and that he, Tina, her grandfather and Jesse were holed up in a hidden weapons bunker and trying to plan their next moves. "In short," he admitted, "the original mission parameters are FUBAR."

"That sounds accurate," Denny said. "What do you intend to do about it?"

Just as he was about to reply, he felt Tina tapping him on the shoulder.

"Don't forget to tell him about Feng Li," she said. "And put your gun away."

Jason slipped the Glock back into his shoulder rig and turned his attention back to Denny. "There's one more thing," he said. "The man behind it all. He's not Russian."

Denny looked surprised. "If it's not a Russian, who is it?"

"A guy named Feng Li," he said.

"What?" his boss said, coming halfway out of his chair. "He's dead!"

"Not as dead as I'd like him to be," Jason said. "Tina positively identified him."

"Hold on a minute," Denny said, sitting back down. "We need to bring someone else in on this one." He tapped at another icon on his desktop and it began to flash an urgent red. A moment later, the Room 59 director, Kate Cochran, appeared at the doorway.

"This had better be the end of the world," she said, striding into the room. "I was in the middle of a sparring session and that emergency page cost me a kick to the head."

"It's not the apocalypse," Denny said, "but it's close."

Kate looked at him soberly. "All right," she said softly. She took a seat next to Jason and glanced at him. "Agent Siku," she said. "Aren't you on a recon mission in Alaska?"

"Yes, ma'am," he said. "But it got…a little complicated."

"It always does," she said. "Give it to me," she added to Denny.

His boss went through everything Jason had told him, including the final bit about Feng Li.

For several moments, Kate was deathly silent. "Damn," she finally said.

"Excuse me, but I'm not quite clear on something," Jason said.

"What would that be, Agent Siku?" Kate asked.

"Well, when Tina told me about Li, she said she was terrified of him. Now you two are acting like his return from the dead is a sign of very bad things. Can you tell me why everyone is so frightened of this guy?"

"Good question," Kate said. "And there's a simple answer. When we started Room 59, we put it together with one agent representative from each of the participating nations. A 'prime' is what they were called. They trained and developed future training methods at one of our facilities here in the United States, then returned to their own countries to train the agents there. Li was a prime. When he got tired of straight fieldwork, he asked to be promoted to midnight teams, and his request was granted without question. If the midnight teams are the best of the best, Li was a perfect fit."

Jason shrugged. "Okay, so he's a tough guy, I get that. But lots of agents are tough."

"You don't understand, then," Denny cut in. "When Li turned rogue, it took us a long time to track him down. And we didn't go in light. Two midnight teams of five and two field agents went in where he'd been cornered. He decided to make a last stand. He killed all but one agent. It was a disaster."

"So why'd you think he was dead?" Jason asked.

Denny shrugged. "I had a sniper—one of our best men—stand away and wait. He shot him," he said. "Twice in the chest."

"And he was dead, right?" Jason asked. "Dead, dead?"

"Yes," he said. "It was a clean, confirmed kill. He was shot twice in the chest from less than two hundred yards away with a sniper rifle using armor-piercing rounds. The sniper checked his body. He was dead."

"Not as dead as one would think," Kate said.

Despite himself, Jason felt a surge of relief wash over him.

"Maybe it's time to abort," Kate continued. "Extract Agent Siku, debrief Tina, take the smaller fish into custody and let things calm down."

"We can't do that!" Jason said. "No way do we let this guy go!"

"Agent Siku!" she snapped. "I'm thinking of your safety. The mission is a bust. There comes a time to admit that."

Jason shook his head. "It's not a bust yet. The sub is still out there—and the Asp. Give me twenty-four hours," he said. "Please."

Kate and Denny exchanged a long look.

"Look," Jason said, "they've got the sub, they have it armed with nukes and they even have the damn Asp helicopter. These small-timers don't mean anything in the big picture. Give me twenty-four hours to finish the mission—including Li and his men. If I come up short, then I'll pull the plug myself."

Denny remained silent. This one was Kate's call. She studied Jason carefully, then said, "Agent Siku, are you really as good as your friends at the CIA say you are?"

"How good do they say I am?" he asked, grinning.

"They say you're the best," she said.

"I hate to be immodest," Jason replied.

"You better be the best," Kate said. "Because if you're not, Li won't give you a chance to pull the plug on the mission. He'll hunt you down and kill you without hesitation."

"Understood, ma'am."

"All right, you've got twenty-four hours and not a minute more. If we don't hear from you by then…" She left the statement hanging.

"Then I'd best get started," Jason said, getting to his feet.

"Your orders are now modified," she said. "Use any local assets you've got available. Sink the sub and destroy the Asp, take them all out. Clean sweep."

He nodded in understanding, then turned to Denny. "Can your offshore team remotely control the Scorpion?"

"Of course," Denny said. "What did you have in mind?"

AFTER WRAPPING UP his report with Denny, Jason logged out of Room 59 and shut down the system. He put his laptop and the other gear into a field pack, thankful that Jesse had found most of his things including the handheld device that would be critical to his plan.

The others were talking quietly at another table on the far side of the room and he joined them.

"So," Tina asked as he approached, "do you still have a job?"

"For now," he said. "Thank you."

"For what?" she asked.

"Finally telling me the truth," he said. "If you hadn't…"

"I know," she said, grinning. "You would have killed me."

"Yes," he said grimly.

He saw the cold finality of his words sink in and the movement in her throat as she swallowed. He had her full attention; now it was time to go to work.

"I've received revised orders," he said, sitting down at the table with them. "And in order to carry them out, I'm going to need some help."

"What do you have in mind?" Jesse asked.

"I have to get back out to that submarine. By the time we make it back to the coast, the Scorpion will be repaired and waiting."

"How's that?" his brother asked.

"There's an offshore team of specialists," he answered. "They called the Scorpion remotely while I was talking with my superiors. They will get it repaired."

"Handy," Jesse said. "If only I could fix cars that way."

"And what will you do with the sub, assuming you can find it again?" Tina asked.

"I have orders to sink it," he said. He turned to Tanuk. "That's where you come in."

"How can I help?" the old man asked.

"I need some explosives," Jason said. "C-4 if you've got it, along with the detonator caps and timers."

Jesse laughed. "You're going to try to sink a submarine with C-4?" He shook his head. "No way."

Tina glanced at Jason, then said, "No, he can do it. From inside the sub. You're going in, aren't you?"

He nodded. "It's the only way. I can get in the sub—"

"Come on!" Jesse interrupted. "You don't even know where it is anymore. They could have moved it all the way back to Russia by now."

Jason pulled the handheld out of his jacket pocket and turned it on. He typed in several coordinates, looking for a frequency response. "No," he said. "They haven't moved it. It's right where it was."

"Let me see," his brother said.

Jason held up the screen, which showed a sonar-style radar. It was pinging the sub and showing its exact location. Whatever cloaking mechanism they had in place was pretty good; he'd had to go to ultraviolet to find it.

"That's…amazing," Jesse said. "How'd you do that?"

"I put a tracer on the sub when I was down there

before," he said. "You remember? When you and Chris and the guys were trying to kill me?"

"It wasn't personal, Jason," he said. "Just work. A man can change, can't he?"

"Yes, a man can change, but you didn't change your heart or your beliefs, Jesse, and that worries me. You just changed sides," Jason asked.

The tension in the small room ratcheted up several notches.

"What do I do with you, if you decide to change sides again?"

Jesse shook his head. "I won't."

"We'll see," Jason said. "But you need to understand something. Tina, I can trust. Tanuk—no offense—is nothing more than a pawn. But you…you were a player. If you switch sides again or try to betray us…I'll hunt you down like a rabid dog and kill you. Plain and simple."

"Harsh," Jesse said. "Considering I saved your life back there."

"It's better for you to know where we stand now, because I'm going to be asking you to do something for me."

"What's that?" Jesse asked.

"Once I'm all set at the Scorpion, you're going to get Tina and her grandfather out of here. I want them as far away as possible. Nome, if you can make it without stopping." He looked at Tina. "I'll catch up to you there."

Jason saw the understanding in Jesse's eyes. "Yeah," he said. "I can get them there, Jason."

"No way," Tina interrupted. "I'm not leaving you out

here to face this by yourself. Have you forgotten Boris? Have you forgotten that Feng Li is out there right now, hunting us?"

"Yes, you are," Jason replied. He held up a hand as she started to argue. "Listen to me, Tina. I care for you and that's a distraction right now. I've got twenty-four hours to get this done or it's all over. You know the rules—it can't be personal. If you're here, it gets personal."

She started to protest, but her grandfather placed his hands over hers. "He is right, granddaughter," he said quietly. "Let him do his job, so you can do yours."

"Mine?" she asked. "What's my job?"

"Keeping me safe," he said, "as well as yourself. You will have more to do in the future. This is not your time to act."

"What are you talking about?" she said. "This is…look, I know I'm just a translator, but I've had the field-agent training. I can help!"

"Possibly," Tanuk said. "But you will have to trust my wisdom and insight in this matter. Jason is right. It is time for you to be elsewhere."

Thoughtfully, Jason considered the old man's words, then grabbed his hand. "The tattoo," he said. "Now I remember."

Tanuk smiled. "It is more often a curse than a gift."

Tina looked at the familiar design. It had always been there. "You told me they gave that to you as a child," she said. "For your first whale kill."

He nodded. "I lied."

"Arrgh!" Tina cried. "Does anyone here *ever* tell the truth?"

All of them looked at each other sheepishly, then Jason cleared his throat. "Apparently, not so much."

"So, what does it mean?" she asked Tanuk. "Where did you get it and why?"

"When I was eight," Tanuk said, "I had my first vision. A bad storm was coming and I warned the people in time. The village elders—you must remember, this was a long time ago—called me a seer. Trained me as a medicine man. The tattoo signifies that, but very few of us are left now who remember those days."

"And how did you know?" she asked Jason.

He shrugged. "I read a couple of books on Inuit culture before I came up here. There was some mention of it, just a line really and a picture of the tattoo, but when I first saw it, I couldn't remember its significance."

"I do not know what Tina's future holds," Tanuk cautioned them. "Only that now is the time for her to keep me safe and be far away from here. I feel that if she stays it could have dire consequences to her or you both. Better to be safe."

"This is crazy," Tina said. "I'm supposed to just walk away and let it go? I have a job to do, too," she said. "Denny authorized it, didn't he?"

"He did," Jason admitted. "But I'm inclined to trust your grandfather on this one. Whatever goes down is going to be very messy. I don't want to see you getting hurt. The basic field-agent training doesn't cover what's going to happen up here."

"I can handle myself," she said. "I kept my cover with you, didn't I?"

"This isn't going to be about cover, damn it," Jason said. "This is going to be fighting and bloody and nasty. People are going to die in ugly ways. That is not your world."

Her shoulders sagged in defeat. "You're right," she said, her voice quiet. "That's not my world. But I still want to help."

"And you will," he said. "But then you have to get out of here." Just knowing that she'd be far away when it all came down caused a surge of relief to wash over him. He cared about her future, which was more than he'd allowed himself to feel for anyone in a long, long time. "No more arguing."

She opened her mouth, then closed it with a snap, nodding.

"Good," he said. "What other weapons and supplies do you have stored away in here?"

"You might be surprised," Tanuk said. "What do you need?"

Jason considered it for a few moments, thinking of the terrain around the Quonset building, then said, "Aside from the C-4, here's my wish list—shrapnel grenades and smokers, Claymore mines, a sniper rifle and rounds to go with it and—in an ideal world—a rocket launcher and shells."

Tanuk smiled and nodded at Jesse, who said, "Let's get to work, brother. We've got a lot of loading to do."

"It will be better this way," Jason said to Tina. "You know we can't allow this to get any more personal than it already has. The mission first. We'll deal with the future if we survive all this."

"What do you mean *we?*" she asked. "Don't you mean *you?* I'm going to be a long way away, remember?"

"You aren't there yet," he said. "And I fully anticipate more arguments before I have to knock you unconscious and have Jesse load you into the truck to get you out of here."

"You wouldn't!" she said.

"In a New York minute," he replied. "Now, let's get to work."

"I could help, Jason," she said. "You know that."

"I do," he said. "But the best help you can give me is getting as far away from this mess as you can."

She nodded. "Want to help me carry some crates?"

"Sure," he said. "But let's not overdo it. We've got some time before the Scorpion will be back and we both took a good pounding back there."

Tanuk joined them as they headed for the larger cavern. "In life there is always heavy lifting," he said to himself. "That is why we have family."

18

Jason looked at the supplies that they had piled into the back of the SUV. His wish list was basically complete. All they had to do was get him back to the Scorpion, and Tina, Jesse and Tanuk on their way to Nome. He pulled out the handheld one more time, reviewing his maps and the new coordinates where the Scorpion was going to land. Then he double-checked his escape routes from the Quonset building. It wouldn't do him a lot of good to succeed in his mission, only to freeze to death before he could make it to safety. There weren't a lot of choices, but it was better to have it all firmly in mind.

"Are you ready?" Tina asked, coming up behind him.

"Yeah," he said. "We're all set. It's time to get out of here and finish this."

He looked her over and realized that she had armed herself like Rambo. While he was still a little surprised that she worked for Room 59, and he knew she could take care of herself, seeing her looking as if she was planning on taking on an army made him uncomfortable. "The plan is still the plan, right?" he asked.

She nodded. "I just want to be extracautious. Feng Li isn't a fool. He'll know you're coming for him, which means he's going to have men spread out all over this area. If we get caught, I want to be ready."

"Tina," he said, stepping closer to her and lowering his voice, "I need you to promise me something."

"Anything you need," she said.

"I need you to promise me that you'll run before you fight. That you'll get yourself and Jesse and your grandfather to safety. This kind of work—it's what I do. You weren't a field agent and you have more than just yourself to think about."

"Don't you?" she asked pointedly.

He nodded. "I think I probably do," he said. "But we have to stop Feng Li now, and I can't do that if I'm busy trying to keep you and the others safe."

"I know," she said, hugging him tightly. "I just don't want to leave you. It feels like…like if I can see you, I can keep you safe."

He steered her toward the SUV as Jesse and Tanuk climbed in. "You can keep me safe by being safe yourself, okay? Promise me?"

"I promise," she said. "Run if I can, fight if I must. You're the agent in charge. I know the drill."

He smiled down at her. Part of him wanted to take her onto the sub with him, if for no other reason than the banter she provided would help ease the tension.

"Good," he said. "Understand that this mission has taught me a lot, including how important it is to have people to care about in my life. It's given me hope that I can allow people to be close to me and still do what I do. But right now, more than anything else, I need to keep you safe. Understand?"

She played with ground at her feet with the toe of her boot. Jason could see her wrestling with her thoughts, trying to come up with a way out of her promise, but knew that he had her.

"All right, but I don't like it very much," she said.

"You don't have to like it," he said. "I don't like it all that much myself. I just need you to do it."

"Stop right there. If you go any further it will turn into an order and then I'll have to defy it just to soothe my wounded pride. I don't take orders very well," she said.

"No orders this time," he said. "Think of them as firmly worded requests."

He leaned forward and pressed a kiss to her forehead. His hand paused on her hair, letting several strands rest between his fingers. He would have loved nothing more at that moment than to take the time to explore every strand of hair on her head. When he got to the end of this he was going to take some serious time to consider that part of his life. To figure out what it meant to truly care about someone for the first time in his life, to figure out if what he felt for her was love.

She climbed into the vehicle, sitting in the back with Tanuk, while Jesse took the driver's seat and Jason the front passenger's seat.

"All set?" Jesse asked.

"Set," he said. "Let's finish this."

THEY DROVE to a cove south of the village, choosing to use a new location. It was a safe bet that the others they'd used before were being watched. Jason went down to the waterline and placed his beacon, and only had to wait a few minutes before the Scorpion emerged from the depths. It had been repaired, and from a quick check, the modifications he'd requested had been made, as well.

He made a mental note to send a thank-you to the offshore team if he survived all this. They had gone above and beyond getting everything done. The others were standing near the front bumper of the SUV, and he turned and said, "Let's get this thing loaded up."

Jesse looked up and Jason could see some level of concern etched on his features, but he nodded. "You're the boss," he said. He moved around to the back of the truck where the cargo was stored, and Tina and her grandfather moved to follow him.

The briefest flare of reflecting light was the only warning they had.

"Cover!" Jason yelled, diving behind some rocks and hoping the others would do the same.

A barrage of shots rang out, the bullets ricocheting off the rocky beach and several hitting their truck with loud pinging noises. Jason peered over the rocks and saw a large group of men, led by Chris and Troy, coming down the hillside. A quick count and he tallied a dozen.

"Status?" he yelled.

"We're okay," Jesse yelled. "But this could get ugly."

Now that they were pinned down, the men coming down the hill had slowed their firing and were taking up positions to surround them. They couldn't all fit in the Scorpion, which meant that they would have to fight their way out of the ambush. He risked another glance and saw that Jesse and Tina were crouched behind a rock outcropping similar to his, while Tanuk was kneeling behind the front side of the truck.

Jason dived out from behind the rock, rolling to his feet, and making a dash for the truck. "Get behind those rocks, old man," he said, yanking open the door and diving inside.

Several shots rang out, but his sudden move had surprised everyone and they missed.

He crawled into the back and found the sniper rifle. It was a fairly new Russian model, the VSK-94, fitted with a silencer and a scope. He grabbed the 20-round magazine and attached it to the weapon, then crawled back until he reached the front seat.

A few shots rang out, but the tinted windows and the angle made it hard for anyone to get a decent shot at him. After a quick look to see where the attackers had taken up position, he lowered himself out of the SUV, then onto the ground. He saw that Jesse and Tina were still in the same place and that Tanuk had made it to a better shelter.

He waited a moment until he caught Jesse's eyes, then mouthed, "Get ready." He offered a thumbs-up.

Jesse nodded and whispered to Tina.

Crawling beneath the truck, Jason found a solid position near the right rear wheel. A large stone provided additional concealment, and he slowly moved the barrel of the rifle to the thin window of space between the rock and the tire. His own angle wasn't great, but all he really needed was to thin their numbers enough to get them to rush his position in a panic.

He peered through the scope and swept it over the hillside. "Come on," he said. "Somebody stick your head up."

At that moment, Troy decided to take a look.

"Wish granted," Jason whispered, squeezing the trigger. The weapon made barely a sound, but the impact of the gas-fired round on Troy's forehead was spectacular. He came completely to his feet in surprise, his nervous system taking over, then toppled backward, the back of his skull removed.

The action caused two more men to peer up from their own cover to see what had happened. Jason fired twice more in quick succession, dropping them quickly.

A few scattered shots were fired in return, mostly at Jesse and Tina's position.

"Stop firing, goddamn it!" Chris yelled. "He's got some kind of sniper rifle."

The sound of his voice was enough to get a fix on his position, but when Jason looked through the scope, he couldn't see Chris. He'd picked a good hiding spot.

Patience, Jason counseled himself. The others will get nervous, make a mistake.

He continued to sweep the hillside, and another two minutes passed before one of the men risked a look. Jason squeezed off another round and the bullet took the man in the throat, spraying blood on the person concealed with him.

"Bill!" the other would-be soldier yelled, coming to his feet.

It was enough and Jason's shot found him in the left ear and he dropped. That made five dead.

"Stay down, damn it," Chris yelled.

"He can't take us all," one of the men shouted back. "I say we rush him."

"Be my guest, you moron," Chris yelled back. "It's your funeral."

That was the moment Jason had been waiting for. He'd been betting that Chris wasn't the kind of leader who inspired any particular loyalty in the men he worked with, but those men would know each other and feel a level of loyalty to each other.

The remaining men jumped to their feet and ran down the hillside, shooting as they moved.

"Now!" Jason yelled, not bothering to look to find out if Jesse and Tina knew what to do. The sound of their weapons firing was more than enough information.

He continued to use the sniper rifle, picking his targets carefully. Eight men rushed down the hill, firing as they went. Four were dead before they'd hit the bottom—two from his rifle and one each from Jesse and Tina, who were using handguns and had to pop off their shots and then dive for cover again.

The others suddenly changed their minds and tried to make a run for it.

"Not today," Jason said, flicking the selector switch to full auto. He mowed down the final four like wheat before a combine.

When silence descended, he could hear Chris cursing up a storm. "Fuck, fuck, fuck!"

"Guess you're out of soldiers—if you can call them that," Jason shouted. "If you surrender, come down with your hands up and no weapons, I won't shoot you."

"Yeah, and I suppose if I leave a tooth under my pillow tonight, the tooth fairy will bring me money, too!" Chris yelled back. "You killed Troy, you bastard! You killed all of them."

"I'm a little cranky," Jason hollered. "Don't make it worse."

There was a long silence, then Chris shouted, "How about I come down there, unarmed, and we settle this like men and I kick your ass for you?"

"Sounds fine to me," Jason said. "Come ahead."

He watched through the scope as Chris slowly stood up from behind the shelter of rocks he'd chosen, then very purposefully dropped his weapons. He held up his arms and turned a full circle. "I'm unarmed and I'm coming down!"

Jason watched him most of the way, then shimmied backward and rolled out from beneath the SUV on the far side. Jesse and Tina had been joined by Tanuk and they held their weapons on Chris as he reached the rocky beach.

Jason moved forward, still holding the rifle.

"Thought you said we could fight," Chris muttered. "Or maybe you're afraid."

Jason chuckled. "Of what?" he asked. "You?"

Chris nodded. "That's the VSK-94," he said. "A nice weapon. You must have visited Grandpa's stash."

"You never know what you can find lying around in the tundra," Jason said. Turning to the others, he told them to put away their weapons.

"You're not seriously going to fight this guy, Jason," Jesse said.

"It's what he wanted," he said. "Are you worried?"

"He's a good fighter, Jason," he warned. "Really good."

Jason turned his attention back to Chris and studied him. He was standing loosely, weight on the balls of his feet. The muscle tension of his body showed that he was coiled to spring like a snake.

"Interesting," Chris said. "Are you worried now?"

Shrugging, Jason said, "Not really."

"Oh, yeah," Chris said. "I can almost smell your fear. Kicking your ass is going to make my whole year." He inched forward. "Why aren't you worried, hero?"

"I'm not a hero," Jason said. "And what you are smelling isn't fear, you idiot. It's burnt gunpowder."

"How's that?" he asked.

Jason lifted the rifle and shot him twice in the chest. "Because I just shot you, moron," he said.

Chris stumbled backward, his hands pressed against the wounds. "But you..." He coughed and spit blood. "You're supposed to arrest me."

"Sorry," Jason said calmly. He pulled the trigger a third time, and the round hit home, taking Chris between the eyes and silencing him for good.

"Jesus," Jesse whispered. "That…that was harsh."

"Saved time," he said. "Besides, I don't have the energy to waste beating him up. There are things to do and we're running out of time to do that."

"Speaking of things to do," Tina said shakily. "Just before they showed up, Jesse was telling us something I think you need to know."

"Oh? What would that be?" Jason asked.

Jesse sighed heavily. "They haven't finished loading the sub," he said. "It's a safe bet that Feng Li is on board, but Boris will still be at the base, getting those minis loaded up."

Jason shrugged. "I'll deal with the base after I've dealt with the sub. Those minis won't have anywhere to go if the sub is gone, and even if they beat me there, so what? A few weapons more or less isn't going to make that big of a difference."

Jesse shook his head. "You don't get it, Jason. There are still two nuclear warheads at the base. They came in with the Asp the last time it landed. If we don't pin them down there, who knows where those will end up?"

"Why didn't you say something sooner?" Jason asked angrily.

"Honestly, I didn't even think about it until we got here," Jesse said.

"All right," Jason said. "Where does Feng Li keep the Asp? I know he's not keeping it at the base and the sub can't hold it."

"I don't know," Jesse said. "But if we can pin them down there, maybe we can keep those nukes out of Feng Li's hands."

"And how do you propose we do that?" he snapped. "I can't be in two places at once."

"No, you can't," Tina said, her voice soft. "But we could go. Hold them until you get there."

"What? No, you can't be serious!" he said.

"Do you see any other options?" she asked.

"It's a foolish risk," he said.

"Denny told you to use us," she replied. "So use us. I can handle myself, so can Jesse."

"I want you safe," he said. "Didn't you hear what your grandfather said? It's not your time to act."

"Maybe it is now," she said. "Isn't this what Room 59 is about, Jason? Keeping the world safe? Sometimes you have to fight—and risk things you care about—to protect not just the world, but your family, your future. The work I do for Room 59 isn't as dangerous as yours, but it's still important to the cause. I can't let some crazed lunatic take off with an advanced nuclear sub and the weapons to use it."

"I don't like it," he said.

"I know you don't," Tanuk interrupted. "But Tina is right. It feels right. This is the way things are supposed to be."

"I suppose you're going to go with them?" he asked. "Risking your neck, too, just because?"

The old man shook his head. "No, I will return to the village. The other elders will hide me and keep me safe until it's over." He glanced at Tina. "I am sorry for all this, my granddaughter. I am too old to fight these kinds of battles."

"I know," she said. She leaned over and kissed him on the cheek. "Get going, old man. I'll see you soon."

"She hates emotional goodbyes," Tanuk said. He kissed her, then shook hands with Jason and Jesse. "Do right," he said to them. "And make our world safe again." Then he turned and in moments had disappeared into the hillside grasses.

"So, new plan?" Tina said.

Jason nodded, feeling more than a little morose. "New plan," he agreed.

"We won't let you down, Jason," Jesse said.

"Good," he said.

He briefly explained what he wanted them to do and, despite their accusations that he'd lost his mind, he eventually got them to agree. They helped him load the Scorpion with the equipment he'd need, and kept the rest for their assault on the base.

They'd need every bit of it. He knew that much. He could only hope they'd still be alive when he got there.

He shook hands with his brother, then pulled him into a rough embrace. "Keep her safe," he said.

"I will," Jesse replied. "Just get to us as fast as you can."

"Done," Jason promised, turning to Tina. She pulled him close and kissed him.

"Get to work now," she said. "And try not to get yourself killed."

"I'll do my best," he said.

He climbed into the Scorpion and guided it into the

murky Arctic waters. It felt as if he'd never see either one of them again, but it didn't matter. He'd found a woman he cared about and a brother he didn't know he had, and somehow that brother had seen that being on the side of good was more important than any pay-check. They were people who made caring easy, the risks of caring worthwhile.

And none of that mattered. The mission had to come first.

For Jason, it always had…and it always would.

19

Jason took a direct route back to the sub, expecting that the minisubs they'd been using were back at the underground cavern, taking on their final loads. The tide had gone out, and with it, many of the largest pieces of ice debris. Closer to the surface, the water was a dark green, almost an emerald with the tiniest bit of light; down where he was, the darkness closed in tight. He relied on both his vision and his radar to avoid obstacles— large piles of frozen rock, huge beds of ocean weeds that floated on the currents, and even whales, which seemed to avoid him almost of their own volition.

One of the things he'd asked the offshore team to do was retrofit the Scorpion's hull, using the same light-bending technology, but to project the image of a barnacle cluster, rather than a school of fish or other marine life. He guided the Scorpion closer and closer to the sub, hoping that his plan would work.

It was in the same location as before—Feng Li must have felt very confident not to move it. He slipped around beneath it to the torpedo tube where he'd previously placed the magnets. Originally, he'd planned to use the special dry suit and swim to the sub, but time was too precious now. He had to get this done and join Jesse and Tina at their main base of operations before they were both killed. Just before reaching the tube, he powered down the Scorpion's engines to almost nothing. He barely had guidance control, but it was just enough.

He eased the craft ever so slowly until the escape hatch of the Scorpion was directly positioned over the torpedo tube, then he extended the ring of magnets he'd had the offshore team install. He shut down the engines and let the magnets do the rest of the work. The magnets drew the Scorpion and the sub closer together, and with a dull thud his vessel locked on to the sub. He had to hope that there was no one in the torpedo room at that moment wondering about the noise.

When he engaged the escape hatch, the field would create an air lock of sorts, allowing him to enter the torpedo tube. He checked his weapons and handheld once more, then opened his laptop. It was time to determine if the line leech had done its job. The computer powered up, and he tapped in the code that would connect his computer, the Scorpion, the handheld and the line leech all together. The software worked silently for almost two minutes before it gave him the message "All connections established."

"Good to go," he said. He left the laptop running in

the Scorpion and used the handheld to override the alert command on the submarine's torpedo tube. He showed it as undergoing routine maintenance, then stepped over the field and reached through. The outer door of the torpedo tube was icy cold, but the seal was good.

He entered a new command into the handheld and the outer door unlocked. He reached down and opened it, then slipped silently through the field and into the tube, going head first.

He made his way down the tube, fervently praying that they didn't choose that precise moment to test fire a weapon or something, until he made it to the hatch where the torpedo itself would be loaded. Once again, he used the handheld to order a computer override— this time a command to open the interior tube door.

After several seconds, he heard the sound of the bolts sliding free, and he watched as the tube door opened. He continued on, sliding out of the tube and into the torpedo room itself, crouching and looking for enemies. The room was empty.

Taking out the handheld once more, he typed in a search command, looking for the set of plans he knew had to be stored within the main databanks. It was tempting to try to sink the sub remotely, but he knew that they could manually override any command he gave their system from the bridge. He didn't want them to be aware of a problem until it was far too late to do anything about it. The handheld was searching, so he slipped it back into his pocket and moved to the doorway.

Jason threaded a small suppressor onto the barrel of his Glock and crept forward to the hatch leading to the next compartment. Glancing down the hallway, he could see that there were three men walking down the passageway. Two stopped and climbed up a ladder to the next level, while the third continued on in his direction.

Jason pulled back behind the door and waited, slipping his gun back into its holster. Jason stood tight against the wall and waited. As soon as the man crossed the threshold, Jason reached out from behind him, grasped him with one arm and pulled him to his chest.

The stunned sailor didn't have time to speak before Jason snapped his neck. He lowered the body smoothly to the floor and pulled him out of view, deep into the torpedo room. Another quick glance down the hallway showed it empty, so Jason took a few moments to remove the Russian sailor's uniform and put it on over his own clothing. The fit was tight and the pants too short, but if someone didn't look too carefully, he might slip by them unnoticed.

After hiding the body behind a rack of torpedoes, Jason looked into the hallway again, and found it still empty. The engine room would be on the far end of the submarine, but most likely on the same level, or perhaps the one above it. He moved confidently down the hallway, trying to look as though he belonged there and knew where he was going.

He'd made it about a third of the way when two sailors came out of a side compartment and almost collided with him in the narrow space. Jason kept his head down and muttered, "Excuse me" in Russian.

One of the sailors said, "Dimitri? What's wrong?"

Without turning around, he said, *"Da?"*

He felt a hand on his shoulder and knew it was too late. He reached up and across his body with his right hand, grasping the one on his shoulder and twisting it, hard. Jason heard bones snap in the sailor's wrist, accompanied by a yell of pain.

So much for quiet, Jason thought, while lashing out at the other sailor and taking him in the knee. The bones made a satisfying crunch and that one went down, grabbing at his leg and calling for security.

Jason removed the Glock from its holster and fired twice. He silenced both men instantly.

Above him, on the next level, he could hear voices shouting queries. He only had a couple of moments at most. He dragged both men into the compartment they'd come from and shut the door. There were splatters of blood along the floor and the bottom of the walkway walls, but there was little he could do about that. Perhaps the dim light would help.

A set of booted feet appeared on the ladder leading to the next level up, and an idea struck him. More confusion might equal more time. Positioning himself in the hall, he lay down on the floor at a seemingly awkward angle and watched through slitted eyelids as the security man approached.

This one was more cautious, moving slowly and looking at each compartment. Jason let out an internal sigh of relief—only one man had come to investigate. Once more, patience was all he needed.

The man knelt down to examine his prone body,

when Jason suddenly sprang to life. One hand reached out and covered the security officer's mouth. The second brought up the silenced Glock and put a round through his throat. The man fell over, dying from lack of oxygen and unable to make a sound. Jason got to his feet and dragged the man into the same compartment where he'd put the others, then continued on his way.

He knew more would follow when the first man didn't return with a report. In a few minutes, the deck would be swarming with sailors trying to figure out what was going on. Moving on quick, silent feet, Jason made his way to the engine-room compartment and peered inside.

Three more sailors were on duty there, watching gauges and manning the computers that controlled the engine and propulsion systems.

Things are about to get interesting, he thought.

At that moment, an alarm began ringing throughout the sub and a voice over the internal address system said, "Red alert! Red alert! There is an intruder on board. All hands to stations! All hands to stations! Security to check all decks!"

So much for the element of surprise, Jason thought. He stepped into the engine control room.

Still reacting to the sudden alarm, the sailors didn't even see him at first, and two were down before the third realized that his companions were dead. He jumped for a switch on one console—obviously an alarm of some kind—and Jason almost didn't reach him in time.

He grabbed the sailor, yanking him backward and

onto the hard metal of the deck. "Don't," he said, pointing the Glock. The young sailor held up his hands in surrender.

Jason gestured with the gun. "Shut the compartment door and lock it," he ordered.

Nodding, the sailor climbed to his feet and shut the compartment hatch, then turned the wheel that slid the lock bolts into place. He stepped away from the door, once again lifting his hands.

"Sit down," Jason told him, motioning to a chair. The young man took a seat and Jason quickly bound his hands with a plastic cord he carried in his pack. "Now, you can sit quietly and live," he told him, "or you can die. Your choice."

"I will be as silent as a mouse," the kid said.

"Good choice," he replied. He took his pack off and began removing the C-4 charges. The engine room was usually a loud place, but since the sub was currently at stop and the engines were shut down, it was fairly quiet.

He began placing charges in key system locations— propulsion, oxygen exchanger, combustion and fuel, as well as near the hull itself. The series of concussions from the explosions might be enough to blow a hole in the side of the sub itself, but either way, once the explosions hit, the sub would remain on the bottom of the ocean.

And the Russians couldn't risk the kind of retrieval mission it would take to get it back.

His handheld beeped softly and he pulled it from his cargo pocket. The screen read, "Search complete. Download?"

He quickly typed in the commands to have the sub's plans downloaded to his handheld and the laptop itself.

"You will…blow up our submarine?" the Russian asked.

"I thought I told you to sit quietly," Jason said.

"I do not want to die," the kid said. "Please."

"There are escape pods built into this vessel," Jason said. "Maybe not enough for everyone, but you might get lucky."

The kid nodded in sour understanding.

As Jason finished wiring the detonators, someone tried to open the compartment door and quickly discovered that it was locked from the inside. "Damn," he said. "I really don't want to go down with the ship myself."

Someone began hammering on the door and Jason risked a glance through the small porthole. Three security officers were standing outside, demanding that the engine crew open up. Thinking quickly, Jason moved to where he had the sailor tied up and drew a blade from a sheath on his ankle.

The Russian's eyes widened in fear. "I'm not going to kill you…yet," Jason said.

He sliced through the plastic cuffs and said, "You're going to answer the door and let them in," he said. "You'll act like nothing is wrong. Don't interfere when they come in, and you may live through this yet." He offered his best cold stare and added, "Understand?"

"Yes," the sailor said. "I understand."

Jason pulled out the Glock again and noted the wear and tear on the silencer. He'd need to replace it after this encounter. He stepped behind the door and motioned for the sailor to open the hatch.

The sailor spun the wheel and stepped out of the way as the three security men burst into the room, all of them talking at once, too busy jabbering about an intruder to notice the two bodies already lying on the deck. Jason fired his first two rounds in milliseconds, needing little time to aim at this distance. The third security man dived for cover, and that was when the young sailor tried to be a make a run for it.

Kicking out with one foot, Jason slammed the hatch shut, which the kid ran into full tilt. There was a dull sound as his head connected with the metal of the hatch and he dropped as if he'd been poleaxed. The momentary distraction, however, was enough for the security man to take a shot, and Jason felt the burning sting of a graze in his left shoulder. The force of it was enough to spin him sideways.

"Damn it," he said, adjusting his position on the fly. He went all the way to the deck, rolled and came up firing. His first round was wide, but the second hit the security officer in the chest, driving him back into the computer console. His fingers squeezed the trigger spasmodically, and the rounds hit the metal plating on the floor and ricocheted several times around the room before stopping.

Jason breathed a sigh of relief. "With my luck lately, I'd have been killed by a ricochet." His handheld beeped and he glanced at it quickly. The screen read, "Download complete."

"Good enough for government work," he said. He looked down at the unconscious sailor on the floor.

There was nothing he could do for him now. Ignoring the stinging pain in his left arm, Jason moved back to the hatch and peered into the hallway.

Sailors were running every which way, trying to figure out where the intruder was. The bodies of the others must have been found. Still, in this kind of confusion and chaos, it was possible he might have a chance to slip through unnoticed.

"Sorry, kid," he said, opening the door and stepping back into the hallway. He left it open and walked ten full paces before he reached into his pocket and pushed the button that would detonate the C-4. He had five minutes before the explosives would blow.

He moved quickly through the crowd, keeping his head down and using his fluent Russian to occasionally shout out responses to questions.

"Where is the intruder?" one sailor asked.

"I think he went up a deck," Jason replied. "Security needs all the help they can get!" He shoved the man in the direction of the nearest ladder.

In a time of crisis, Jason knew people often want to be told what to do, and this man was no exception.

Once, a security officer grabbed him and said, "Have you seen Vladimir?"

Jason nodded. "He went to the bridge to report something."

The security officer ran off, never looking back.

It took him the better part of four minutes by his count to reach the torpedo-room hatch. Glancing behind him and seeing no one following, he opened it and stepped inside, pulling it shut behind him.

He didn't see the massive fist that slammed into his already tender ribs, nor the one that followed it, which connected with his jaw and sent him flying to the deck. He grunted in pain as he hit, rolled and came up shaking his head, trying to clear the cobwebs.

20

The man in front of him looked just like Boris, but he had been given the benefit of a full head of hair.

"You must know Boris," Jason stated, stepping away from the giant. "They say that after a long time together, married people begin to look alike. Are you the husband or the wife?"

"I am Vladimir Ambros," the man said. "The Siberian Tiger." He spun the wheel on the hatch door, locking it closed. "My brother is Boris. I understand that you two have already met."

"Recently," Jason said. "Though he failed to mention you during our discussion. You must not be all that close."

"Boris and Feng Li send their regrets," he said, stepping closer. "They wanted to be here to see me kill you. They knew you would come. *I* knew you would come."

"You know, Boris already tried to kill me," Jason said. "He didn't do a very good job of it."

Vladimir laughed. "You are a foolish man, Mr. Siku," he said. "My brother was only playing with you. It was not his place to kill you, but Feng Li has given me that honor. Had you remained captive, he would have killed you himself."

Jason risked a glance at his watch. "I'd love to stay and visit, but things are going to get interesting in five."

"Five?"

"Four," Jason said.

"Four?"

Vladimir was obviously the slower one of the two.

"Three," Jason said.

Vladimir moved in, ignoring him, and Jason skipped away. "Two," he called, avoiding a sloppy but undoubtedly strong roundhouse.

"Why are you counting?" the Russian yelled.

"One," Jason said.

The explosives detonated on the far end of the sub, and the reverberations and noise could be felt all the way to the room they were standing in. "It's just something I like to do," Jason said, feeling the deck begin to pitch beneath his feet, "when an explosion is about to happen."

Vladimir roared like an angry bear and crossed the space between them in three quick steps, lunging to grasp him in a crushing hug.

Jason ducked beneath the swinging arms and threw a solid openhanded blow into the man's crotch. He heard him gasp in pain, then scream as Jason grabbed a handful and pulled, twisting at the same time.

Vladimir slammed both of his meaty arms into Jason's shoulders and for a moment, he wondered if his collarbones or his shoulders were broken…or both. As he scrambled away from the huge Russian, the sub lurched again, and Jason suspected that his plan had worked better than expected. There was a hull breach.

The thought had no sooner crossed his mind than the alarm began ringing again, and a voice ordered all hands to abandon ship. Only a few would make it, he knew. The icy waters of the Arctic would take the rest.

"You fight like a woman," Vladimir said, ignoring the call to abandon ship.

Knowing he was almost out of time, Jason got to his feet, trying to ignore the stabbing pains in his ribs and his shoulders. "You're right," he said, stumbling a bit as the sub lurched yet again. He pulled the Glock. "But I shoot like a man."

He squeezed the trigger three times, driving Vladimir back against the rack of torpedoes and sending them crashing to the floor. The giant fell to the ground, sitting, and stared up at Jason with a look of surprise on his face. "A real man kills with his bare hands," he said, blood dribbling from his mouth and nose.

"Maybe," Jason admitted. "But while I'll go on being at least a pretend man, you'll be fish food." He turned away and felt the Russian grab his pant leg.

"Don't…leave me to die like this. To drown." The man's eyes were pleading.

Remembering the beating he'd taken at Boris's hands, Jason said, "Would you or your brother show the same mercy to me?"

"Yes," he said, nodding painfully. "We are not without honor."

"Bullshit," Jason said, "but who am I to argue?" He raised the Glock and put the man out of his misery.

The rushing sound of water could be heard in the hall behind him, along with the screams of sailors as the icy ocean took them. Most would die even before they reached the few escape pods. The submarine was on its way to being an underwater relic, and if he didn't get a move on, he'd be joining them.

He climbed into the torpedo tube and began to shimmy his way back to the Scorpion.

If everything was going according to plan, Jesse and Tina were already at the base camp and beginning their assault. His only sorrow in all this was that Feng Li and Boris weren't on board to go down with the ship.

But his gut told him he'd be seeing them both before this was over.

JASON SLIPPED BACK into the Scorpion and blew the locks on the docking collar. He could feel the pull of the submarine as it sank lower into the icy black depths below as he fired up the engines. If the suction grew too great, he would be pulled down right along with it.

For a brief, panicked moment, he thought that was exactly what was going to happen as the Scorpion struggled against the underwater vacuum created by the massive, sinking submarine. He hit the engine boosters and breathed a sigh of relief as the small craft pulled away, leaving the sinking submarine and her crew to their fate.

He pushed the Scorpion to its limits, trying to get back to the underwater cavern where the minisubs had been loaded. Only half his mission had been accomplished, and Jesse and Tina by now had to be in position, if they weren't already fighting for their lives. The tide was coming in, which made the job of piloting his submersible more challenging as once more, chunks of ice flowed in closer to shore. The sun had gone down, so he was operating with only the lights of the Scorpion and radar to help him avoid obstacles.

As he neared the cavern, he turned on the tracking radar, which would send signals into the cavern and bounce them back as three-dimensional images of what was going on above the surface.

"Damn," he muttered, seeing the outlines of Tina and Jesse hiding behind a large stack of crates and firing their weapons. They were making their stand right where he'd told them to and fighting for their lives while they were doing it. Each passing second made it more likely that one or both of them would be wounded or killed.

He scanned the rest of the cavern and counted heads. At least a dozen or more guards were opposing them.

He pushed the engines even harder, dodging a large cluster of ice and skirting a rock outcropping. The images on the screen flickered as the extra power went from the computer to the engines. He could make it inside the cavern and join them within two or three minutes if he pushed the machine to its limits.

Suddenly, alarms began to blare inside the Scorpion, and Jason saw that the two minisubs were on his radar and moving in on his position. This time, he knew, he would sink them both. If Jesse and Tina had done their jobs, they hadn't been loaded with the nuclear weapons yet, and he didn't want to give anyone who survived this operation a free means of getting any other weapons away from the area.

"All right," he muttered, guiding the Scorpion toward the two minisubs. "Let's see how the new and improved Scorpion fares this time."

He punched up the controls for the weapons system, and the Scorpion's extendable arms rotated, bringing up an underwater launcher and a gas-powered minigun that fired .50-caliber rounds. A voice said, "Targeting system online. Voice-activated fire control at your command." This time, he fully intended to fight in ways they didn't have any means to counter.

The first sub closed in on his right and he spun the Scorpion on its axis. "Target acquired," the computer said.

"Launcher, fire!" Jason said.

There were two dull thumping sounds as the launcher fired, and in the short distance between himself and the other sub, he saw the rounds closing in on their target. The operator of the minisub tried to turn, but his momentum took him directly into the path of the shells, which impacted the side of his craft and stuck. The outside covering of the shells was magnetic.

A second later both of them exploded, and in the flare of underwater light, Jason saw the hole blown in the side of the craft. The operator was already dead from the blast and his vessel spun wildly out of control, sinking rapidly.

He felt the other sub ram him at nearly full speed and he heard the sound of bending metal.

The controls suddenly felt sluggish in his hands.

The computer was flashing repair warnings all over his screen. His right wing had been damaged, and he didn't have nearly the maneuverability he really needed in a fight. He could go up or down, forward or back, but he could only turn to the left.

"Marvelous," he said. He yanked on the controls with all his strength and revved the engines, causing the Scorpion to spin to the left while ascending toward the surface.

"Target acquired," the computer said. Then it corrected, "Target lost."

"Oh, shut up," he said. "Minigun, fire!"

The computer may not have understood the "shut up," but thankfully, it did open fire. As he spun, the other minisub came briefly into view and he saw the .50-caliber slugs slam into its view screen and burst through it, killing its operator instantly. The slugs must have damaged his controls, as well, because it veered wildly, then began to sink as the engines failed and water poured into the open cavity.

He pulled once more on the controls, feeling a bit dizzy, and allowed the Scorpion to continue its ascent. He eased into the cavern, and managed to get the three-dimensional radar working again. Jesse and Tina were still holding their own and he breathed a sigh of relief.

He guided the wounded Scorpion into the minisub docking bay nearest to them, but when he tried to rotate the arms and have it climb out of the water, the computer said, "System failure. Retractable land arms unavailable."

"Well, so much for clearing the area with the .50-caliber," Jason said. He moved to the top hatch and opened it, then ducked back down as a shot ricocheted off the metal hatch door.

"It's me, damn it," he yelled at Jesse, who'd seen someone out of the corner of his eye and was in full instinct mode.

"Come ahead," his brother yelled back.

He climbed out and ran for their position, dragging his gear bag with him and zigzagging among the boxes and crates to narrowly avoid being shot.

"You're alive!" Tina said, throwing her arms around him.

"Ouch," he gasped.

She held him at arm's length. "You're hurt," she said. "How bad?"

"Bad enough that hugging is really out of the question right now," he said. He looked around and realized where they had positioned themselves. Their backs were to the wall on one side and the water on the other, barricaded behind a large stack of crates. They were cornered.

He looked down at the crates Tina and Jesse were using to kneel on. "I know I said to sit on the nukes, but I didn't mean it quite so literally," he added.

"What are you talking about?" Tina asked, ducking down between shots.

"That crate that you're kneeling on holds a nuclear warhead," he replied.

Tina stared accusingly at Jesse.

"Hey," he said. "All I knew was they were in this room. I didn't know you were going to choose one as your personal sofa, but it's as good a place as any to die."

Jason peered over the boxes and saw that the guards were getting closer and closer to their position. They were also shooting more rapidly, forcing all of them to stay under cover rather than shoot back.

If they didn't do something fast, the front door wasn't going to be an option at all—and they needed to get out. There were still two nuclear warheads to get rid of, as well as Feng Li and Boris to deal with.

He moved closer to Jesse, leaning in so he wouldn't have to shout. "Is there another way out of here?" he asked.

His brother shook his head. "Just the way we came in from upstairs and the water—neither of which look like a great option at the moment."

"We've got to get rid of the nukes and get out of here," he said.

"I'm all ears," Jesse replied. He peered around one end of the crate stack and fired off a round. A man screamed in pain. "There's one less to deal with anyway."

Jason thought rapidly, then an idea came to him. It wasn't perfect, but it would do for now. "How deep is the water here in the cavern?"

Jesse shrugged. "It goes down a ways," he said. "Maybe two or three hundred feet. It's a long way—I can tell you that."

"Perfect," Jason said. "Do you have any of those smoke grenades left?"

"A couple," he replied, handing him one. "Why?"

"Good," Jason said. He opened his bag and pulled out the sniper rifle, popping in a new clip and switching it to full auto. "When I tell you, give Tina and I some covering fire, okay?"

"It's your show, man," Jesse said. "Run it the way you want."

Jason didn't bother with any additional explanations. He moved back to Tina and gave her a gentle shove off her perch. "Hey!" she said, landing on her butt. "That's my nuclear couch!"

"Funny," he replied dryly. "Grab an end and get ready."

She grabbed the crate handles on her end and Jason pulled the pin on the grenade, then counted off almost every second the fuse had before he tossed it overhead to land on the other side of their crate pile. Smoke began to billow upward, filling the air and making it hard to see more than a few feet at best.

"Now," he said, and Jesse peered around the corner and fired off a quick burst. To Tina, Jason said, "Lift!"

She did and between them, they dragged the crate along the ground, and Jason thanked God that it wasn't the full rocket, but just the warhead itself. They were barely able to lift it as it was. He guided them toward the docking bay where he'd left the Scorpion.

Nearby, Jesse continue to fire off 3-round bursts, and between that and the smoke, the guards were keeping their heads down pretty well.

"No time for anything fancy," he grunted. "Push it into the water."

"The water?" she said. "Won't it sink?"

"That's the general idea," he said.

They both moved to one side of the crate and shoved it into the water. The container was airtight, but the pure weight and density of it caused it to sink quickly out of sight.

The air began to clear and bullets began to fly closer to the Scorpion, pinging metal and forcing Jason and Tina to dive back to their makeshift cover. "Drop that last smoker on 'em!" he shouted at Jesse.

Jesse used his last grenade and once again, smoke billowed out.

"Let's get this last one moved," he said, feeling every muscle in his body cry out in protest. He didn't mind the bumps and bruises, but the bullet graze on his arm was stinging like a bitch and was still bleeding. He knew for a fact that he had a least one cracked rib and the others were badly bruised. Thinking on it, he wouldn't be the least bit surprised if he had other injuries he hadn't even noticed yet.

Tina helped him move the last crate over to the water and shove it in. It sank as rapidly as the first one, and Jesse did his part by continuing to keep them covered with short bursts. They dived back behind the crates just as the smoke began to clear again and Jesse loaded a fresh clip into the rifle.

"Okay, the nukes are taken care of, at least for now," Jason said. "It's time we got out of here."

"You won't get any argument from me," Tina said. "Just tell us how."

"We can use the Claymores," Jesse said. "As they

start getting closer, they're going to bottleneck some. I've been saving them for last."

"Good call," Jason said. "But we've got to get them in closer, so it's time to do a little acting."

"Acting?" they both said.

"You'll see," Jason replied. "Where do you have the switches for the Claymores?"

Jesse shoved one crate to the right, and Jason could see all the lead lines running to a set of four switches. "The whole area in front of us is covered by the arc," he said.

"Okay," he said. "Tina, when they fire their next barrage, I want you to let out a scream, and, Jesse, I want you to start cursing. Keep your hands on those switches and wait for my signal."

They both nodded and Jason took the rifle back from his brother and put it to his shoulder. There was no point in wasting shots. He peered through the scope and looked for someone of rank. He finally found the man, talking rapidly into a microphone.

He exhaled and took the shot, then cursed as it went wide, only hitting the man in the shoulder. "The damn scope is off," he muttered. It must have gotten knocked around some. Still, the man went down, cursing, and Jason heard him order the others to open fire.

He dived back down just as the barrage hit. Tina took a deep breath and screamed while Jesse began to curse like a sailor on shore leave. Both of them were quite convincing.

"Now," he whispered. "Be silent."

Both of them went quiet.

"I think we got 'em, sir," one of the guards yelled.

"Move in and check it out," the wounded officer called. "Nice and easy."

Jason found a space between the crates and eased the barrel of the rifle through it, adjusting the scope slightly once it was in place. The sound of cautious steps approaching could be heard.

"Hold," he whispered.

He sighted in on the man farthest away.

"Hold," he repeated, his words barely a whisper.

The guards moved closer and were now inside the Claymores' arcs.

"Ready," he said, his finger tightening on the trigger.

"Now!" he shouted, his shot taking the guard in the chest.

Jesse pressed down on the switches and the Claymores went off with loud *whuff*ing sounds, followed by the screams of dying and injured men as shrapnel filled the air.

Jason used the cover of the crates and the confusion to continue taking shots, piling up the bodies behind them, even as they turned and tried to escape. As his brother had predicted, there was a bottleneck and the men went down easily.

The way ahead was all but clear, and Jason gestured for them to follow as he stepped around the crates and began the cold process of finishing off the injured. They couldn't risk having one of them creep up behind them.

Both Tina and Jesse seemed appalled at the carnage they'd wrought, even more so as Jason gunned down a young soldier trying to crawl away.

"Why?" she asked him. "Why?"

"Because to leave them alive puts all of us at risk," he said.

The words had no sooner left his mouth than a nearby rifle sounded and Jesse went down, cursing for real as his blood began to flow.

21

"Jesse!" Tina cried out, rushing to his side.

Feeling a wave of cold wash over him, Jason tracked the source of the shot without thought and fired in the space of a heartbeat or two. The guard he'd wounded earlier had propped himself up against a crate and waited for them, much as they had waited for his men.

Jason's shot took him in the heart, killing him instantly.

He scanned the area for any other dangers and, seeing none, turned back to his brother. "How bad?" he asked, kneeling down.

"I'm okay," Jesse said. He held up his left hand, which was bleeding profusely. "It passed right through me."

"Yeah, and took several bones with it," Jason said. He pulled out his knife and cut a long strip away from his shirt. "It's a good thing you're right-handed."

"It's a good thing he's not dead," Tina snapped.

There was an unspoken accusation in her voice, as if Jason had done something wrong. He could feel the waves of anger coming off her.

Jason didn't respond to her tone, but nodded his head in agreement, then wrapped the hand carefully. "This is going to require a lot more medical care than we can give it here," he said. "Try not to bump it on anything—it will hurt like hell if you do."

"Can we get out of here now?" Tina asked.

Jason got to his feet and helped Jesse to his, holding him steady while he caught his breath and his balance returned. A nearby guard had a canteen on his belt and Jason took it, pulled the cap and handed it to his brother. "Take a drink. You can go into shock later if you feel like it," he said. "Right now, you've got to stay focused."

"How can you be so cold?" Tina asked. "Look around you!"

The high-tension wire inside him frayed a little bit and he turned on her. "You don't get it, do you? You were an analyst and it wasn't real to you. You do all those translations, but they don't connect to what happens if you pass on certain information. This is my life. This is what I do. I kill people, Tina, bad people who will hurt others for pay or power or even those just stupid enough to work for those kind of people. And if I don't do it just right, people die—but the wrong ones."

He jabbed a finger in her direction. "You've switched back and forth between treating me like a schoolboy to treating me like a lover to being my partner and back again, but, Tina, this is who I am. Now, I'm getting you two out of here, then I'm going to hunt down Feng Li and put an end to all this once and for all. Until then, I'd appreciate it if you'd do less talking and more shooting!"

Even as he finished his sentence, he raised the rifle once more and fired it over her shoulder, his shot taking a guard in the back who'd been trying to sneak away.

"Is that understood?" he finished.

Her sullen glare was frosty, but she nodded. "Yes, sir," she said.

"Good," he replied. "Now let's get moving."

They met little resistance on their way to the stairs leading out of the cabin, and as they reached it, Jason noted a large crate marked Phosphorus Grenades. He stopped and pried open the lid using his knife. "These will do nicely," he said.

"What do you have in mind?" Jesse asked.

"A lot of these crates are wood," Jason said. "Phosphorus burns real hot. We'll toss a few of these in here before we go, and with all the ammunition and the fuel, all of this will be so much useless ash in a few hours."

"Sounds good," Jesse said.

They each took three, with Jesse using his teeth to pull the pins. They tossed them in random directions, and as they turned up the stairs, the bright glare of the burning chemical lit the cavern behind them. The crackle of flames and heat was already starting by the time they reached the main floor of the Quonset building.

"Head for the front," Jason said. "I'll take point, just in case we run into any more guards."

Tina chuckled dryly. "I'm pretty sure you've killed just about everyone," she said. "What's your body count for the day?"

Gritting his teeth at her jibe, he moved forward, his eyes searching the darkness for any sign of a guard who might stand between them and freedom. They reached the door without incident.

"Must have sent pretty much everyone they had on hand down there," Jesse said.

"Guess so," Jason replied. He eased open the door to the icy air of night and they stepped out, moving past a truck and in the direction of where Tina said they'd left the SUV.

As they cleared the back bumper, a heavy gust of wind passed over them, and Jason turned to see the Asp landing next to the building. In the copilot seat was his old friend Boris, and at the controls was an Asian man that he assumed was the infamous Feng Li.

"Well, well," he said. "I guess I won't have to go hunting for him after all."

Feng Li shut down the silent, twirling blades, but his eyes never left Jason's. Boris climbed out of one side, while his boss climbed out of the other.

"Maybe live to fight another day," Jesse suggested. "You can't take them both and I'm not exactly a hundred percent myself."

"Let's run for it," Tina said. "You can hunt him down later with a…a flamethrower or something."

Jason shook his head. "The Asp was part of my mission, too," he said. "And there may never be as good a time as this one to take him out."

Tina tugged at his hand. "Please, Jason, let's just go."

"She's right, brother," Jesse said. "We've done enough for one day."

"You two have, anyway," Jason said. "Get in the SUV and get out of here." He pulled his hand out of Tina's. "I have to stay."

"Have you lost your mind?" Tina asked. "You're already wounded, exhausted, and those two are as fresh as daisies. What am I supposed to tell Denny if he kills you? That I stood aside and let it happen?"

Jason grinned down at her. "He won't," he said. "Now get going."

He turned away from them and walked toward the Asp. As he did, Feng Li and Boris moved as well. The moonlight was bright enough to light up the area almost as well as stadium lights. It was a beautiful night—cold and the air was clear and clean. He felt alive, his nerves tingling with anticipation and, he admitted to himself, no small amount of fear. Feng Li had a reputation and he'd already seen what Boris could do.

It was time to show them what he could do.

He heard the crunch of shoes on the snow behind him and glanced backward to see Tina and Jesse walking in his wake. He stopped and turned. "I thought I told you two to go," he said. "Get out of here and get to safety."

"What is it you say?" Jesse asked. "The mission comes first, right? I didn't go through all this just to quit five yards before the finish line."

"Neither did I," Tina said. "We'll see it through with you."

He looked at both of them carefully, then nodded once. "Tina, you stay out of it." And before she could object, he said. "I mean it. I'm going to try to take Boris out of the picture first, then Feng Li. Keep him off me as long as you can, Jesse."

"He doesn't look all that scary to me," he said.

"Trust me," Jason said. "You'll have your hands full. Try to keep moving and don't let him get close. There won't be any weapons. This is…personal now."

"I thought it was the mission," Tina said.

"It is," he replied. "Sometimes, the mission is personal. It has to be."

He turned back around and said, "Let's go."

The three of them started walking forward once more. The tundra grass and the frozen snow crunched beneath their feet, and their breath steamed in the air.

Jason wondered if he would die, if the others would, then put it all away. All of the feelings and emotions that could distract him from what he had to do.

So that Boris and Feng Li had to die so the world— the world of those he cared for, and the world of those who deserved to be safe—would be safe again.

And that was a mission he could believe in. Even if it meant his own death.

The two groups came to a stop about ten feet apart and spent several long seconds staring at each other— assessing strengths, searching for weaknesses.

Jason spoke first. "Boris," he said, using English, "I've missed you. I did get a chance to meet your brother, however. I did give him my very best."

"For that," Boris replied in Russian, "if for nothing else, I will kill you."

The cold spark of anger flared toward uncontrollable rage. That was good, Jason knew, and one of the reasons he taunted those he was about to fight. Rage burned hot, but it caused mistakes in combat. Only in a state of cold calm could one avoid the mistakes that led to death.

He flicked his eyes in the direction of Feng Li. The man was lean, with sharp, almost pinched features. His stance was one of loose readiness, and his dark-brown eyes were frozen—his was the look of a predator, a man who knew how to fight and kill. "You must be Feng Li," Jason said. "I heard you were dead."

Feng Li grinned and there was a white flash of teeth. They almost looked pointed. He offered a small half bow from the waist. "You are correct, Mr. Siku. I *was* dead. The sniper sent by Mr. Talbot made a mistake, however, leaving me in the jungle so quickly. The ancient medicines of my home country were able to bring me back." He offered the shark's grin once more. "I do not think you will be so lucky, here in the frozen wasteland of Alaska."

"I promise you, Feng," Jason replied, "that as soon as I'm done killing Boris here, I will be a lot more thorough than that sniper was."

"We do appear to have a problem," Feng said. "You are three and we are two. Would you have our fight be unfair?"

"I don't think—" Jason began, but Feng's hand moved in a sudden blur, producing a small-frame

Glock, aiming and firing it so quickly that it cut off the rest of his sentence, like some strange form of punctuation.

He heard a pained gasp from behind him and spun. Tina's face was ashen, and blood blossomed like a winter rose high on her chest. She staggered back a step, then sat down in the snow. Jason knelt down beside her. "Tina?"

"I think…" she began, her voice a whisper. "Going to faint."

Jason clasped her hand and said, "Just hold on." He got to his feet and turned his attention back to Feng. "This won't take long," he finished.

He heard her fall over, knew she was unconscious. He pushed his fear for her aside. "She wasn't a threat to you," he said.

"All of my dead soldiers downstairs would disagree," Feng replied, "if they had the voice to do so. The dead are silent in this place."

"Well," Jesse finally spoke, "I'm all for you shutting up." He leaped forward, diving at Feng's legs and hitting him in the knees. They went rolling through the snow and the grass—Jesse trying to use his greater weight to keep Feng pinned on the ground, Feng fighting to get to his feet where he could do more damage.

Jason turned his attention to Boris just in time to see the massive man closing in on him. He stepped sideways, driving a knee into the man's midsection. It felt like a brick wall, but he followed through on the move, slamming an elbow into the back of the man's skull.

Boris staggered a step or two, then spun to face him. He really did resemble a bear, Jason thought, skipping backward. "You hit pretty hard for such a small man," the Russian said.

"Yeah, your brother mentioned that," Jason said, dancing out of reach. "Right before I killed him."

That did it, he saw. The ice had turned to fire. Boris roared and came at him again, catching him with a shoulder in the ribs. The world spun as he was lifted into the air, then flashed by in a moonlit blur as he was slammed into the ground. The air left his lungs with an audible sound, but he found the strength to roll away.

Speed and agility were his best allies in this fight. If Boris got hold of him, he might just snap him in two, like a human pretzel.

Still snarling, the Russian followed after him.

Jason gained his feet, ignoring the pain in his battered rib cage, and caught Boris with a roundhouse kick square in the jaw. He staggered, spitting blood, then surged forward once more.

Jason moved away, circling, waiting for an opening. Out of the corner of his eye, he saw Feng gain his feet, and felt a surge of pride for his brother who'd held him down for so long. The pride quickly turned to concern, however, when he saw Jesse staggering.

He looked as if he'd been in a threshing machine. Blood ran from his nose, mouth and ears. Feng wasn't fighting him. He was toying with him.

"Come on, you little rice cake," Jesse said, his chest heaving with exertion. "You call that fighting? We've got a village grandmother that hits harder than you."

Sadly, Jason could see that his brother's words were bravado, and he would be quickly spent.

The slight diversion of his attention was all Boris needed, however, and he turned back to his own battle in time to feel the Russian's arms wrap around him and lift him off his feet.

"I will crush you like a grape," he said as he squeezed.

This time, Jason knew he had broken ribs because he felt them give beneath Boris's arms. Pain shot through him, running up his spine and slamming into his skull. Lights flashed before his eyes.

Acting on instinct, he raised his arms and brought his hands down as hard as he could on the man's ears. Boris grunted, staggered, but held on.

Jason did it again, and this time, he felt the Russian's hold on him loosen. Off balance and deafened, Boris dropped him to the ground. He backed away, shaking his head.

Gritting his teeth, Jason closed in. He needed to end this and quickly.

Boris saw him coming and tried to move away, but his strength wasn't speed. Jason moved with him, grasped his left wrist and twisted and yanked the big man toward him. Using all the muscle he had, he spun and smashed his own elbow into the Russian's. It broke with a dry snap and Boris screeched in pain, going to his knees.

End it now, Jason thought. He circled around and drove a snap kick into the huge man's nose, driving his head up and leaving his throat exposed. Dropping down, he planted a knife hand into his opponent's throat, trying to crush his larynx.

But Boris wasn't quite finished and managed to duck his head down, taking the blow on the mouth instead. He drove an uppercut into Jason's chin with enough force to send him flying through the air and managed to gain his feet. He wasn't steady, but the man was a machine. He would keep fighting as long as he could.

Jason lay on the ground, trying to catch his breath when he saw Boris's shadow looming over him. Still deafened, the man was shouting as he said, "Now you will die!"

Rolling, Jason lashed out, sweeping the man's legs out from underneath him. Already lacking balance, he toppled to the ground.

Knowing that time was getting more precious by the second, he leaped to his feet, then jumped in the air, coming down on the man's sternum with his elbow. He heard a faint crack as it broke beneath the force of the blow.

Jason got up and did it again before Boris could catch his wind. This time, the bone shattered completely. The Russian coughed weakly, blood flowing out of his mouth. His lungs had been pierced by the bones and he couldn't breathe.

Getting up once more, Jason looked down at him and said, "You're done." He pulled his combat knife from the sheath at his boot. The blade's edge glittered faintly as he grasped it firmly and drove it into the Russian's heart. He twisted it, shredding the big muscle.

Boris shuddered once beneath him, then died, unable to speak whatever hateful final words he might have said. He had joined his brother in whatever hell awaited them.

Jason climbed slowly to his feet, feeling as if he'd been through a threshing machine himself. He really did prefer a clean assassination mission. One shot, one kill, move on. "Damn complications," he muttered, turning to where he knew Feng and Jesse were fighting.

His eyes widened as he saw the Chinese man twist away from a clumsy lunge and come in behind Jesse. His arms circled Jesse's neck and their gazes met for a brief moment, then Feng snapped his neck with one easy move.

Time seemed to slow as Feng released his hold and Jesse toppled over into the cold snow, dead before he hit the ground.

Feng didn't even look all that winded, though it appeared as though Jesse had given a good battle. Blood trickled from a cut on his lip and even in the dim light, Jason could tell that Feng was favoring his left side slightly.

"And then there were two," the rogue agent said, straightening his lean frame. "He fought well, for a civilian. A pleasant enough diversion."

"I'm going to kill you, Feng," Jason said, his blood turning to ice. He felt nothing. His brother was dead. Tina probably was, too. People he cared about, the closest thing he would ever have to a family, and he felt nothing. "If it's the last thing I do, I'm taking you with me to hell."

Moving forward with catlike grace, Feng smiled once more. "Better men than you have tried, Mr. Siku. For the destruction you have brought down upon my little operation here, I promise you a painfully slow death."

"Bring it, then," he said, circling away from the man and gauging his opponent. "Let's find out if you're really as good as they say you are. My guess is your reputation is probably a little bloated."

"I promise you, Mr. Siku," Feng said. "I am better."

The real fight, Jason knew, was about to begin.

And worse, he realized something else as the distance between them closed. Feng was better than he was and he was about to die. So be it, he thought. But I won't make it easy for him. Not by any measure.

Feng suddenly leaped into the air, and Jason met him halfway.

22

Spinning wheel kicks sliced through the air, and Jason stepped inside of them, taking one on the shoulder but driving a hard right into Feng's inner thigh. Instead of tumbling to the ground, however, the Chinese man sprang backward, landing on his hands, then flipping once more to right himself.

He didn't pause, but drove forward again, and Jason found himself backing up, blocking twice as many punches as he was able to throw. His opponent was rattlesnake fast and knew where to place each blow to cause the most pain and damage.

Trying to give a little in return, Jason gave up on blocking and stepped into a punch that caught him directly on the cheekbone below his right eye. The pain was excruciating, but worth it as he managed to put a knife hand into Feng's left collarbone. It wasn't enough to break it, but there was at least a crack, and the Chinese man backed off once more.

Remembering that Feng was favoring his left side, Jason pressed the attack, aiming for Feng's ribs this time and driving a hard kick into his side. Feng danced away, but not fast enough to avoid it entirely. He increased the distance between them and began to circle.

"You fight well, Mr. Siku," Feng said. "Better than I expected, considering your condition."

"I'm tougher than I look," Jason said, turning and moving to his left.

"You already know you cannot beat me," Feng said. "I can see that knowledge in your eyes."

"Maybe, maybe not," he said. "But even if I can't, I can hurt you. Maybe hurt you bad enough for you to crawl back under your rock for a while."

Feng laughed softly. "You would die an extremely unhappy man should you fail. Your life is all about the mission. I know—I lived it once."

Jason nodded. "So I've heard. Still, the charm of all this punching and kicking has worn off." He reached behind his back and removed two push daggers from his belt. They weren't his favorite weapon, but they required him to get up close and personal. Feng was a little less dangerous when he wasn't leaping and spinning through the air like some kind of tiger.

"Weapons, Mr. Siku?" Feng said. "I am disappointed in you. I thought we were going to do this the old-fashioned way."

"Screw the old-fashioned way," Jason spit. "I'd rather just kill you and move on with my day." He lunged forward, capturing Feng's right arm in a twist lock. He jabbed his right hand forward, but Feng twisted, and the blow slipped off the flexible body armor he was wearing beneath his clothing.

Using his left arm, Feng wrapped Jason's right, twisted sharply and dislocated his elbow. The dagger in that hand fell from nerveless fingers and he tried to move, but the Chinese man was faster, slamming his forehead into Jason's nose, breaking it with a horrible crunching sound.

He stepped back, leaped into the air and slammed both feet into Jason's chest.

"That sounded painful," Feng said, circling once more, even as Jason struggled to get to his feet. Blood poured from his shattered nose, and pain radiated from his elbow in sickening waves. "I promised you it would be slow. I am a man of my word."

Spitting blood and staining the snow, Jason managed to get to his knees and then his feet. With no way to put his right elbow back in place, he knew he was in deep trouble. That was his primary hand and now it was useless.

He spit once more and realized that in the last exchange, he'd dropped both his weapons. "Guess we're back to the old-fashioned way," he said. "Sure you don't prefer pistols at ten paces?"

"I enjoy the personal touch of hand-to-hand combat," Feng said. "Don't you?"

"Not as much as I once did," Jason admitted. He began to circle once more, looking for an opening of some kind, any kind that would let him harm this killing machine. Even as Feng tried to close the gap once more, Jason moved away, letting patience be his guide. In truth, he didn't have much left in him and he felt as if the next exchange would end it—one way or the other.

Feng leaped into the air once more and Jason feinted to his left, then moved right. Unable to adjust, Feng landed awkwardly, just enough to put him off balance. Seeing his opportunity, Jason made his move and closed the gap.

Screaming in pain, Jason forced both arms forward, driving his fingers beneath the man's floating ribs on each side. He grabbed them with his remaining strength and yanked as hard as he could. His right hand slipped away, but the left held and he felt the rib break. He released it, then tried to back away, but it was too late.

Truly angry, Feng grabbed his right arm and twisted him around once more. Jason felt the loop of wire slip around his neck, and tighten, cutting off his air supply.

"A very nice move," Feng hissed in his ear. "My left lung will be punctured on my next breath."

Jason tried to reply, but with no air and the wire getting tighter and tighter, he couldn't force out the words. Lights began to swirl in his vision, and he knew it was over.

He heard Feng inhale, then gasp in pain as the broken rib bone turned inward, stabbing into his left lung. It was a shame he didn't manage to get both of them. That might have been enough to change the outcome.

"Goodbye, Mr. Siku," Feng said, the wire tightening even more. "You lose."

"No, he doesn't," a voice said.

Jason felt Feng's body tense, heard the unmistakable sound of a harpoon gun, and suddenly he was free. He slumped to the ground and rolled. Behind him, Feng stood, staring in horror at the long harpoon sticking out of his shoulder.

Searching the darkness, Jason spotted Tanuk standing nearby. Behind him, lights began to flicker as more and more people became visible. By all appearances, the old man had brought half the village population with him.

Slowly, Jason struggled to his feet. His right arm hung useless at his side, and blood continued to drip from his nose. His throat burned with each breath of icy air he took. Nothing had ever felt quite so good.

"You were saying?" Jason gasped.

Tanuk moved to his side, helping to hold him up.

Feng stared at Jason as though trying to figure out a particularly difficult puzzle, then he began to back away, moving slowly toward the helicopter. "This is not over, Mr. Siku," he said. He grasped the harpoon, groaning in pain as it tore muscle and scraped bone, but he managed to get it free. He tossed it on the ground. "Men like us do not like leaving enemies behind."

Sinking to his knees, Jason looked at Tanuk. "Quickly," he rasped. Blood vessels had been ruptured in his throat, and he spit, trying to clear his airway. "In the back of the SUV. There's a green metal case, rectangular. Get it for me."

"Let him go, son," Tanuk said. "We need to get you to a hospital."

Jason shook his head and his eyes blazed. "Get it now."

Tanuk moved away, and Jason watched as Feng tried to climb into the Asp. His battered body wasn't cooperating very well, and he had to pull himself inside the helicopter and crawl into the pilot's seat. He rested for a moment, leaning his head back. Jason knew that the rogue agent was losing a lot of blood, but the man was tough as nails. He needed to be stopped, here and now, before he could do any more damage.

He heard a stirring behind him and saw Tanuk and another man carrying the case toward him. Feng began the start-up sequence, and the Asp's nearly silent engines began to cycle. "Hurry," he told them.

They set the case on the ground and all of them began to open the latches. Inside, cradled in foam, was a Russian-made Kornet-E antitank weapon. It was the infantry model, which used a laser-guided warhead. In combat, they could be used to penetrate concrete barriers and take out ground units who dug in behind protective shields. Inside the case were three warheads.

Lifting the Kornet out of the foam, Jason got it loaded, but putting it on his shoulder proved to be a bit too much. That collarbone was definitely cracked or broken. "Help me," he ordered Tanuk. "Get it on my shoulder."

The old man helped him lift it, while in the distance, Feng finished the start-up sequence. The Asp's rotors began to turn, and the blades started to spin rapidly as he prepared to take off. Looking through the glass, he saw what Jason was doing and started to lift off.

Flicking the switch to turn on the laser guidance system, Jason said, "Get everyone out of the way. I don't want anyone hit with the back blast."

Tanuk turned and started yelling for everyone to move.

Jason peered through the optic sight, and for a moment, his gaze met Feng's. The Chinese man nodded in acknowledgment, gaining altitude. He was perhaps fifty feet off the ground when Jason fired the rocket.

Using the laser, it tracked a path through the night and slammed into the Asp's cockpit, exploding on impact. The glare was blinding at this range and in the dark, and everyone's eyes began to water as the helicopter crashed to the ground in a burning, ruined heap.

Jason dropped the Kornet, groaning in pain. "Help me up," he ordered Tanuk. "I have to make sure it's finished."

"No one could survive that," the old man said. "No one."

"I have to be sure," Jason said. "Get me there."

Tanuk helped Jason up and the two of them slowly crossed the snowy field to where the Asp was burning on the ground. Even as they got closer, Jason saw movement near the wreckage and he used his left hand to awkwardly take the Glock out of its holster. Personal my ass, he thought, holding the weapon. I should have just shot him and been done with it.

"There!" Tanuk said, pointing.

Sure enough, burned and horribly injured, Feng was trying to crawl away, using the wreckage as cover. He must have jumped from the Asp milliseconds before the warhead impact. Both of his legs were broken and he was dragging them behind him like broken sticks of wood.

"Feng!" Jason shouted.

The Chinese man rolled onto his back, slowly raising his hands. "You…win, Mr. Siku," he said. "I surrender."

"You don't understand," Jason said. "There are no winners, no losers. Surrender is not an option. You've forgotten what Room 59 was created to do. We keep the world safe from people like you, no matter what the cost."

"What…will you do, then, Mr. Siku?" he asked, panting for breath. "Will you become what they made me? A cold-blooded killer of men?"

Jason shook his head and raised the Glock. "No," he said quietly. "I will be more. I will finish the mission you forgot. The mission you walked away from." He squeezed the trigger three quick times, using the time-honored pattern of two to the chest, one to the head. At this range, even left-handed, he didn't miss.

"And I will help keep this world safe."

Slowly, he slumped to the ground. The warmth from the burning helicopter wreckage felt nice, and he knew he was drifting away. The last thing he saw before the darkness took him was Tanuk's face, the last words he heard were, "You can rest now, son."

JASON WOKE to the smell of woodsmoke and a scent that reminded him vaguely of cinnamon. He could hear hushed voices nearby, and he slowly opened his eyes. Above him, he saw a wooden roof with all kinds of symbols and signs hung from the rafters.

"He's awake," a cracked voice said.

Jason turned to see Tanuk and an old woman, her face wrinkled with time and years, move toward him. She was ancient, but her voice was strong and sure. "You're going to live," she said. "Though I wondered for a time if you still had the will to fight."

Remembering, Jason looked at Tanuk. He was confused and still a bit groggy. "Tina?" he asked.

A broad grin split the old man's face. "She, too, will live. The cold actually helped her survive," he said.

"Where is she?" Jason asked.

"A small hospital in Nome," Tanuk said. "It was decided to keep you here might be the safest course of action. You have many enemies."

"Jesse?" he asked.

"I'm sorry," Tanuk said. "There was nothing we could do for Jesse but release his spirit to the next world. Tina is waiting for you to come to her in Nome. There is much you need to discuss."

He had no sense of time. "How long have I been out?" he asked.

"This is the third day since they brought you here," the old woman said.

"Damn," Jason said. "I need my things, I have to…let people know what's happened here."

"I think they know," Tanuk said. "Your people arrived yesterday."

"My people?" he asked.

"Yes," he said. "The ones with the hard eyes and winter stares. One waits for you outside."

Pushing himself upright, Jason took a better look at his surroundings. He was in some kind of medicine hut, by all appearances. He felt better than he had any right to, though he was still sore. His right arm was in a sling. He looked at the old woman. "You took care of me?"

"Yes," she said. "I am a healer, though few come to me anymore. My art will soon be lost."

"That is sad," Jason said. "I feel much better."

"Good," said a voice from the doorway. "Denny is expecting a full report from you within two days, but I'd like a summary now if you're up to it."

A broad-shouldered man with long dark hair was standing in the doorway, looking a little out of place in a heavy parka. "You can call me Adrostos," the man said. He had a slight Greek accent. "When you didn't report in, Denny assumed the worst and sent me with a team in case things had gone to hell. Feng Li is—was, rather—a very dangerous man."

Jason laughed. "That's an understatement if I ever heard one."

"They tell me you killed him," Adrostos said.

"I had help," he replied, using his left hand to gesture toward Tanuk. "Really, everyone up here helped."

"And the submarine?"

"Bottom of the ocean," Jason said. "I'll send the co-ordinates to the offshore team today, so they can get it marked and start recovery, if they want to."

"Did you get the plans for it?" Adrostos asked.

The old woman made an eerie sound that flittered

somewhere between a crow and a bear. "Enough!" she said. "You can talk more later. Now, he needs to rest and get his strength back. He still has a long journey ahead of him."

"I do?" Jason asked.

"He does?" the man echoed.

"Yes," she said, making a shooing gesture with her hands. "It should be enough for you to know that this bad man is gone and his evil weapons with him. You'll know more—in two days. Now go!"

Adrostos smiled ruefully and nodded. "Two days, Jason," he said. "In Denny's office. And check your system messages. Full debrief on any witnesses, clean-up if needed." He paused, then added, "Understand?"

"I got it," Jason said, watching as the man stepped back out the door. Even from inside, he could hear him telling the rest of the team to pull out. What Adrostos had meant was that if he had to, he was to eliminate anyone who knew too much. One thing he knew for certain—Adrostos was every bit as dangerous as Feng Li. He carried himself with the steady assurance of a man who had killed many others and slept well at night. Briefly, he wondered if Adrostos was part of the midnight teams, then dismissed it. There was no point in speculating about ghosts.

The old woman brought him a bowl of soup and placed it with a wooden spoon on a tray next to his bed. "You must eat all of that, if you are to get your strength back quickly. You have far to go."

"Where am I going?" he asked. "I did what I came up here to do. Now I go home."

"And where is home now?" Tanuk asked quietly.

Jason stared into the bowl of soup, his mind working on the problem. "I don't know," he finally admitted. "I just don't know."

"Eat your soup," the medicine woman said. "Not every answer is in your head or your heart. Some are elsewhere."

"Where am I going?" he asked her.

"In the long run," she said, "that is up to you. But first, you must go to Nome and visit Tina. When you see her, you may have more answers than you do right now."

"I hope so," Jason said. "Right now, I'm just confused."

"You're doing fine so far," Tanuk said. "It's not complicated really. It's just love."

The old woman laughed softly. "You should've been a storyteller," she scolded him. "You open your mouth and all kinds of bullshit comes out."

They both laughed again and Jason ate his soup, thinking of Jesse—a brother found and lost—and of Tina. What did she think of him now, knowing the cost of all this? What did he really feel for her?

What kind of life could he offer her?

A dangerous one, his mind answered. At the best of times.

And that, he knew, was precisely the problem. He couldn't offer her anything that she hadn't already walked away from.

This mission had been one of too many complications and too many questions already.

He finished his soup and allowed himself the luxury of falling into sleep again.

Sometimes, it was better to dream of a world he could never have, rather than try to live in the one that he couldn't change.

23

To call the facility in Nome a hospital was a bit like calling a goldfish a shark, Jason thought. With less than twenty-five beds, it served the Inuit and other native populations in a huge area—mostly with local clinics. Still, the facility itself appeared decent enough and the staff was professional.

After waking from his nap, Jason had decided to leave right away, rather than stay any longer. There was little point in putting off what he needed to do. He thanked the old medicine woman and shook hands with Tanuk, who offered him some words of advice before he left.

"Do you know, son, what the difference is between a man alone and a man with a family?"

Jason had shaken his head. "Not really," he answered.

"Wisdom, maybe," Tanuk replied, then turned and went back into his small home.

Adrostos had done him a kindness, leaving him a floatplane that he could fly down to Nome, rather than use an ATV over the rough countryside. The flight itself had been fairly short and by early morning, he was in Nome, wandering the streets and waiting for a diner to open so he could get some breakfast and a cup of coffee.

What he was really doing, he knew, was putting off seeing Tina.

She'd put her trust in him, done everything he'd asked, and nearly lost her life in doing so. People in her village, people she knew, had died. Sitting in the dingy little diner, he finished off the last of his coffee and paid his bill. He couldn't wait any longer, and headed for the hospital.

He stopped at the main desk and asked the young lady there what room she was in. "Just down the hall and then to your left," the woman told him.

"Thank you," he replied, then turned away and headed in that direction. He felt funny inside, almost wooden or as if nothing was real. He thought he had a handle on how he felt about Tina, but he didn't know what to do about it. If, that was, there was anything to be done.

He reached her room and stopped at the threshold. The door was open and he peered inside. Tina was propped up on a handful of pillows, her head turned away from the door as she stared out the window. He wondered what was going through her mind, what thoughts she was thinking.

Jason tapped lightly on the door frame and she turned to look at him.

"I guessed it would be you," she said quietly. "My grandfather called and told me you were alive."

He didn't speak, just nodded his head. It was as if seeing her had robbed him of his voice.

"Come in," she said. "I figure we have some things to talk about."

He stepped into the room and held out the small bouquet of flowers he'd picked up on the way in. "I…I thought you might like these," he said.

She smiled and he was struck once more by her beauty. "They're beautiful," she said. "Thank you."

He set them on the bedside table, then moved to stand near her bed. The silence between them felt like a chasm he'd once seen in the mountains in South America. There was no possible way across, no way to bridge the gap. Still, he had to say something. "I wanted to apologize," he blurted.

Tina's eyes widened slightly. "Apologize?" she asked. "I don't understand."

"I should have protected you better," he said, the words coming out in a sudden rush. "I shouldn't have let you get hurt."

She smiled once again and took his hand. "That was my choice, remember?" she asked. "I'm not very good at taking orders, so even if you'd told me to take off, I would have stayed."

He shook his head. "Still, I should have expected…" He sighed, letting his words trail off. "I should have expected something like that."

"Really?" she said. "Do you think that somehow you should know how every battle will be fought? Is that how you usually operate?"

"Not exactly," he admitted. "Usually, I plan everything down to the last detail. I'm not big on the battles. I'm more of a 'one shot, one kill, move on' kind of guy. They sent me on this mission because they thought I'd have a better chance of fitting in with the locals."

Tina burst out laughing, then grabbed at her chest. "Ouch," she said when the pain subsided. "Don't make me laugh. It hurts."

"You don't think I fit in?" he asked.

"Not even remotely," she said, shaking her head. Her hair was beautiful.

He chuckled. "Not everything went according to plan," he said. "But the mission got done, so that's something."

"So I heard," she said. "Someone named Adrostos— a very scary man, by the way—came by and debriefed me late yesterday. He told me you killed Feng."

"I did," he said. "With some help from your grand-father."

Her thoughts turned inward, and her face went still. "Jesse didn't make it," she said.

"No," Jason said. "He didn't."

Images of the fight flashed through his mind. Maybe if he'd taken on Feng to begin with Jesse would still be alive. But when it came right down to it, Jason knew that Feng was the kind of tiger who liked to play with his food. He'd bought the time he needed with Jesse's life. "He fought well," he finally said.

"I imagine that he did," she said. "There's something else that didn't go according to plan. Something…I'm not sure how to tell you this."

Concern filled him. "What is it?" he asked. "You're okay, aren't you?"

She nodded. "Yes, I'm okay, but…there's something you need to know."

"All right," he said. "You can tell me anything."

"I guess we'll see about that," she said. She pointed at her belly. "I'm pregnant, Jason. I'm going to have a baby."

A strange ringing sound echoed in his ears. "Baby?" he repeated. "What baby?"

"*Our* baby, Jason," she said. "Yours and mine."

"But…well…how did that happen?"

She allowed herself a small smile. "How soon they forget," she said.

"No," he said. "I mean, yes, I remember. I know how it happened, it's just…"

They were both quiet for a moment, then she said, "Just?"

"I…" Words failed him for a moment, and he tried again. "I don't know what to say, Tina. What to feel. What you feel."

She started to speak and he held up a hand to stop her. "You have every reason to hate me," he said. "With everything that's happened, a lot of people killed. Jesse dead. And you certainly didn't expect to get pregnant."

"No," she said. "I didn't. But that's how life works, really. You want everything in your world, every mission, to go according to some plan, but it doesn't. Life happens and things change and get in the way of your plan and you adjust. I will have to adjust."

He nodded in understanding. "What do you want me to say, Tina? I nearly got you…and…and our baby killed. What can I offer you?"

"Tell me how you feel about me," she said. "What's in your heart?"

Jason stood up and started pacing the room. "I care about you, Tina," he said. "I really do. I don't know if what I feel for you is love, because I haven't ever allowed love to be a part of my life. It's all too fast, what we've had, and I'm not a good candidate for being a family man."

"No," she admitted. "You haven't had much experience with that anyway."

"To be honest," he said, "I'm afraid to love you. It wouldn't be fair. We need…I need time to think. To figure out what I'm feeling, what I should do."

"I appreciate your honesty, Jason," she said. "Really I do. And I understand. We practically just met and now I've sprung this on you."

"No, it's not that," he said, then chuckled. "Well, it's that a little. But I'm not the kind of man to walk out on you," he said. "If you never want to see me again, I'll…I mean we can work out some kind of support. I would understand. But then…" Once more, he ran out of words.

"But?" she pressed.

"I'd like to know the child," he said. "The baby. I don't…I mean I didn't have a father or a mother. I didn't have a family. I think it's better for kids to have that. I don't know what it means to be a father, but I'm willing to learn."

He stopped pacing and faced her. "What do you feel about me?" he asked quietly. "Do you love me, Tina? Have you fallen in love with me?"

The silence grew between them again for several minutes, then she said, "I think you're right, Jason. It's been too fast. I don't really know what I feel. I care about you, and I won't cut you out of the baby's life. I think we both need time."

He didn't reply right away. At least they were both being honest with each other. There'd been more than enough lies between them.

She looked at him thoughtfully for a minute, then said, "What do you fear?"

Startled, Jason said, "I'm not afraid of anything."

"Yes, you are," she said. "I'll ask you again, what do you fear? Think about it."

He did as she asked, and after a moment, he said, "Failure. Love. Family. All of it, I guess."

"Go on," she said.

"I don't know how to be good at what I do for a living, yet be the kind of man you deserve as a husband, if that's something you even want. If it's something I want. I don't know how to be a father—I never had one of my own."

She laughed lightly. "Do you think there's a manual or a book you can buy that will really teach you how to be a good husband or a good father?"

"If there was," he said, "I'd sure buy it. But the fact is that I'm…what I do for a living…it's not very good for a family."

"No," she admitted. "It isn't. That's why most of the Room 59 agents that are hired don't have one. The missions, if you will, don't mix. And families can become liabilities if your true identity is known."

He nodded. "And maybe that's why it would be better if I just…went away. If I never came back and the only thing you ever saw from me again was a check once a month."

"Is that what you want to do?"

"No," he said. "But I don't see a lot of other choices."

"As my grandfather says, there are always other choices."

"He's a good man," Jason said. "But I don't think he really understands what my work is." He looked at her, his gaze catching hers. "I don't think you really understood until you saw it up close."

Tina held her silence, thinking about his words, then she said, "You're right. I didn't understand. Not really."

"Why did you leave the Room 59 offices and come out here?" he asked. "You've got the talent, if not the full training, to do what many field agents do."

"It just wasn't my world," she said. "I would look at all this information—pictures, reports, videos—and think *this can't be real*. Yet they still wanted me to wring some kind of sense from it. And the problem was that it never made sense to me. I knew some of the field agents and would talk with them, but it never sank in that much of the carnage I was looking at belonged to them. It was like they owned it somehow. Does that make any sense?"

"Yes, it does," he said. "And we do own it. We have to."

"And that's why I left," she said. "I couldn't imagine a world where people would own that kind of behavior.

Where they would kill someone else—another human being—without mercy. It wasn't the kind of place I wanted to live in, so…I left."

"And now I'm here. You know what I do. You've seen what I do."

"Yes," she said.

"So where does that leave us?" he asked. "Do you want me to stay?"

"To be honest, Jason, I don't know," she replied. "I've been lying here trying to figure it out for the past three or four days—however long I've been in here. I care for you, but what you do is dangerous. Every time you walked out the door, I'd be worried sick that you wouldn't come home to me, to our child. You talk about making the world safe, but the world is a big place. I don't know how you'd make *us* safe." She sobbed quietly, hitched a breath, then said, "I don't know what I want or what you should do."

He sighed. "I guess that makes two of us," he said. He looked at his watch. "I think we both need some time. I'm supposed to be catching a flight soon. Denny has a lot of questions that still need answering."

"I know, I know. The mission comes first," Tina said.

He leaned down and kissed her on the cheek. "Sometimes, family is the mission."

"We'll see," she said, trying not to cry. "Stay in touch, okay?"

"I will," he said. "You can count on it."

Then he turned and walked out of her room.

JASON'S FLIGHTS TOOK him back the way he'd come— from Nome to Anchorage, Anchorage to Seattle and

Seattle back to Minneapolis. It was late when he arrived home, and rather than deal with Denny and Room 59 business right away, he tossed his suitcase on the sofa, his laptop on the desk, showered and crawled into bed.

He slept for almost ten hours, and woke no more certain about what to do in regards to Tina and their baby and his job than when he walked out of the hospital in Nome. He made himself coffee and ate a half a grapefruit and some toast, then did some light stretching. It was going to be a while before he was back to full strength again.

Once his morning routine was completed, he sat down at his desk and fired up his laptop. The glasses he used were right where he left them. He put them on and went through the log-in process that confirmed his identity.

Using his avatar, he entered the Room 59 offices and headed for Denny's door. He noticed several people giving him long, wondering looks as he passed through, but ignored them. He stopped in front of Denny's door and knocked politely.

"Come in, Jason," Denny called out.

Jason opened the door and stepped in, surprised to see that in addition to Denny, Kate was also present. "Shut the door, please," Kate said.

He did as she asked, and Denny motioned for him to sit down.

"How are you feeling?" his boss asked.

"I'm on the mend," Jason said. "I should be mission ready within a week or so."

Kate chuckled. "I think we can manage a little more

downtime than that. You've had quite an adventure from what I understand."

Jason just nodded, then turned his attention to Denny. "You know what happened on the mission?"

"Yes," Denny said. "Kate and I were just discussing it. Under the circumstances, we're both very happy with how you handled things. There was a little cleanup involved with the locals, but Tanuk helped with a lot of that. And we've got a team down at the sub right now, and another looking over the plans. You did well. Congratulations."

"Thank you," Jason said. "So why do I feel like there's another shoe about to drop?"

"Isn't there always in our line of work?" Kate asked.

Jason couldn't help but laugh. "Yes, I suppose there is. What's this one?"

Kate leaned back in her chair, studying him carefully, then motioned for Denny to take the lead. "There is one complication from your trip that we have to address," he said.

"Tina," Jason replied. "And the baby."

Kate nodded. "That's the complication, by the way," she said. "Not the shoe. We'll get to that in a moment."

"I don't see how she enters into this," Jason said. "She works for the agency and from what I gather, you and Denny knew of her involvement from the beginning."

"No, no," Denny said. "That's not it, really. The complication is that—as you know—agents who have families tend to run into problems. We don't encourage it, and we prefer to hire people who don't have a wife or a husband and children to deal with. There are too many risks. When the mission gets personal, bad things can happen. They have in the past. Even the best agent can lose sight of what he or she is supposed to be doing if someone they care about is put at risk."

"I'm aware of the preference," he said. "But at this moment, I'm not even sure if I'm ever going to be more than a monthly check to them. We're both aware of the complications."

"It gets worse," Kate said.

"Worse?"

"Yes," Denny said. "Tina has requested that she return to her work here as an analyst. She wants back in to the main office work."

As Jason started to speak, his boss held up his hands. "Strictly an office job," he said. "We're considering it, but we've never had two people who were…involved… both working for us. It's a unique situation."

"She didn't mention it to me," Jason said. "I assumed she'd be staying up there." He turned to Kate. "Is this the shoe?"

"Not exactly," she said. "You're very good, Jason. Better, in fact, than I thought. The fact that you were able to do what you did—including taking out Feng Li—was very impressive. The other shoe is that we're wondering if you would consider a different position with Room 59."

"But you just hired me to be a field agent," he said. "You said the work was good."

"We did," she said. "But we think there's a way to

utilize your unique talents to benefit Room 59 even more."

"How so?" he asked, intrigued despite himself.

"Would you be interested," Denny asked, "in being a prime?"

"You mean training other agents?" Jason asked.

"A prime is more than a trainer," Kate said. "They are the best of the best, and aside from training, they also do some fieldwork on occasion. Usually with the midnight teams."

"It's a tough job," his boss said. "Different than straight fieldwork, more hours and responsibilities, less downtime." He thought for a moment, then added, "And the pay is better."

"Why?" Jason asked.

"I admit it was my idea," Kate said. "It solves several problems at once."

"Which are?"

"First, if you're a prime, it means that other than field assignments—once or twice a year, usually—you'd be working pretty regular hours. Our training schedule is rigorous, but a prime trains the trainers. You won't be on banker's hours, but it will be close."

"And?"

"Second," Kate continued, "we need a new prime for the U.S. region. Our last one permanently moved to taking over one of the midnight teams last month."

"That's a promotion?" he asked. "Sounds more like a permanent mission."

"It is," Denny said. "They have the worst job in our agency. Hands down."

"Other than get me out of the field, what does this do for me?"

"If you decided to continue your relationship with Tina, being a prime would make that more…comfortable for us. And it would undoubtedly make it more comfortable for the two of you. We could bring her back here, and your relationship could continue unhindered, provided both of you observed the usual rules about classified information."

"I see," he said, considering the implications of the idea. "It's an interesting proposition."

"What do you think?" Denny asked.

"I'd like to think it over," Jason said. "Can you give me a little time?"

Kate and Denny both nodded. "Of course," she said. "Take a few days and consider it."

"You'd make an excellent prime, Jason," Denny said. "But this isn't a one-way ticket, either. If you don't want to do it, or you don't like it, we'll respect that, too."

"Thanks," Jason said. "I was sort of wondering about that."

"It's hard to leave the field," he said. "I know I struggled with it at first, too. But there are some benefits to it, as well—not the least of which is a longer life expectancy."

"I'll give it serious thought," he said, getting to his feet. "Thank you for the offer."

"You've earned it," Denny replied. "Anyone who can kill Feng Li deserves a promotion. Especially since I thought he was dead myself."

"If I hadn't looked through the wreckage, he'd have probably survived again," Jason said. He thanked Kate again and left Denny's office, then made his way back out, and logged out of the system.

JASON SPENT DAYS recovering physically and considering his options. Was it time for him to give up being in the field? To become a teacher of future assassins, rather than be one himself? Would this allow him to be with Tina?

He didn't know the answers, but at the least, he knew where to direct the questions.

Jason stood up, went to the kitchen and poured himself a cup of coffee. Staring out the window into the Minnesota autumn, he thought of all the things Tanuk had told him about family, the things he'd learned about family during his mission.

What was it the old man had said while he was getting ready to get on the plane to Nome?

He thought about it for a moment, then it came to him. "The ties that bind a family together are more complex than love, son. Having a family, a real family, means knowing that for the rest of your life, there is nothing you will have to face alone, no mountain or challenge you must conquer on your own. It means being there for others before yourself, because someone else is doing the same for you. Home is always where they are, where you are. It's not the place, my boy— it's the people that count. That, son, is a family."

"I don't know how to be that," Jason had told him. "I never have."

Tanuk had put his hand on his shoulder and squeezed gently. "We're never too old to learn, son. Not even me."

Jason thought of the old man fondly, then reached for the phone.

There was a beautiful woman in a little village in Alaska. She spoke flawless Russian. She was tough and smart and had already sent him a message by asking to return to Room 59.

He dialed the number and waited as the connection was made. He heard Tina's voice and she sounded so very far away. In his heart, he knew that wasn't right.

"Tina Kanut," she said.

"Tina? It's Jason," he said.

"It's good to hear from you," she said, after a long silence. "What can I do for you?"

"I heard you want to come back. Work as an analyst again."

"Yes," she said. "I don't know why, but I think I can make a difference now. Be better than I was before. So I want to come back."

"I don't want you to come back," he said quietly. "I want you to come home."

"Home?" she said, a hitch in her voice. "What do you mean?"

"If we both try," he said, "I think maybe we can be a family. It will take a lot of work, and a lot of time, but we can go slow, you know? There's no rush." He suddenly realized that the silence on the other end of the line was because she wasn't there anymore. He felt a wave of disappointment wash over him. Didn't love start with caring, with commonalities? How was he ever going to get this right?

Suddenly, Tanuk's voice came on the line. "Jason?" he said. "Are you still there?"

"Yes," he said. "Yes, I'm here. What's going on? What happened to Tina?"

"She's on her way," Tanuk said. "Welcome to the family."

James Axler
Outlanders®

PANTHEON
OF VENGEANCE

War machines and rebels clash in ancient Greece…

In his human skin, Baron Cobalt nearly destroyed Cerberus with his quest for power. Now evolved into his godly Annunaki form as Overlord Marduk, he's reconsolidating his power and claiming the Mediterranean. As Marduk's Nephilim-led forces challenge the ruling Hera Olympiad and her legion of cybernetic demigods to a death dance, Kane and the Cerberus warriors harness the power of a cyberarmy eager to bring retribution and justice to the real monsters of antiquity.

Available in August 2008 wherever you buy books.

JAMES AXLER

DEATHLANDS®

JAMES AXLER

DEATHLANDS

Plague Lords

In a ruined world, past and future clash with terrifying force...

EMPIRE OF XIBALBA, BOOK I

Plague Lords

In a ruined world, past and future clash with terrifying force...

The sulfur-teeming Gulf of Mexico is the poisoned end of earth, but here, Ryan and the others glean rumors of whole cities deep in South America that survived the blast intact. But as the companions contemplate a course of action, a new horror approaches on the horizon. The Lords of Death are Mexican pirates raiding stockpiles with a grim vengeance. When civilization hits rock bottom, a new stone age will emerge, with its own personal day of blood reckoning.

In the Deathlands, the future could always be worse. Now it is...

Available December wherever you buy books.